About the A...

Born in Dublin in 1959, Dermot Bolger's nine novels for adults include *The Woman's Daughter*, *The Journey Home*, *The Valparaiso Voyage*, *Temptation*, and, most recently, *The Family on Paradise Pier*. His first crossover novel for a young adult readership, *New Town Soul*, was published in 2010. He is the author of over a dozen stage plays, including *The Lament for Arthur Cleary*, (which received The Samuel Beckett Award), *In High Germany*, which was filmed by RTÉ television, and *The Parting Glass* – a sequel to *In High Germany*, which explores the lives of the same characters twenty years later. His recent *Ballymun Trilogy* of plays – *From These Green Heights*, which received the Irish Times/ESB Irish Theatre Award for Best New Irish Play of 2004; *The Townlands of Brazil* and *The Consequences of Lightning* – explored the rise, demolition and regeneration of a green-field working-class Dublin suburb over four decades.

A poet whose eight volumes of poetry include *External Affairs*, he devised and edited the bestselling collaborative novels, *Finbar's Hotel* and *Ladies Night at Finbar's Hotel*, published in a dozen countries, to which many of Ireland's most famous novelists contributed chapters. The editor of numerous anthologies, including *The Picador Book of Contemporary Irish Fiction*, he has been Writer Fellow in Trinity College, Dublin and Playwright in Association with the Abbey Theatre. Between 1979 and 1992 he founded and edited the Raven Arts Press in Dublin, which championed new Irish writers, and he is a regular contributor to most of Ireland's leading newspapers.

A SECOND LIFE
This renewed, revised edition published 2010 by
New Island
2 Brookside
Dundrum Road
Dublin 14

Original version first published by Penguin Books, 1994

www.newisland.ie

978-1-84840-070-2

British Library Cataloguing Data. A CIP catalogue record for this book is available from the British Library.

Book cover and typesetting by redrattledesign.com

Printed by CPI Antony Rowe, Chippenham, Wiltshire

New Island received financial assistance from
The Arts Council (An Chomhairle Ealaíon), Dublin, Ireland

10 9 8 7 6 5 4 3 2 1

Dermot Bolger

A Second Life

A Renewed Novel

**NEW
ISLAND**

Author's Note

When I first wrote *A Second Life* in 1993, my life – as the father of two small children the same ages as the children in this book – was probably as chaotic and pressurised as Sean Blake's life seems to be until the car crash on the opening page of this novel prompts him to take stock of that life. The similarities end there, because good fiction is about throwing yourself into the mindset of people who are unlike you, although you always bring or discover surprising parts of yourself on that journey. Unlike Sean Blake, I had not been adopted, although the death of my mother when I was ten undoubtedly left an absence and a yearning, which echoes something of the void Sean feels at never having known the woman who was his birth mother.

Adoption is the central theme of this book, but *A Second Life* did not set out to be about the ongoing searches that were becoming more visible in Ireland in the early 1990s as adopted children desperately tried to unearth the truth about their birth mothers and to understand the plight of those young mothers who felt they had no option left but to sign away their children born out of wedlock. They were mothers who later found every door closed in their faces if they tried to make contact with – or discover the least bit of information about – the children who were perpetual absences in their new lives;

children whose existences they were often too scared or ashamed ever to speak about to anyone, even to their own husbands.

This novel had a different starting point. In 1992 my fifth play in three years was staged, a production in the Peacock Theatre during the Dublin Theatre Festival. So much was happening in my life back then that my main memory is not of the production itself, but of the play being 'teched' one afternoon in the darkened the-atre. During the blackouts, as the lighting man reconfigured his settings, the only lights visible were two illuminated (and ignored) 'No Smoking' signs on the wall and the glow of a dozen cigarettes littering the darkness as an anxious cast and crew puffed away.

The cast talked a lot that afternoon, as casts do during the slow business of a technical set-up, and one elderly actor started to de-scribe being in a car crash some years previously. The accident was so serious that his heart had briefly stopped and suddenly he found himself observing the accident scene from above, so detached from his own body below that he had time casually to observe the tiny detail that small flecks of dandruff were sprinkled on the hat of the paramedic who was trying to cut him free from the wreckage.

From such seeds are novels born. This odd image – and also his comment about how he initially possessed a sense of feeling almost cheated at being brought back to life inside his badly injured body – haunted me over the following months. When I finally found the time to sit down and start work on a new novel, I knew that I had my opening. I'd never had an out-of-body experience, but a desire for research led me into the situation where one Friday night a state-registered nurse legally administered a powerful dose of hal-lucinogenic drugs into my left buttock in a deconsecrated Protestant church in the grounds of a former mental asylum in Dublin. This experience was sufficiently terrifying later to make me as wary of method research as Sir John Gielgud was of method acting.

Some authors meticulously plot their novels in advance, skilfully bringing readers on pre-ordained imaginative journeys. I work at the opposite end of the spectrum: what draws me to my desk each morning is a combination of anxiety, stress and curiosity, in that, quite simply, I have no idea what is going to happen next.

A novel may start by being about one thing, but as a citizen you always have your antennae open to the discourse starting to seep out in your society. During the early months of writing *A Second Life,* often, when I turned on a radio or simply overheard conversations on buses, I realised that an ever-growing number of mothers and children separated during the 1940s, 1950s and 1960s were now desperate to find out about each other. Despite huge obstacles, people were attempting to find ways to take the first tentative steps towards seeking out the stranger who was their parent or child, never sure if these approaches would be welcomed or rebuffed.

Adoptions gradually became a backdrop and then the central theme of this novel as it began to echo some of the hidden stories within Irish society that were finally starting to be told around me. People once silenced by shame were no longer being silenced. Irish society had never been ruled by any real obsessive devotion to religion, but more by a fetish about respectability – the main facet of which involved keeping family secrets secret. The wall of silence caused by this mindset was being eroded by individual voices in 1993 – a decade before films like *The Magdalene Sisters* were made – but the physical walls behind which the adoption files were kept remained as high and impenetrable as ever.

As a novelist I was trying to absorb the undercurrents rippling through Irish society and to weave them all into the backdrop of the novel. At around that time I attended a one-act play by the great Jennifer Johnston. It was lunchtime, a meagre house, a bare set with just one chair. The superb actress Rosaleen Linehan entered, sat down, and commenced her monologue. But after ninety seconds she stopped and did something incredibly brave. She looked at the audience and said, 'Excuse me; I got off on the wrong note. I think

A Second Life was hardbacked by Viking in 1994, softbacked by Penguin in 1995, sold well and was translated. But I never allowed it to be reprinted when it went out of print because, as the years went on and I would occasionally glance back over it, I kept thinking of the courage of Rosaleen Linehan on stage that day saying, 'I got off on the wrong note.' I know that – amid all the pressures of my busy family life, my myriad writing and other commitments at that time and the fact that I was trying to capture a moving object by tapping into the psychic mood of the period as birth mothers and adopted children started to make their voices heard – I also had got off on the wrong note, because in the white heat in which I wrote the original novel, I had burdened Sean Blake with too much anger and too many scores to settle.

At thirty-four I had needed a good editor and so at fifty-one I have sat down and – half as editor and half as writer re-imagining each scene – I have tried to re-engage not only with characters like Sean Blake and Lizzy Sweeney, but also with my younger self whom I kept questioning as I cut away chunks of dialogue, added or removed scenes and rewrote almost every paragraph in some way.

Therefore this is not the old novel and nor is it fully a new one. I like to view it as a renewed novel, as the novel that I might have written if – amid all that was happening in my own life and the changes occurring in the society around me – I had taken a deep breath and said, 'I'm going to start again.'

Sean Blake, as I say, is not based on me, but his children in the novel – aged three and aged six months – were based on my own children, and Sean's wife, Geraldine, was very much based on my own wife, Bernie. Rewriting the book in the early months of 2010 allowed me the chance to remember her again exactly as she was as a young mother. I looked forward to her re-reading it when republished, to giving her the first signed copy as I always did. Tragically, several weeks after this renewed version was completed, while radiant with good health and energy, she collapsed when swimming with one of our sons and died without warning from a ruptured aneurysm.

Several of my books were directly dedicated to her, but *A Second Life* had originally been dedicated to our two beautiful sons. This renewed edition is dedicated to her memory, because no matter what name appeared on the dedication page, she was always the person for whom my novels and plays were written, in the hope that she might like them, in the knowledge that she would recognise so many tiny moments transformed by fiction, because she was the centre of my life.

The Ireland of 1993 was changed utterly from the Ireland of a decade before and is almost unrecognisable from the Ireland of today. One small change is that when a commissioned novel is now finished it is sent to a publisher within seconds as an e-mail attachment. Back in 1993 manuscripts still needed to be posted.

In 1993 the order of nuns who had run the High Park Magdalene Laundry in Drumcondra applied for an exhumation license to remove the remains of one hundred and thirty-three women who had died while incarcerated in their laundry, because they wished to sell the site to a property developer. They could only provide death certificates for seventy-five of the one hundred and thirty three women and, during the exhumation, the remains of yet another twenty-two nameless and forgotten Magdalene women were unearthed. All but one of these women's bodies were cremated and reburied in a mass grave in Glasnevin Cemetery.

By chance, on the day that I walked down to the General Post Office in O'Connell Street in Dublin to post off the manuscript of this book, three survivors from that Magdalene laundry were seated outside the entrance, visible at last in the most historical site of Irish rebellion, defiantly collecting signatures for a petition to have a monument erected to the nameless woman cremated and transferred to that mass grave. I stopped to sign the petition and talk to them. At one stage I even held aloft the jiffy bag containing the manuscript and was about to say, 'This book is about you and about women like you. It tells one of your stories.'

But wisely I said nothing: this book could not be about them, because nobody could tell their stories that they uniquely owned. All I could hope to do – in 1993 and again in 2010 – was to echo something of their lives within the parallel imaginative world that is fiction. No novelist could so eloquently and honestly tell their stories in the way that so many of them have done in interviews and memoirs and documentaries in the years since, when the walls of silence have finally been breached and so many ageing mothers and now grown-up children have tentatively made contact with each other and started to fill in the missing gaps of secrets that could once never be spoken about.

Dermot Bolger
September, 2010

In loving memory of Bernie

Chapter One

28 December 1991

Whoever repainted the ambulance had missed the top rim of the doors. From above, the flaky cracks in the original paint-work looked like a dried-up riverbed. The top of the paramedic's hat was speckled with flecks of dandruff and, when he lifted his head from my chest, I could see my own face staring upwards, criss-crossed with streaks of blood. The two ancient trees that overshadowed the main gates of the National Botanic Gardens were bare. Yet from somewhere within their depths a blackbird was calling.

How long was it since I'd felt this serene? It seemed hard to remember the petty agitations at breakfast time, the newspaper photo-desk ringing about deadlines, my three-year-old son Benedict refusing to eat, slowly becoming bored of his Christmas toys. All of this had occurred only minutes ago, but I no longer felt any connection to my former life. I was surprised to feel no pain either or any sense of grief or loss. Instead I was observing the scene of the crash below me with casual disinterest.

Moss was clogging the gutters of the house in flats on the corner. Cracked roof slates there would cause problems in winter. A young student peered out through lace curtains at an attic window. I could see party balloons sellotaped to the windowpane and the top of her hair, still wet from the shower, as she leaned forward to stare at the

1

cars stalled in both directions. How stressed those drivers looked as they stared out through their windscreens. Where were they all travelling to, in this limbo between Christmas and New Year, with offices and factories closed? I felt sorry for the drivers forced to stare at my dead body. I did not feel sorry for myself. Indeed I felt no particular emotion towards my body, which lay half in and half out of the crushed car.

The bus driver looked to be in shock. He lay on the pavement beside the gates into the Botanic Gardens, his face white, tufts of black hair in his nostrils. His legs kept twitching involuntarily. It was not his fault. It had been my fault, late as usual for a photo shoot, taking the corner wide to avoid the cars parked outside the Addison Lodge pub.

Two security men from the Botanic Gardens came to the gate to watch. One was prematurely bald, a ridge of greying hair circling the freckles on his skull. The ambulance man managed to get my body on to a stretcher. They worked frantically, thumping at my chest. All that futile effort and concern: why could they not just let my corpse be? Already I was moving away from them, the morning light darkening and then dissolving into night. I felt my body glow, like before a sexual climax, the heat becoming intense and all-consuming. I had drifted high above the gates of the Botanic Gardens. There were gnarled trees below me, Victorian glasshouses to my left, the white glint of water beyond. I saw Glasnevin Cemetery to my right and thought of all the people I knew who were buried there. Then it became too dark to see; the old trees became shapes, then their shapes turned into faces. The moon had risen suddenly, cold and brilliantly bright in the blackest of skies, and, as I was gradually drawn towards it, I began to recognise those faces.

I was only three years old when my grandfather died, yet I knew him at once, along with other faces I had never imagined I would see again. They crowded towards me, growing more numerous. My two children seemed to be present too, except they had the faces of adults, faces older than mine, faces that smiled in welcome. I did not feel any need to question their presence because I was possessed by a sense of total wellbeing, as if I had finally arrived home. What had I been afraid of before now? Why had I waited this long to die?

'You'll like it here, son.' I recognised my father's whisper and sensed myself smiling. The white moon was no longer cold. It dazzled and spun, radiating heat as it drew me in. I had only to pass through the moon and my hands would be able to touch those faces. The faces began to spin: merging together like a vibrant whirlpool. But one young man's face stood out from the others. I could not put a name to him and yet I knew his features intimately; his surly, almost menacing sneer that was so out of kilter with the joyous, welcoming throng. The others faces were suddenly gone and there was just that sneering face, blocking my path as if telling me that I did not belong there. He seemed to suck all the brightness from the moon and turn everything dark.

Ding, dong, dell: pussy is in the well. How far do I have to fall down this dark well shaft, catching glimpses of the life I once knew, flecks of disconnected memories like on a television being flicked between stations. I have a wife and two children: responsibilities summoning me back down inside that body. I have pain to face and business to finish. I need to get back to who I once was: a man who took photographs for a living. I hear the click of a shutter and picture myself lying face up on a stretcher. I zoom in on that stretcher when I really want to sweep back up towards the weightless freedom I had felt. But I cannot climb back up, because I can not make peace with the one unfriendly face blocking my path there. Where do I know his face from? *Go back down to hell; go back to your own life.* Am I saying these words to him or is he saying them to me? If it is my own voice, why does it sound so strange? I try one last time to climb up and reach that moon made of shimmering faces, but the moon keeps soaring up in the sky, with him spitefully pushing me away, making me fall down through this dark tunnel.

But as I plummet downwards, the moon also seems to suddenly fall from that vast height. It spins towards me, brilliantly luminous, and then strikes my face and splinters apart, turning everything white and then grey. I see a grey pavement with cracks, a grey morning with grey mist, a paramedic with greying hair thumping on my chest. I experience the same awful thud as when you fall in your sleep and jerk awake. I'm screaming and now I recognise my voice, though it is barely audible. I'm screaming so loud that the sound fills up my head, yet still it can't expel the pain. The sky begins to blacken as the paramedic bends down to listen. A voice from the darkness says, 'He's breathing again. His heart was stopped for so long – how the hell can this man start to breathe again?'

*

I'm breathing. The curse of God on the interfering paramedics who got me breathing again. I don't want to breathe; I want to fly to the moon. I want those welcoming faces back, I want to be weightless and return to that sense of overwhelming bliss. The ambulance keeps jigging from side to side. I imagine the lines of traffic we are hurtling through; the harassed drivers with lists of appointments, deliveries, deadlines, all chasing their tails. Briefly I had been free from that stress. Two figures lean across me, adjusting straps. Which of these bastards brought me back?

My body feels numb. The painkilling injections have done their work. But can they not give me a drug to stop me from thinking? How do they honestly expect me to fit back into this life? Maybe I'm paralysed and facing forty years of vegetating in a hospital ward. Give me back my death, I try to scream at them. We sway sharply left. There is the sound of another siren, a police escort. I am filled with inconsolable grief, though my tears lack the strength to run down my face. They lie on my eyes like coins. Moments ago I had been wrapped inside a blanket of love. Now I am crying for myself, forced back to face this pain.

A Second Life

The ambulance stops. The doors open and there is grey, lacklustre daylight. A nurse leans over me and says something. I do not remember being carried from the ambulance.

*

My hospital bed was besieged by flowers. Bizarrely I seemed to know their Latin names during the moments when I drifted towards consciousness. Yet I never had any interest in horticulture. During one moment of clarity I recognised my wife, Geraldine, sitting alone beside me. In another moment, Benedict was hesitantly touching my bandaged hand. I sensed his fear of the tubes and masks. I knew he was torn between wanting to be with me and desperately wanting to get away. He would block this bad memory from his mind as soon as he left the hospital. If I did not survive, would he have any real recollection of me when he grew up? I would not even be a photograph on the mantelpiece because I had never let myself be photographed. I tried to feel concern for Geraldine, yet I felt nothing. 'You're so lucky,' Geraldine whispered during those conscious seconds when I recognised her. I could have tried to say something in reply, but it was too much effort. I felt her kiss on my lips long after she had left.

I woke again to find it was night. Nurses tended to me. I was suddenly suffused with absolute pain. I had possessed a life once, I had known ordinary happiness or unhappiness or whatever those terms meant. On Christmas morning we had knelt by the decorated tree: Sinéad in her rocker, Benedict almost as mesmerised by the sparkly wrapping paper as by the presents inside it. Had that been three days or ten days ago? I had no concept of time anymore, no notion of how I could ever leave this bed.

When I moved my head I could see a drip feeding down into my arm. I had stopped cursing the medics who brought me back to life. I knew whose fault it was: that surly faced young man who had blocked my path. His face came between me and every waking thought. I knew his features, but could not remember from where. Was he a schoolmate or somebody I had photographed in a crowd, somebody who found their image stolen and printed in a newspaper? How far back did I have to go to find him?

On one occasion I awoke to full consciousness. I could see my own body, not indifferently from a height, but by just tilting my bandaged head to glimpse my smashed shoulder and plastered arm. I am using his face, I thought, as a shield to keep reality at bay. I need to focus on the present tense, on my responsibilities, on the three people who need me. I have a life to rebuild… But my mind was already scavenging back through the past in search of him. When I blacked out into sleep I saw his head turn towards me. I woke up to hear sounds outside the hospital: church bells ringing, car horns, the New Year being rung in. I felt his name about to come to my lips. I passed the short eternity until my next blackout like a man choking on some forgotten word that was obstructing his throat.

*

Mostly I did not know the difference between day and night. I knew only a limbo of white ceiling and faces passing across my vision like clouds. Or else I slept, experiencing the most vivid dreams. There was no year in my life I did not relive. Communion on my tongue, bare knees offering up their pain for the souls in purgatory. Stained glass in winter, brass plaques on varnished pews… *Pray for the souls of the Miss Healys.* The first taste of an ice-cream cone purchased from the van parked outside Tolka Park, and being held aloft there on my father's shoulders among Shelbourne fans as they celebrated a goal.

Often I returned to my two earliest memories. In the first one I am sitting on a ridge of mud, hungrily staring at a worm wriggling in my hand, with a sickly feeling on my tongue as if I had just swallowed something vile. In the second memory I am standing on the flagstones of a cramped cottage where my family once holidayed.

The cottage stinks of mildewed thatch and I am terrified of a local woman staring spitefully at me. I tried to drift back further in time, but I stopped myself because, even when unconscious, there were parts of my past where I refused to go. They belonged to someone else, someone whose pain I refused to bear.

I jolted awake to find Geraldine sitting by my bed. I sensed her anxiety and tried to say something, but instead I drifted back to sleep and dreamed about being seventeen again. It is a summer's evening. I am standing with a girl beneath the bridge over the Tolka beside the Botanic Gardens, the pair of us hidden from view of the road overhead. 'How did it feel when you discovered you were adopted?' The girl can sense my resentment at her question; how I curl up emotionally into a protective shell, destroying any intimacy by kissing her roughly.

My dreams pitch me forward in time to when our first child is being born. They have taken Geraldine away and I am alone in a filthy waiting room that stinks of trapped smoke. It is an hour since her waters broke, since I ran down the frosted street in the night to find a taxi. The driver had joked about having never seen me anywhere before without a camera. I want to be with Geraldine, to share her pain in whatever way I can. I have never felt so sick with nerves. My body feels like glass which any movement could shatter. I am filled with intense love for our child to be. I try to pray but am too scared to remember any words.

Then, as the midwife summons me in to join Geraldine, I suddenly think of the anonymous woman whose features may echo my own: my birth mother who once experienced the pain I am about to witness. Nobody would have been there for her in whatever isolated rural convent I was born. There would only have been other girls in the same predicament: young mothers allowed to hold their children for a few seconds before the nuns took us away. In the delivery suite Geraldine tries to smile. I want to be strong for her sake, but I am haunted by something I have not thought about in years, my ignorance about my own birth. I try to imagine my mother's face, her conflicting emotions. Had she been frightened to feel love for the child she would be forced to give up? How could I know what she felt? Maybe she had cursed me at birth as an unwanted ball of flesh the nuns would dispose of? The only facts I knew about her were that she was from Laois and she was nineteen years old. My wife gasps at a quickening contraction and I hold her hand and forget everything else, caught up in the miracle of seeing my child being born.

My wife's face is replaced in my dreams by the face of that unknown young man. He looks around twenty-three years old, with black hair and sallow skin. His face scares me. He is my real father, I think, suddenly, the nameless bastard who must have run away. I feel a quivering excitement, the exhilaration of release. I have placed him now: the man who still may not even know that I exist. Perhaps this was how he looked on the night I was conceived; sly and boorish, deceit in his heart and lust in his balls. He looks familiar, because these are an echo of my own features I am staring at, distorted but borne forward by genetics.

But I as stare at him in my sleep his sneer only broadens. He is not my father, I realise. I will not be rid of him so easily. Who are you? I try to ask, but he turns away, his hair becoming the dark blur that draws me back into unconsciousness.

*

I am being lifted on to a trolley by two men. I know that I have just had an injection. There are lights overhead, voices. Try to stop breathing, I think to myself.

'We cannot put you out fully,' a male voice says.

Then there is a denser and more luxuriant darkness than I could have ever conceived. Slowly I begin to traverse through that darkness towards colours emerging in the distance. But I am merely an observing eye now, an unleashed pupil cruising inside my own brain. I could be floating through outer space, yet I know that I am travelling inwards, through the magnified layers of a patchwork universe of blood cells and infinitesimal fibres.

I know that this time I am not dead and I will meet no waiting faces here. I am trapped inside the power of the drug. My initial euphoria fades. This journey is inescapable and impersonal; a dog, given the same drug, would experience these same wonders. This is what makes the experience more frightening than dying. Because I am no longer even a soul: I am a speck free-floating through a chemical fantasy landscape. I sense that masked surgeons are working at my skull, yet I cannot think of myself in proportion to them. Palpitating coils of colour interlope around me, waterwheels of dazzling sparks, the rings of arid planets majestically turning. It is impossible to fathom how quickly or slowly they rotate and then dissolve before my eyes. If I could think in human terms I would feel utterly lonely, but this landscape is bereft of emotion. I can only drift impetuously past each imploding star, straining to connect back to the body I had once lived inside.

I try to focus on the memory of my wife's face, on Sinéad's birth, on carrying Benedict up a flight of darkened stairs, on unlocking the back door to fetch coal on a frost-sparkled night. But I feel so removed from those memories that they are meaningless. It seems impossible that I will ever fit back into my body again. I begin to sense a cold white light. I am lifted on to a trolley, but it cannot be the same trolley as before because I feel that I am the size of Gulliver now: a blubbery giant who dwarfs everyone. I cling to the trolley, terrified that if I fall I will crush the passers-by in the hospital corridor, who stop to stare at me and then scatter in fear of getting crushed by the tyres of the trolley that revolve like huge Ferris wheels.

*

I woke at night in a new room in another hospital. I could not tell how much time had passed. The pain in my head was fierce but bearable. My mind was clearer than any time since the accident. I could see my injured shoulder and arm. My body ached. A mobile touch pad beside the bed had a red button embossed with the outline of a nurse's head. I tried to reach out with my good arm but the effort was too much. I opened my mouth, thinking that I needed to strain to make the faintest sound. To my surprise a cry emerged. Footsteps came and the door opened.

'You're back with us, Mr Blake,' the night sister said. 'Rest yourself; you're after a serious operation. They had to drain fluid from your brain, but you'll make a full recovery.'

My mouth was parched. I realised how blurred my voice sounded.

'What else did they do to me?'

'The doctor will see you in the morning.'

'Can you tell me now, please?'

'You mightn't feel this way now, but you got off lightly. Any scars will be above the hairline. Nobody will see them unless baldness runs in your family. Some ribs are cracked, you have a fractured arm and a fracture of the shoulder. It will take time, but you're going to be fine.'

There was a television and a crucifix on the wood-panelled wall of the room. A plastic bottle of holy water with a blue cap looked incongruous among the drips near the bed. The lights of north Dublin were below. I recognised the blazing floodlights of Dalymount Park.

'It's the Leinster Senior Cup Final,' I said. 'January the fifth. Bohs are playing at home. I always hated Bohs.'

'Why is that?'

'My father was a die-hard Shelbourne fan: a particularly small, obscure tribe of eternally disappointed men.'

She smiled at the description as she turned to leave. 'Somehow I think you're going to be all right. Try to go back to sleep.'

'Sister…?'

I needed to talk to someone but I didn't know what to say. She turned.

'I was dead, wasn't I?'

'The chart says that your heart stopped briefly. It's not so uncomm-on.'

'How do people feel…afterwards?'

'There was a priest here earlier. I think he hasn't left if you'd like me to…'

'I don't really have much time for priests. But you must have met people like me before.'

She looked behind her. The corridor was empty. I could see the desk where she had been sitting.

'There's proper counselling you can get,' she said quietly. 'We can arrange for it tomorrow.'

'Talk to me, please.'

'I'm not trained to…' She hesitated, and then shook her head as if slightly baffled. Her low voice was almost conspiratorial. 'A lot of patients initially seem to feel cheated to be alive. Don't ask me why, I hate the thought of death, but when the brain gets starved of oxygen it throws one last great party to give itself a hallucinatory send-off. Maybe during that euphoria people feel released from all their problems and then suddenly they are brought back to face them. But you're one lucky man. I've seen people left paralysed from the waist down after car crashes, being fed through a straw for the rest of their lives. You've had a miraculous escape, Mr Blake. Thousands of people never get this second chance at life. Now try to sleep.'

She closed the door. I felt less alone for her words, for the thought that others had felt similar bewildering emotions. I knew where I was: a room in the private hospital run by Bon Secours nuns on Washerwoman's Hill. This was only two hundred yards away from where my car had crashed into a bus outside the Botanic Gardens. One of my last memories was of passing this hospital. Moments later I had been clinically dead. It had only taken a few seconds for that crash to occur, but in my head I could break it down into a protracted sequence of events. Firstly I had taken the corner way too wide, so that I was on the wrong side of the road. Secondly I saw a woman step off the pavement with a baby in her arms and I had needed to swing the car back towards my own side of the road to avoid hitting her. Thirdly the bus came out of nowhere. If I had not swerved to avoid the woman I would have ploughed headlong into the bus, instead of glancing off the side of it. I would now almost certainly be dead. I thought back over my memories of finding myself floating above the crash site, serenely observing everything. I had no recollection of a woman and child among the hushed crowd, watching the paramedics frantically try to resuscitate me. But I possessed a fleeting sense of her face as she stepped off the pavement, so anguished looking that it was almost as if she didn't care what happened to her. Yet her arms had been protectively cradling the child.

I needed to stop thinking about that crash, but I found it hard to dwell on anything else. The Bon Secours Hospital was close to my home; convenient for Geraldine and the children. I could imagine Geraldine teasing that, despite all my talk of being an atheist, the nuns had finally got hold of me in the end. I smiled and then my smile faded. This was not my first time to be in the care of nuns. But there had been no wood-panelled private room back then, no call bell to summon nurses. Just pregnant girls on their knees scrubbing floors or put to work in the laundry; infants lined up in iron cots like post waiting to be dispatched from a sorting office; the beeswax scent of shame and disapproval. At this moment I desperately wanted to know my birth mother's name, why she had given me up, what became of her. I pressed the call bell.

'Could I have some water to drink, please?' I asked the night sister. 'And, if you don't mind, could you take that bottle of hocus-pocus holy water out of my room?'

She held the glass to my lips, then eased my head back onto the pillows. She went to close the curtains and I asked her to leave them open. A taxi passed the hospital gates beyond the long sweep of the lawns. A few lights shone in the apartment blocks by the river. A crane was discernible to the left of the black shapes of the arboretum in the Botanic Gardens. The memory of gazing down at the Victorian glasshouses there seemed more real than my conversation with the nurse a moment ago. Behind the arboretum lay Glasnevin Cemetery where my adoptive parents were buried. I had always hated the desolation of that graveyard. But now it felt welcoming, like a doorway behind which I knew faces were gathered, wondering what was keeping me so long from them.

A mile away, in an old estate off Griffith Avenue, a woman lay alone in the bed in which we had conceived two children. Surely I had been given this second chance for Geraldine and the children. Then why could I not focus on the love I felt for them? My eyes kept being drawn back to the dark expanse of the Botanic Gardens below my window. The memory of that young man's surly face returned and it seemed to belong out there. *Aesculus*. This word came to me unbidden. I did not know its meaning, just that it was linked to those dark gardens.

I closed my eyes and the yew-tree walk in the oldest part of those gardens came into my mind: two lines of gnarled, intertwined trunks that had withstood centuries of storms. The place seemed to call out to me. I knew that I was traumatised from the crash, but amid my confused, scared state I sensed that something linked me to that narrow yew-tree walk; something I refused to remember. If I could unlock this memory, then maybe my confused emotions would begin to make sense.

Chapter Two

Elizabeth heard the crash and woke. It was so close that she thought a car must have taken the corner wide, sliced through the railings and struck the wall of her bungalow. The bedside clock told her that it was two minutes past ten in the morning. If any of her family called in to spy on her they would know, from the fact she was still in bed at this hour, that she had gone walkabout the night before. It was Sharon's husband, Steve, who had coined the phrase: 'Your mother's Irish, not Aborigine. This is Coventry. She can't just go walkabout with her spear.'

She pulled back the curtains to stare out. The estate looked deserted. Lights of Christmas trees flickered in some porches. The daily procession of older neighbours had already departed for the shops, wheeling their shopping trolleys. The younger couples who had moved in more recently would still be off work with the Christmas break, yet there was no sign of their children playing out on the street. How different things had been thirty years ago, with skipping ropes, the thud of footballs and the excited shouts of young boys forever haunting her.

There was no sign of a crash, yet Elizabeth knew that she had heard one, so close and loud that her nerves were jangling. It had not been a dream because, with the drugs they gave her, she no longer had dreams. It had been something real, a fearful noise that cut into her. She took her hand away from the window, watching the moist outline of her fingers vanish from the pane, and she knew that she simply had to get away from this house. It did not matter what the nurse, who was due to check in on her, might say, or what threats her three daughters made. Elizabeth needed to be out walking. She dressed with furious concentration to overcome the pain. The street was empty, but few neighbours still spoke to her anyway. The old ones had died off, and to the new families she was just the crazy woman who went walking every night.

The school playground by the main road was empty. This allowed her to pass by it quickly, because if children were playing there, she would often stop to watch them, so trapped inside this habit that she would be unable to move on until her presence unnerved the teachers. She walked quickly now, her hair blowing about in the slipstream of passing trucks. She needed to keep walking so she could find the crash site and make sure he was all right.

Eight hours later, when the police discovered her wandering along the motorway in her slippers, the policewoman wrote down the only words she could discern amid Elizabeth's intense mumbling; 'It was Francis. I know it was. My baby is dead and he'll never find me now.'

*

What frightened her most when she first arrived in London was the underground, the way that people pushed forward on the platform as the lights of the train emerged from the tunnel. It was so tempting to think of simply letting herself fall onto those tracks during the seconds it took for the carriages to shudder to a halt. New Year's Eve was no night to be alone. Girls of her age regularly left the Slieve Blooms for London, but they often married back into them. They met neighbouring boys from home – fellow emigrants from Roundwood and Dunross and Ballyfin and Coolrain – at the Galtymore Dancehall or the Big Top in Cricklewood: couples whose two families would meet on market days in Mountrath, to stand amid the tractors and ponies and racks of boots and greatcoats and marvel at how their offspring had found each other in a foreign city and at how wise they were to marry one of their own.

These young girls left home but recreated home elsewhere: the *Carlow and South Leinster Nationalist* coming through the letter-box every week and calls made from phone boxes across Britain on Christmas Eve to Dunross post office, where ageing parents gathered in the hope that their banished children might get through.

Lizzy Sweeney boarded the tube and tried not to stare at the black man sitting opposite her in the carriage. When she reached her stop she climbed steps into the night amongst a shoal of alien voices. The dancehall had jazz music and a balcony. A globe of mirrors sprinkled coloured light over the dancers. She wanted to be alone, yet she needed to be among other people. Her body still hurt below the waist, she still winced every time she passed water. But it was a hollow ache that consumed her, an absence inside her stomach begging to be filled. She had chosen this dancehall because there were unlikely to be any Irish here, nobody who might recognise her.

'Everybody onto the floor,' the MC was saying into the microphone. 'There's only three minutes to go to 1957.' A nervous young man grabbed her arm. He smelt of Brylcreem and sweat. Before she turned her head Lizzy Sweeney decided that – provided he wasn't Irish – she would give herself to him.

*

In Coventry the maternity hospital was cold. The convent in Sligo had been warmer, despite its harsh regime of reproach. In Sligo she was a sinner, but she had been among her own kind, her cries mingling with the sobs of the Roscommon girl in the next bunk. In this half-rebuilt city of Coventry she had nobody to confide in. She could not tell what Jack's family thought of her or of the fact that nobody from her family had attended their hastily arranged marriage at the registry office. On Jack's instructions she now called herself 'Elizabeth', because no wife of his would have a skivvy's name.

'Elizabeth is a Catholic, you know,' she heard someone say at the wedding breakfast, as if that single word explained everything strange about her. Elizabeth had held in her stomach and tried to understand their accents. When my second boy is born I will feel different, she had told herself, because nobody can snatch him from me this time. She had not expected Jack's offer of marriage. She had not expected to see him again after his few thrusts in that London laneway, with a cold stone wall against her buttocks while a single green firework exploded in a slot of sky between the two dark buildings and the bells rang in the New Year. One hand grasping his shoulder and her other hand holding aloft her skirt while she turned her face away every time he tried to kiss her. When his breath came shorter her nails had dug into the seat of his trousers so as to thrust his seed deeper into the empty void in her womb. The pain had not mattered anymore, or the stains on her skirt, or how he looked at her when he stepped back after he finished and said, 'Christ, you're no more than nineteen, are you? I bet it's your first time. I can tell by the tightness of you, girl.'

On the Sunday after they were married he showed her a photograph printed twice in the *Sunday Express*. It was of Joseph Stalin with a group of Soviet generals. 'Look at how simple it is to make somebody vanish,' Jack said. In the second version of the photograph one general was airbrushed out with a pillar superimposed in his place. 'That poor blighter was either shot or he's in a gulag.' Lizzy had half-listened to Jack talk about show trials, knowing how he loved to present himself as a knowledgeable man of the world. She thought of all the homes in Dunross where there were framed photographs of her communion class. She wondered if a space had miraculously appeared in the back row where she had once smiled shyly.

'I don't look thirty, do I?' Jack used to ask before they were married, during the weekends when he came up to London to visit her. 'Nobody would ever know there's eleven years between us. I promise I'll look after you if anything goes wrong. Let me unbutton your blouse. I love it when you blush like that. Everything is a sin for you Catholics, isn't it? But you lie back and I'll show you just how much fun sin can be.'

Lizzy had done what she was told, because she had learned to do what she was told. She would close her eyes and imagine the nuns' car ascending the crumbling mountain road across the Slieve Bloom Mountains, with glimmers of light coming from distant milking sheds at dawn. She would remember the silence in which she sat, squashed in the back seat between Sister Theresa and her father in the grainy half-light where the only colour left in the world was the red bruise on her check from her father's belt.

She knew that Jack could not truly love her because he could never truly know her. But he loved the way she obeyed him; he loved the notion that he had taken her virginity on New Year's Eve, when he attended that dance because he had missed his train home to Coventry. He loved her unEnglishness – although he hated all foreigners. She was different; obedient and undemanding, unlike cocksure English girls who wanted everything, who came from families who made him nervous that he would not be able to keep up with them. He loved Lizzy's sense of absolute isolation, her lack of history and, most especially, he loved her body.

And she loved the feel of their son growing inside her and even if Jack had abandoned her she was determined to keep her son this time, even if she needed to claw at strangers with her nails. Nobody would force her to sign away her own flesh again. And she came to love Jack because he did not run away when she told him her news. He stopped coming to London and made her leave her cheap digs and her job scrubbing floors and take the train to Coventry instead. When he showed her the bungalow he had bought, and the bedroom he had done up for their son, Lizzy had cried on his shoulder, unable to stop while he hugged her, looking awkward and masculine and pleased with himself.

'The first baby is always the hardest,' the midwife in Coventry said. 'Forget everything you've been told, because nothing can prepare you for what's ahead.' The delivery ward was filled with English accents. The nurses were helpful and reassuring, but Lizzy longed to have one of those frightened girls from Sligo for company. She wondered where the girls were who had worked with her in the convent kitchens and scrubbed laundry floors, only stopping work when the labour pains came. Or the other girls sent by the nuns to work in rich homes in Dublin and Cork – girls who cooked and cleaned and were never let outdoors. Where were all their babies now, she wondered. And – though she tried to prevent the thought – where was her own child, Francis, that boy with the bluest eyes who had cried while she struggled to teach him to suck at her breast?

'Little Boy Blue,' Lizzy said aloud in the delivery ward, 'my little Boy Blue.'

Something about her made the midwife ask, 'Are you sure this is your first child?'

Lizzy ignored her. She pushed through the pain and screamed. When she closed her eyes she could see Sister Theresa's face. She started to panic and shouted: 'Give him back!'

'Shout any nonsense you want,' the midwife encouraged, 'shout with the pain and push.'

'Bitches!' Her scream was loud. Amid the searing pain she saw Francis's face on the morning she last placed him in his cot, the morning when she had not known he would be taken away by the nuns to be prepared for his journey, when she had returned from working in the laundry to find his cot empty and the blankets cold.

'The head is out,' the midwife said, 'One last push … there it is … you have a beautiful, beautiful baby girl.'

*

Elizabeth's eldest daughter Sharon was waiting at the doorway of the bungalow when the police car arrived. This part of Coventry had changed greatly since she was a child. She didn't even want to think about the things that could happen to her mother wandering around the streets at night. The bungalow was as spotless as it had always been. Sharon could not remember any room in it ever being untidy. As a child she had hated the perpetual inspection of hands and nails, how her mother refused to let her go out to play if her skirt was even flecked with dirt. If any relatives of her father called without warning they were left standing on the path while her mother frantically inspected the already gleaming house, polishing things that were already clean, scrubbing her daughters' faces so hard at the sink that their skin felt red-raw, working herself up into a state before she finally opened the door.

For Sharon it seemed like her mother's life had been a constant inspection, but an inspection largely carried on inside her own head, as if something in her past gave her a fear of authority. Her father was a quiet man. She only saw him weep once, when Coventry finally won the FA Cup. He had never once been able to discipline his three daughters, leaving everything to their mother, turning the tool shed in the garden into his private refuge. She remembered an avalanche of old washers and screws spilling out from wooden presses when she cleared out the shed after his sudden death. She had found pipe tobacco mixed with orange peel to keep it fresh, the picket he had carried in the 1972 strike carefully wrapped in plastic. Snapshots of his grandchildren were tacked to the shelf at head height. There were wood shavings on the floor from the rocking horse he had been finishing for her youngest child. Something told her that she should stop, place his ashes in that shed and then set the place alight like Aunt Ellen told her Irish tinkers did when someone died. Using a black refuse sack, she had started to clear the old tins of congealed paint from the higher shelves, biting her lip as she unearthed the mildewed copies of pornographic magazines.

Sharon had never asked her father about her mother's disappearances, but four times during her childhood she woke to find that Elizabeth was missing, her father shaking her shoulder and telling her to mind her two younger sisters. The first time Sharon had been only five, but she remembered neighbouring women coming in to cook their dinner that week, while she recited their ages like a nursery rhyme to everyone who asked; five years, three years, eight months. She had experienced a terrifying sense of abandonment, retreating from reality to play with her toys in the front room, even on the night her mother was brought home by Aunt Ellen. She had refused to kiss or be kissed by her mother. The only response she felt able to make was to wake every night for weeks afterwards, feeling a revengeful thrill as she allowed the warm gush of urine to soak the sheet of her bed.

It was Aunt Ellen who found her mother every time she disappeared; Aunt Ellen who healed that first rift between mother and daughter by coaxing Sharon to climb over the wall and steal all the daffodils from the garden next door. Sharon could remember presenting them to her mother and Elizabeth trying to scold her but also laughing as she wrapped Sharon in her arms with the child finally asking, between sobs, *Where were you Mama? Why did you run away from us all?*

Aunt Ellen had always come up from Birmingham to stay after every disappearance. It was Aunt Ellen who gave their mother a past; who called her Lizzy and transformed her into a girl like them, only ten times bolder and wilder. She told them outrageous tales of Lizzy racing with their brother Tom through fields full of weeds and sheep shite, or daring each other to swim in the lake where their father dumped the carcasses of stillborn calves. After each new story Sharon and her sisters would race indoors to ask their mother if it was true. Elizabeth would glare angrily at Aunt Ellen who would light another cigarette and cackle with such laughter that soon Elizabeth would join in, with the children amazed at how utterly different – young, carefree and unknowable – their mother became during those moments.

The squad car came to a halt now and the door opened. Sharon came forward to take her mother's arm.

'You haven't taken your tablets for hours, Mummy. Are you trying to kill yourself?'

Elizabeth's eyes were very clear. She stopped on the path and looked back down the road.

'Maybe he isn't dead,' she murmured. 'Maybe my Little Boy Blue survived after all.'

Sharon's resentment was gone. She gently coaxed her mother indoors.

'Daddy's dead, Mummy,' she said softly. 'You're ill enough as you are, Mummy, please don't lose your mind fully on me as well. Daddy is two years dead now.'

*

They would summon Ellen down from Birmingham, like they always did when there was trouble. Ellen was the only one who could bring her back to herself, the only one with knowledge of the two worlds she lived in. Ellen would be here in the morning. The agency nurse Sharon had hired to stay the night was reading her paperback in the kitchen, with the television sound turned off in case it disturbed her. When the nurse looked in on her, Elizabeth would feign sleep, so as to be left alone.

She remembered how, as a child, old Packy Maguire used to scare them whenever they lingered at his forge at Clonincurragh in the wintry dusk to stroke the horses that steamed with sweat while he hammered out the shape of shoes. Lizzy would always be thinking about the unlit road home they needed to take up into the hills as Packy Maguire – who dug graves for Protestants – told them his favourite story about digging up a man with splinters of wood embedded in his finger nails. He claimed that you could still hear that man scrambling to escape from his coffin if you listened closely at night outside the local graveyard. Lizzy could still recall Ellen and Tom holding her hands as they ran past the winking trees on the mountain road, their bare legs cold and their stomachs empty, shrieking to frighten each other while dogs barked at every isolated farm they passed.

Elizabeth now knew what that man trapped in his coffin had felt. She was desperate to escape from this bed and be back walking the streets, striding through the headlights of trucks, standing outside the locked school in the dark or simply wandering down the centre of quiet streets on this estate, where late-night drivers were so accustomed to her that they no longer even beeped. This room was suffocating her because it was out on those streets that she would encounter her son when he came to Coventry to find her.

She knew this because she had dreamed it. Ten years had passed since she first had this dream; waking beside Jack to find her arms outstretched in greeting, her body swamped with exhilaration. She had longed to wake Jack and tell him that she was certain Francis was coming to find her. But she said nothing because, during all their years together, she had never been able to tell Jack the truth. For the next seven nights in a row she experienced this same dream where a young man passed her on the street at night and stopped to ask her directions to her estate. In her dream she knew at once who he was and why he was seeking her estate. In the dream he had always walked past her before she called out the name she had given him at birth, that name that she was not certain he would know. But he recognised the name because every night in the dream he turned and when he did she would wake in a sweat, knowing it was not a dream but a prophesy. How often had she crept downstairs to phone Ellen in Birmingham the middle of the night?

'I know he's coming to find me, I know he is.' Keeping her voice low so as not to wake Jack, she used to half-cry and half-laugh on the phone while Ellen tried to calm her. This dream first occurred in the year when the last of her daughters left home. Jack, who spent most of his time after work in his tool shed in the garden, did not even notice at first how, when Elizabeth slipped out for milk, she was gone for hours. Because she always encountered Francis in different street corners in her dream, Elizabeth never knew exactly where she was meant to wait for him. She just knew that she could not be indoors, because she was always his guide in the dream, the stranger from whom he sought directions. Therefore she had started to spend hours wandering the streets every evening, always wearing the coat she was wearing in the dream, even though when winter came she caught a cold because it was so light.

Those walks became her obsession. She refused to yield to disappointment, even when exhaustion would eventually force her to go home, because every night brought him a night closer to finding her. Sharon's husband had no right to start following her in his car. Elizabeth remembered the family conference, her three daughters and their husbands all dropping in as if by accident. Elizabeth had told them that if she wanted to go walking in her old coat, it was none of their business. Jack had said nothing, dwarfed by his sons-in-law, longing to be allowed escape into his den in the shed. Elizabeth could remember looking around at her daughters and feeling a disappointment that she could never confess to them. They were her flesh and blood, yet they were foreigners, dulled by dull marriages. She had cared for them when they were young, gone without sleep when they were sick, rocked them in her arms when they first discovered the fickleness of boys, cried at their weddings. Apart from the times she had disappeared she had been a good mother. Yet none of them had ever replaced her firstborn.

Elizabeth heard the nurse switch off the kitchen light and curl up in her sleeping bag on the sofa, with the alarm clock set to give Elizabeth her next set of painkillers at 6 a.m. How long more before they forced her into a hospital. The doctors who opened her up had found a cancer so advanced that they closed her up again. Six months they had said. Sharon kept trying to persuade her to live with her where she could be properly looked after. But Elizabeth was insistent: let me die at home. Her impending death was her last weapon against her daughters, and she was using it to make them leave her alone.

Ellen would be here in the morning and Ellen would make her laugh. Ellen who would bring three months of back issues of *Ireland's Own*.

'Come up to Birmingham and visit the Irish Club,' Ellen would say. 'You might even bring me luck at the bingo.'

'Francis is going to come for me, Ellen. I know it. I can't leave here. I have to wait for him.'

She would know by Ellen's face that her sister did not believe her.

'Lizzy, you're dying. Come back to Ireland with me for one visit. Come down to Dunross. It's a changed world and nobody judges you anymore. Sure half the babies born in Laois these days wouldn't know a father if they fell over one. Everyone would welcome you with open arms. We could even visit Father Tom in Cavan. There have been enough rows in our family; it's time to put things to rights. You have not been back in Dunross since Mammy's funeral and none of us were even allowed to see you on that day. Will you not come back with me this once?'

Elizabeth would give Ellen the same reply she always did; that she would not go home without her son. When Francis found her she would hire a car from Dublin airport to take them to Dunross, even if her cancer was so advanced that she could barely walk. She would not care what pain she was in, but she would not go home without him.

The drugs were drawing her under. There would be no dreams tonight and Ellen would be here when she woke. She would tell Ellen about hearing a car crash in her mind and beg her to phone every hospital in Dublin. She did not know what name her firstborn had been given by those strangers; all she had was a date of birth. She could only pray that he was not badly hurt and whatever pain he was suffering might be passed on to her to endure. But in her soul she knew that he was not dead: Francis was one day closer to finding her.

Chapter Three

If I were to frame an imaginary self-portrait from those weeks immediately after the crash I would shoot it – using no flash and with a long exposure – down the hallway of my terraced house, lit only by moonlight filtering through the fanlight above the front door. The foreground wall would be lined with framed photographs leading to the small downstairs toilet where I sit, barely discernible amid the shadows, occupying only one corner of the lens as I stare out into the hallway. The weak shaft of moonlight would draw the viewer's eye and only on a third or fourth glance would they notice my indistinct figure, gazing out with haunted eyes, barely in the picture at all.

That was how I felt in those first weeks at home. This self-portrait was imaginary because I had never taken a portrait of myself or willingly allowed anyone else to take my picture. I was superstitious about which side of the lens I belonged on.

But throughout that January I wasn't sure where I belonged anymore, because my old life no longer seemed to fit. Geraldine was told it was vital to my recovery that I try to rest, at least until I returned to hospital for more tests on my heart. So I slept in the spare bedroom where there was less chance of being disturbed. Sinéad was teething. I regularly woke to the noise of her cries that stopped when Geraldine's footsteps reached the cot. I wanted to get up and take my turn, but my body was so exhausted that I would drift back to sleep instead. By the time I woke the house would have already risen, with Benedict being dressed downstairs before Geraldine rushed up with my breakfast on a tray after Sinéad had been fed.

The spare bedroom doubled as my storeroom, crammed with discarded lens boxes, contact sheets and unanswered correspondence. It felt strange to wake up amid the bric-a-brac of my previous life, possessions that had seemed too important to throw out, though they would never be used again. I told Geraldine that I was too weak to see anyone, but in truth I was in hiding in that spare bedroom, listening to the sounds of life continuing downstairs without me. My medication meant that I regularly drifted into unconsciousness and would wake, disorientated, as Geraldine entered the room with a tray. I didn't want to see anyone except her and the children. I didn't want to have to discuss the miracle of my survival, to talk about the experience of being clinically dead. When callers came to the door my breathing would quicken and tightness would grip my chest. Panic attacks, the doctor called them. My body would shake before Geraldine would close the door and run upstairs to take my hand, fighting her own fear as she calmed me down.

My life before the crash had been neatly divided in two. For three days each week I had worked under contract for a national newspaper. This regular income purchased me the time to work on my own projects and private obsessions; taking sequences of pictures that were regularly exhibited in photographic galleries at home and abroad, but could never generate enough income for my family to live on.

I knew I had deadlines and commitments; a forthcoming exhibition in Berlin that I had been obsessed with before Christmas. But I found it impossible to concentrate on my work now. I could not even properly discuss my feelings with Geraldine, although I knew how my silence hurt her, how every time she closed my bedroom door her smile surely faded into a look of glazed exhaustion. Some nights I woke to find her kneeling by my bed, wanting me to wake so that she could put her arms around me. Her smile when I opened my eyes was filled with relief and elation. This was the time to talk to her, like we used to talk so openly when our bodies were first drenched with sweat after sex, but I did not have the words to explain my new sense of dislocation.

But sometimes I woke alone and made my way downstairs to sit in the dark in that spare toilet and try to think my way out of my malaise. This house had been built in the 1920s. I sometimes wondered if the ghosts of previous owners still existed here; if they had been among the welcoming faces I saw when my heart stopped. Perhaps the painkillers were disorientating me, but some nights I sensed that the walls were breathing back out these past lives; that, if my eyes could readjust, this empty hallway was a blur of continuous movement. Black-booted children stomping across lino; a toddler shuffling in his father's shoes; a woman opening the door to allow her husband wheel his bicycle through the house; a girl allowing herself to be pressed back against the hall door and kissed. The past lives that I could only guess at by the names and dates on the deeds. I should be gone too, but I had been given this second chance. So why could I not rejoice instead of sitting in the dark, framing imaginary self-portraits as if I desperately need to prove that I still existed?

*

For me the hardest part of putting together an exhibition of my work was writing the programme note, because I have never been able to summon concise definitions of the themes that pervade my work, even though I know what I am after in my head. My photographs are moments snatched from the chaotic randomness of life. They are about control and ownership of memory: brief skirmishes in an ongoing war against the headlong slippage of time. I will never win the war, but occasionally, in how I manage to encapsulate one split second, I win a tiny battle by creating an image that I can stand over, that tells the truth as I see it instead of the version of truth being fed to me. The only time I ever feel truly in control is when I am behind a camera. Even as a child I broke the world down into frames for safety's sake. Confronted by a teacher or a bully, I would put my hands up to my face and cut him down to size, framed between my fingertips.

None of my father's photographs were displayed at home. But once, when he lifted me up into the attic as a young boy, I glimpsed the neat stacks of old negatives and the darkroom chemicals that he no longer used. However, I had little idea of how he spent the years before my birth up in that attic, using developer and fixer to play with the alchemy of light and shade in intimate streetscapes of Dublin that were never appreciated. The few examples of his early work that survive are like mirrors held up to the Ireland of his day. If that Ireland had seen them it would have done what any primitive tribe does when forced to confront themselves in a mirror – run away screaming. To adopt a child from the Catholic Protection Agency you needed to show that you were a responsible adult with a proper job. By the time I grew up I simply saw my father as a man who drove a van for a company that sold postcards.

When I was nine I started cutting out coupons from the back of the cornflakes boxes and storing them in my bedside locker. It was several weeks before my mother realised that I saving them up to buy a cheap camera on offer from the cereal company.

'Sure, your father used to be a photographer,' she said. 'Why didn't you ask him? I'm sure he has an old camera somewhere in the attic. He might teach you how to use it.'

But I went on collecting the coupons. My father's name was never credited on any of the postcards he sold, just the Italian name of the small company he worked for. However, occasionally if we passed

a postcard rack outside a shop he would point out some image that
was his. Those clichéd images of Ireland held no interest to me: cliffs
at sunset, O'Connell Street with dark green open-deck buses. The
printing process had rendered them artificially garish, with bizarrely
inflated colours adding to the static sense of unreality. Maybe the
original images had been good, but they were carefully doctored
by his boss – the famous Enrico Pezzani – to represent an Ireland
that had already vanished before they were taken; an Ireland that
had never really existed; a carefree landscape of red sunsets where
anything awkward could be airbrushed away.

This was why I wanted my own camera to take my own photographs. I didn't want Dad to have them developed at work and
brought home to be spread out for inspection like a school report.
As I waited for the cheap camera to arrive I kept visualising the shots
I wanted to take. When it finally came in the post it contained a free
film. I used up the film within an hour, but I went on pretending
I had film left, getting neighbours to pose in their gardens, waiting
at the corner for the bus to pull out and the conductor to toss a
ticket-roll to the shouting boys, my finger clicking away as I framed
the long ticket-roll fanning out in the wind.

The chemist had a display of Old Spice and talc in his window
against a backdrop of red crêpe paper. A machine told your weight
for a penny. There was a smell of dust and dried wood. He was
never visible when I entered his shop. I had to wait, beside trays
of combs and barley sweets, while he counted pills into coloured
bottles behind the partition.

'Can't your father develop this for you free in work?' he asked
when I handed him the film. When I said nothing, he winked.
'Secret documents, is it? You're not spying for the Russians?'

It took four days for the film to be developed. Each afternoon I
called to the chemist in case it came early. I had my pocket money
saved up in a small pile of coins beside the Sacred Heart lamp at
home. The pictures were bitterly disappointing. The objects that

my eyes had focused in on were only tiny blurs in the background. The chemist told me that they cost four shillings and seven pence. There were grey threads of hair on his white coat. His face looked like granite. I promised to bring him the money the next day but instead I used my stash of coins to buy another roll of film from a chemist in the village. I torn up the original photographs on the way home and told my mother they had not come out. When the second roll of film was as bad as the first I told no one. The camera was junk. It could never capture what I wanted. I smashed it and buried it in a hole in the back garden, with no stone on top to mark the spot.

*

This would be my second self-portrait, taken in a converted attic over a shop. It has blackout blinds which can be pulled down to make it a darkroom. I kneel cross-legged on the floor as if totally immersed in the piles of contact sheets spread around me It is only when the viewer stares closely that they see the glazed, withdrawn look in my eyes.

By the 1st of February I still wasn't working. I was hiding: I wasn't sure from what. The newspaper kept up my contract, the odd small cheque arrived in the post, and every day I walked to this private studio with the aid of a stick, trying to break through my lethargy and get back into the swing of my busy life. But I felt disconnected from everything. In movies men wake up from accidents with amnesia. They stare at women who claim to be their wives, at children who call them father. If only they could remember some names and dates, they think, everything else would come back as before. I could remember every detail of my life before the crash, but it was as if they had happened to somebody different from the person I now was.

The deadline for the Berlin exhibition had passed, as had the date for the photo supplement for a magazine in Sweden. I had always thrived on deadlines, never missing one, but now I felt becalmed, unable to respond to the urgent reminders that arrived every day in the post. I would go into the studio every morning full of resolution, but slowly be sucked into endless sifting through reams of contact sheets, searching for one face that had to be there.

Amid all the rooting I managed to unearth the negatives from the roll of film I had taken in the Botanic Gardens when I was ten. I had always presumed them long thrown out, until I found the scratched negatives carefully preserved among my father's papers after his death. I had not visited those gardens since the crash, yet they frequently featured in my dreams in vibrant colours.

My studio was near the fruit markets behind Capel Street. Forklift trucks filled the narrow street outside, sacks of carrots and onions being loaded into vans. Plywood cartons lay smashed on the pavements. One evening I stood up from the piles of contact sheets and walked to the window. A businessman in a Crombie coat emerged from a doorway, pausing to joke with two suppliers. I watched him take a roll of banknotes from his pocket and count them carefully into the palm of one supplier. The other supplier passed around cigarettes and they all lit up, their heads framed by the electric light coming from the warehouse loading bay in the dusk. Their confident masculine world brought back the memory of my father with a sharp and painful sense of loss. I could visualise him at a bar counter in Donabate during the summer when I worked with him, laughing at a shopkeeper's terrible jokes and agreeing that Neil Blaney was the man to put manners on the Brits. He would have agreed to anything to get that shopkeeper's order; he had the true salesman's ability to change his opinion a dozen times a day. And I could remember us driving over the humpback bridge by the railway station as we left Donabate and how he winked at me and kissed the crumpled order in his hand.

'You'll like it here, son.' It was his voice that I had heard in the limbo after the crash. 'You'll like it here.'

Where was 'here'? With no oxygen getting to my brain, had my nervous system simply gone into overdrive, releasing hallucinogenic endorphins, having a farewell party before oblivion? This was the logical chemical reason for what I had experienced. The word endorphin was concocted from two words – endogenous and morphine; in full flow, natural endorphins could be a hundred times more powerful than any man-made analgesic. They had allowed me to hear the voices I wanted to hear, to see the faces I had loved. They had granted me the final perfect dream, the chance to fool myself on the precipice of oblivion. They could explain everything, except the identity of the one face which kept haunting my sleep.

The businessman climbed into his car. Lights were being switched off, steel shutters clanged down. How could I go back home to Geraldine and the children and try to focus on nappy rash and teething? I wanted my father back as he had been that summer when I worked as his van boy; the certainty of that male world of salesmen; the thrill I had felt at being allowed to illicitly ride on the open foot-plate as we careered past hedgerows in small lanes with insects crashing into my face and my hair blown back.

It was time to go home, but I couldn't seem to leave. Instead I resumed my search through old boxes of photographs, scanning contact sheets and negatives for the face that had confronted me when I was clinically dead. Finally I glanced up in my empty studio; unable to articulate what was disturbing me. My breath started to quicken, my chest grew tight. The first symptoms of a panic attack. My doctor had told me how to counter them, but I was terrified of being trapped alone there, at the mercy of some illusory presence. I left the studio, leaning heavily on my stick as I limped down the stairs towards home.

*

On the afternoon of my eleventh birthday a bus turned over on the main street of the village. My class had been unleashed from school and we ran shouting through the church grounds to push through the crowd. There were shards of glass everywhere. A woman screamed hysterically while the ambulance driver tried to reassure her that her daughter would be all right. A man with his head bandaged sat on the pavement with his back to a lamppost. His eyes were closed as the cigarette smoke came out from his nostrils. He inhaled with intense concentration. From the way his foot hung it was obvious that it was broken.

A man in an anorak was walking slowly around the scene. People made way for him, the police and ambulance men never stopping him like they did with everyone else. When he reached the figure slumped against the lamppost the injured man straightened himself up. His hand unconsciously tidied back his hair as he stared up into the camera lens. The man in the anorak clicked three times, then lowered the camera. Both men grinned, as though sharing a private joke, before the photographer moved on.

'Which paper?' the injured man called after him.

'*The Evening Herald*. I'll make sure you're in it.'

'Do you want my name so?' The injured man shrugged off the ambulance men who were trying to lift him on to a stretcher. But the photographer just kept walking towards his next subject, his silence making the man's question seem childish. Watching him, I knew who I wanted to be when I grew up.

That evening I waited for my birthday present, growing more excited as I realised the gift was so significant that my mother was waiting until my father came home before she gave it to me. Yet although they had a cake for me with candles and sang 'Happy Birthday', no present was produced. Instead there was a nervous tension between them all evening. I was dressing for bed when my parents entered my bedroom. By now my excitement was replaced by anxiety. I could sense how they were both waiting for the other to speak.

'You know that we love you more than anything in the world,' my father began.

I had always taken their love for granted. Something in his tone made me feel deeply uncomfortable.

'And you know how proud we are to call you our son. That's what you are and that's what you'll always be. And in years to come, when we are dead, this house and everything else we own will belong to you alone.'

My father hesitated and looked at my mother sitting at the end of the bed. She took my hand but said nothing, leaving my father to continue.

'Remember when you were small and you asked us where you came from? We always said you were found among the leaves in that potato bed in the back garden. You're older now, I know the way lads your age talk in school, you probably know a lot by now.'

'From Mammy's tummy… I know.'

I was embarrassed. I did not want a present anymore: I wanted them to leave. This was the sort of dirty talk that belonged in the school shed where Joe Sheridan from my class kept a copy of *Titbits* hidden.

'No. Not from your mammy's tummy.'

My father stopped, unsure of how to continue.

'I mean, yes. Yes, from a woman's tummy, but… son, I'm no good at this sort of thing. But listen, we have to tell you now because many people on the street know and we don't want you to be hurt by finding out from their children. The thing is that sometimes men and women want children with all their heart, but God's a peculiar class of being… He has his own reasons and we don't know what they are… but often He doesn't let those men and women have children of their own. And then there are other women, you see, who don't want children at all and those women only have to spit sideways before God blesses them with the gift that He wouldn't give to us.'

My father was not a man to say much at home. I watched him stand awkwardly before me. I knew that he didn't want to be here.

I also knew that what he was trying to say would change things between us forever.

'Do you understand what I'm trying to tell you, son? You are as much our son as if you came from your mother's tummy… I mean… we love you just the same, it makes no difference to us…'

'But I have another mother?' I asked.

'No, not anymore. I mean you once had…'

My mother gripped my hand tighter.

'And you still have,' she said. 'You always will. You have two mothers and I can't tell you who she is or where she is, except that she was nineteen when she had you and from Laois and I was never even meant to know those facts. But I pray for her every night because she brought you into the world for us.'

'And why did she not want to keep me?'

The hurt in my voice startled me. My father was silent, anxious to shift the responsibility for this conversation onto my mother. I suddenly realised that these terms were inaccurate: I was no longer sure what I should call them.

'Maybe she did want you,' my mother said. 'Maybe she just couldn't keep you. We're trying to be as honest with you as we can, Sean. I know this is difficult, but you're eleven years of age now. We don't know why she gave you up for adoption. She was a young girl; she must have been in trouble. She had no husband probably or there could have been a dozen other reasons. All we know is that you were six weeks old when the woman from the agency gave you to me, you were wrapped up in a blue blanket in a blue outfit and you were the most beautiful sight I had ever seen. We were able to give you a proper life here, you see. That poor girl could give you nothing except shame and disgrace.'

'Who was the woman? From what agency?'

'Mrs Lacey… you know, the nice woman who calls to see me every six months.'

'Mrs Lacey gave me to you?'

My voice was scared. This was too vast to take in. Twice a year Mrs Lacey came to visit my mother and I would be summoned into the sitting room to stand before her. Mrs Lacey would praise how well I looked but I hated those visits because my mother seemed nervous for days beforehand and her anxiety always made me uneasy as I stood there, feeling somehow under inspection.

'Mrs Lacey works for The Catholic Protection Agency. It's part of her follow-up work to check that you're happy, that you're being looked after.' My mother squeezed my hand tighter.

'Could Mrs Lacey take me back? I mean, who owns me? How do you know this other woman won't find me again?'

'Your other mother knows absolutely nothing about us, not even what your name is. It's been eleven years since she signed you away. Even if she could find you she has no legal claim on you. You're our child. But she has her own life now, her own family maybe. She would never dare to tell her husband that you exist.'

'We have a present for you,' my father butted in as though he could no longer bear this conversation. 'That cheap camera you got was no good. If you're a big enough boy to know secrets, then you're big enough to work this.'

He went out to the landing and came back with his old camera which he placed on the bed. He must have spent hours polishing it up. The lens glittered in the light. There was a steel shutter and all kinds of markings and lettering like on a telescope. It felt heavy in my hand and solid. I raised it up to my eye. My parents stood caught in the viewfinder, distant and reduced to adoptive parents now, trapped into hesitant smiles.

Chapter Four

The next imaginary portrait I would take of myself occurs outdoors in late February. The shot is lit by a slant of early morning sunlight casting long shadows across the grass from a mishmash of half-capsized tombstones. The side gate is open to the small burial ground that surrounds Drumcondra Protestant church. Even older stones lie against the wall, listing indecipherable virtues of eighteenth-century Dublin gentlemen. A gravel path twists past the small church and I lean against the tumbledown wall there, balancing my weight carefully, as I hold a small boy on my shoulders. In one hand I hold the walking stick that I now use more from habit than necessity. The child points with intense concentration at mechanical diggers working on the foundations of a new apartment block being built in the derelict site beyond the wall.

Even at three years of age Benedict knew there was something mysterious about the graveyard. On our morning walks he would often stop outside the Cat and Cage pub and point down Church Street, pulling at my arm and asking to go to what he called 'the strange place'. I never told him precisely what a graveyard was, because for now death had no place in his vocabulary. He just loved to play on the gravel path, making mounds of small stones and breaking them up again with a stick. Or sometimes we stood at this wall to watch the construction work and the workmen with hard yellow hats might pause to call out and wave to him. He would bury his face in the safety of my hair, suddenly shy but also thrilled at being addressed by them, because his greatest desire was to be a builder one day.

During my stay in hospital he had grown whiney, wanting to keep a nappy on all day even though he had worn one only at night for the previous three months. At bedtime he had cried for me, hanging out of Geraldine and sobbing 'give Daddy back'. Yet when she drove with him to the hospital to collect me, he had not wanted to talk about my injuries, but merely announced in an excited tone that he had seen a tractor on the way there. His only acknowledgement of the crash was that he went out to the garden and found himself a stick to match the walking stick I was using. For the first few weeks that I was back home I watched him walk to the shops beside Geraldine, leaning on his stick in the exact way that I did, refusing to be parted from it.

Now some mornings before I went to my studio I brought him for a walk around Drumcondra. We would sit on the bench outside St Patrick's College, immersed in spotting motorbikes and big trucks with trailers among the heavy traffic on the main Belfast Road. Or else we searched Griffith Park for men working on the two tractors in use there. He was obsessed with tractors. His concentration when he searched for them was total; the delight when he found his favourite red one completely illuminated his face.

During the last week in February I finally developed the last shots I took before the crash. They had been intended for a feature on homelessness in Dublin, a look at one day in the life of a man sleeping rough in winter. The images were stark and technically skilled. In one, a burst of light poured through a crack in a sheet of corrugated iron over the window of the derelict joinery where the man slept under a pile of newspapers. In another I had experimented with a long exposure to avoid using a flash and yet compensate for the absence of light under a railway bridge as he raised a flagon of cider to his lips. In the last shot he had lifted his face to stare with cold eyes into the heart of the lens.

With that stare, the man had ceased to just be himself. His mixture of resignation, loneliness and defiance made him momentarily represent every man who ever crouched in despair in the rain. Yet, looking at the contact sheet, I knew I had failed. There had been no real communication between us as I worked and he waited to be allowed to disappear back into his loneliness. The feature on homelessness had been due to appear opposite the fashion page in the newspaper. My shots were a sop to sentimentality by the editor, something different to fill the space between advertisements. I had children now and responsibilities, with my camera lens for hire. That was what made the man's stare so haunting: despite my alleged concern he knew that he had my measure.

Ten years ago I would have spent the day with him: I would have lifted his flagon to my own lips and drank without wiping it. And he would have talked openly about his life, not through any sense of shared experience, but because I would have arrived on an old bicycle, obviously working only for myself. He would have grown relaxed and a little contemptuous as he let me click away, convinced that my photographs would never be seen by anyone else.

But on the day I photographed him I was working against a deadline, trying to remember to collect a cream for the baby in the chemist on my way home. I had shied away from his misery, so focused on catching the light and on how the curvature of the bridge echoed his bent head as he drank, that I had ceased to focus on him as a human being. After I developed the shots I set fire to them, watching the flames splutter into blues and greens in the half-light of the studio. Then I burned almost all every photograph I had taken in the months before Christmas. They all looked stale and bogus now, because everything felt stale, except those morning walks with Benedict.

As he sat on my shoulders in Drumcondra churchyard, his fascination with everything he saw was infectious. The webbed wheels of
a JCB glinted in the light, with rainbow slicks of oil in the puddles
formed among the mud on the building site. I was teaching him the
names of the objects we looked at, but he was teaching me how to
see them anew. His world possessed an eternal freshness without the
shadow of death. These misshapen tombstones were no more than
crooked stones to him and only when alone with him did I feel fully
at ease, in a world where all questions could be answered by naming
a new object. With him I was never suddenly swamped with loss at
having been brought back to life again.

When I was with Geraldine, however, it was more complicated.
For the past two months she had been trying to shield me from the
pressure of decisions, but there were everyday problems we urgently
needed to discuss: car insurance, hospital bills, our bank overdraft
with little income coming in, choosing a school for Benedict. I tried
to engage with these problems, but my comments were only half-
hearted, putting all the decisions back on her shoulders. I knew this
was unfair, but I seemed unable to be drawn back into the present.
I was hiding in my own world, engaged with my own preoccupa-
tions. One night she finally broke down.

'Sometimes I think you wished you'd never survived that crash.
Apart from the scare about your heart and a few minor injuries, you
walked away scot-free. It was a miracle, yet half the time you just sit
there, barely bothering to talk to me.'

How could I explain how I had come back to life changed, no
longer able to focus on the small republic of love we had carefully
built up? I was too haunted by the gaps in my knowledge about a
totally different life, about which she knew nothing. I was
lying awake at night, dwelling on the mystery surrounding my
birth mother. For six weeks that nineteen-year-old girl must have
nursed me, probably sleeping with me in a wooden cot beside her
bed, being woken by my cries and feeding me at night in some

dormitory. I knew that she signed me away more than three decades ago, but no matter what new life she had made for herself, could she have forgotten me?

Was I born of rape or incest? Had she seen the eyes of some man she hated whenever she looked into my pupils? Or had my birthday been celebrated secretly in the years since then, a woman alone in a locked bathroom furtively eating a slice of cake while her family moved about the house, oblivious to her tears and her secret? Perhaps she never married, had drifted into drink and loneliness until found frozen to death under cardboard behind a railway station in some foreign city? Maybe that was why I had not been able to focus emotionally on that homeless man during the shoot before Christmas, maybe subconsciously he reminded me too much of the gaps in my own life, of loose ends and a secret shame that I had spent years shielding myself from.

I remembered Peter McHugh, a hard-edged self-made millionaire I once photographed, talking to me about being reared in an orphanage. 'Your mothers were all prostitutes,' a nun told him repeatedly. 'If you ever meet your mothers after you leave the safety of this orphanage, you should spit in their faces.'

When I was young, my feelings towards my birth mother were dominated by a fear that she might return and snatch me away from the new parents who loved me. I had rarely allowed myself to think about her because I could not bear the sense of abandonment. I blocked her out, like Benedict had already blocked my crash from his mind. I had not wanted to understand what may have happened to her, because I was too busy proving that I was someone else. As a helpless child I had possessed no control over my fate, so as an adult I had determined to be totally in command of my life. Before Benedict was born I had rarely thought about her, although once when I was accepting an international press photographer award in Brussels, I remember being surprised by an overwhelming longing that – whoever and wherever she now was – she would see me being acclaimed on the television news that night, even if she could not possibly know that the man making an acceptance speech in broken French, with the taste of calf's brain and champagne on his tongue, was actually her son.

Occasionally in the past I had wondered if she wished to contact me, but although I knew it was impossible for her to find me, I still convinced myself that she would have found some way to make herself known, if she did wish to do so. Generally though she had rarely entered my thoughts, partly because of a fear that, if I did ever find her, she might reject me again. It was simpler to file her away in my mind as an invisible woman who had long since forgotten about me.

Only when I became a parent did I start to imagine what my absence from her life might feel like. During the first months of Benedict's life I often woke and knelt beside his cot, holding my breath as I strained to hear him breathe, and feeling such elation and relief at the faint sound of his breathing that nothing else in the world seemed of any consequence. Even though she had signed me away, whenever she woke for years afterwards she must have instinctively listened out for my breathing. She had been nineteen years old and from Laois. This was all the information my parents ever told me. Laois was the one county in which I avoided taking assignments: even when driving through it I was ill at ease until a roadside sign welcomed me to Kildare or Tipperary. Twice I got speeding tickets on the long straight of road between Portlaoise and Mountrath. 'What are you running from?' the traffic cop asked when he flagged me down the second time. 'Have you held up a bank or something?'

Beyond the wall of Drumcondra churchyard the JCB tilted its bucket down into the loose muck. The sun disappeared behind rain clouds. I lifted Benedict off my shoulders and hugged him suddenly, so tightly that after a moment he complained that I was hurting him. I put him down and he knelt to play with the loose pebbles on the path. I wanted to pick him up again and hug him and never let him out of my sight. Instinctively I knew that at least once during the first six weeks of my life, my birth mother had felt a similar protective surge of emotion towards me. Previously I had wanted evidence and proof, I had prevaricated and distanced myself, but at that moment I knew, from my intense love as I watched Benedict playing, that for decades she had been waiting for me to find her. I knelt beside him and he handed me a small twig, permitting me to take part in his game.

'Can we go walking tomorrow?' he asked.

'Yes. Where would you like to go?'

'Where you never bring me,' he said. 'The garden with the big gates.'

*

The first gull landed on the concrete and tore at the plastic Downes' Bakery wrapper. The gull had worked the crust of bread out when another gull snatched it away from him. The two birds rose, squabbling in the air, as other gulls landed to devour the scraps left after lunch in the schoolyard. While this was going on, my class was being arrayed by height into five rows on the steps, boys pushing each other and pulling faces as the teacher bent to speak to the photographer who had come to take the annual class photo. The man was crouched over his tripod when I stepped away from the back row. I walked a few steps towards the prefabs, sensing the other boys turning, the whole class dissolving into disarray. Even when the teacher screamed at me to step back into place I refused. I was scared of the attention, terrified of the leather in the teacher's pocket. But my new fear of staring into a lens was more overpowering – the fear was both irrational and primitive. Only the presence of the photographer was saving me from being beaten, but still I refused to be part of that photograph.

The light was dim in the headmaster's office. My legs would not stop shaking. The headmaster kept his back turned to me. I could imagine my mother in the hallway of one of our few neighbours who possessed a phone, her fright at having been summoned from across the street to take the call.

'So you only told him the news recently?' the man said. 'You think he might be reacting to it? I'll have to consider this matter.'

Everybody had always known, I realised; people had talked behind my back in the shops, at school, in church. That's why the chemist had said nothing when I never paid him for developing the photos: what else could he expect from a boy who came from God knows what class of people? Outside in the school corridor a brass bell was ringing. I knew that this time I would not be beaten.

The headmaster put down the phone and looked at me in silence for a long time. Then he said there was now a black mark against my name and he was going to write a note to my parents saying that I was not to return to school for three days. I walked out the school gate and down the main street. I walked down the dual carriageway where the forest had once been. I was an outlaw, a loner, the boy with the black mark against his name. I reached the Tolka River. There was a slaughterhouse on the far bank, opposite the pitch-and-putt course, with offal and bright blood splattering from an open waste pipe down into the river. I watched the note I was meant to give my parents bob in the stinking blood-smeared water. I waited all afternoon among the trees until the other boys were released from school. Then I walked home, surrounded by an excited cluster of boys. Two of them had money. Everyone crowded into the small shop where they chose sweets from the jars on the counter. I kept my hands behind my back; rifling chocolate bars, chewing gum, matches; putting anything I could get my hands on down the seat of my trousers. I had never stolen before. In the laneway I distributed them. 'I'm adopted,' I said. The boys nodded as though this excused me everything.

The old family album was kept in a press in the living room. The night after I was suspended, I crept downstairs and waited to see if the click of the living room light would wake my parents. I opened the album. My life was laid out there, dutifully recorded in black and white snaps. On the second page there were three spaces where photographs had been removed. I ran my finger over the grey cardboard on that page as if it could give me a clue about what was being kept from me.

I had always trusted these photographs, badgering my mother to take out the album and retrace each year of my life. I turned to the first page, which held the first ever photograph of me. It was taken among the sand dunes on Dollymount beach in summer. My mother is wearing a swimsuit and a bathing cap. I am three months old. She holds me up for the camera, her face showing pride in her son but also an anxiety to make me smile. Now I knew that this photograph was lying, because I was not her son. Her anxiety had been not just to make me smile but to maintain this illusion that we were an ordinary family. I felt no anger towards her or my father: it was the photograph that I blamed for lying. None of those photographs would ever fool me again. I tore up each one in turn and left the shredded pieces on the table for my parents to find. I went back to bed and then changed my mind. I ran back downwards to draw the bolt on the front door and stand in my bare feet in the garden, watching the wind scatter the torn photos beneath the crooked street lamps.

The Botanic Gardens was the one place that I was never allowed to visit. The next morning I left at house, as if going to school, but I went there instead. A guard was reading a newspaper in the hut inside the gate. I kept my head down as I walked past, in case he asked why I was not at school. I came to the Tolka and watched it fork out into a millrace which joined the river again opposite the rose garden. There was a slope down to a pond with water lilies and a small metal bridge. A gardener with an armband pushed a barrow past me. I stopped on the bridge and lifted my father's camera. I felt both excitement and control as I framed the shot carefully and squeezed the shutter. The click sounded loud and absolute.

For years before this I had been asking my mother to bring me to the Botanic Gardens, but she always made excuses. Because for some reason this place was forbidden, it had become like a secret garden in my mind. A squirrel bobbed through the grass beneath the trees on the slope behind the pond. I knelt like a hunter, drawing him in, patiently waiting until he was only feet from me before I pressed the shutter.

In the past I had wasted film, but during that morning I set up every shot with a precise passion. These pictures were my declaration of difference. I intended to give this roll to my father to have developed in work, so that they would see how I had disobeyed them by going here. I stalked every corner of the Botanic Gardens, finding paths that looked oddly familiar but always finding my way back to the tunnel of gnarled trunks that formed the yew walk. I sat there, waiting for the shouts of girls from the nearby convent to let me know when it was time to go home.

Three nights later my father placed a paper folder on the oilskin cloth of the kitchen table. The photographs spilled out. My mother picked them up, her hands growing agitated as she flicked through them. She glanced at me, her eyes hurt and confused.

'Why weren't you at school?' my father asked.

'I was suspended.'

'Why did you go here?'

'I just did. Why shouldn't I?'

My father looked at my mother and then down at the pictures.

'You have a knack for using a camera,' he said, 'but you're developing a knack for getting into trouble also. These are good pictures, I'll give you that. But if you upset your mother again I'll give you the back of my hand too.'

*

This is my last imagined self-portrait from those becalmed months. I would shoot it from high up near the ceiling of the crowded spare bedroom which I seemed unable to leave. A spur of streetlight comes through a gap in the curtains. My body is curled up in sleep. My rhythmic breathing grows deeper. My body twists again and abruptly I wake. My mouth is open. I begin to suck in air as if drowning. This is where the shutter should click, with my eyes staring up, sharply in focus. But the image breaks free of my control.

As always when I wake, I feel an echo of the incalculable disappointment I experienced at being dragged back to life. But this time my breath comes faster. My chest hurts as I open my mouth wide, trying to snatch in oxygen. My arms are sore, my fingers knotting into cramped shapes. This is a panic attack, I think, trying to remain calm. But it feels different from the other recent attacks, more like a heart attack. They're coming back to claim me, I think; the faces I saw when clinically dead.

My stomach is like a piston, expanding, exhaling. I feel convinced I am going to die. My chest is a tight wedge of pain, my heart feels about to burst. I feel myself being pushed towards those dead faces with each deepening breath. But now I know that I want to live. I'm struggling against the blackness, but it seems to take me over. My torso is lifting itself off the mattress, as if my back is about to break. Suddenly I'm no longer fighting against these deep painful breaths; I'm going with them, hearing the sound of my own breathing as if from a long way off. There is an all-prevailing whiteness and then the whiteness turns blue.

It is the blue of the sea. Physically I am still in the spare bedroom but I am also swimming through dense blue water. I am weightless. I turn my head and a seal swims beside me. I turn the other way and another seal noses against my naked shoulder. A whole shoal swim around me and my body moves with them automatically, surging up towards the green light above the waves, and then plunging

down again towards the seabed where flat fish glide. I am part of
something greater than myself, my companions sensually brushing
against me.

Then I hear Geraldine's voice above the waves; her fear as she
calls to me. I am cresting the waves too fast, my body buckling like
a diver with the bends. I break through the waves and feel the air
crash against my forehead like a blow. Geraldine's arms are trying
to hold me. I want to reach out to her, yet something forces me to
plunge back down into those waves: my mouth frantic to suck in
air. I feel myself sink through the water. Her anxious voice sounds
like a radio being slowly turned off.

All is quiet suddenly as I make out the shape of moonlit trees.
I am high up, gazing down at the gnarled line of ancient trees on
the yew walk in the Botanic Gardens. I am watching myself down
there. I know it is me, only my face is different. My face is the same
face of the surly young man I saw after the car crash. My feet are
bare. There is loose gravel instead of tarmac on the path between
the sloping branches. What age am I? Seventeen perhaps, my head
lolling back, my mouth slightly open. I lean against the knotted
bark of a yew trunk, my arms stretched behind it as if tied. But they
are not tied. I raise them up and slowly place them down on the
cropped hair of the older man who kneels below me. I am inside
this body, staring down at the dark roots of his hair, and yet also up
among the yew branches watching myself playfully push him away.
I turn, trying to straighten my breeches as I begin to run. The man
is behind me, gaining. I want him to catch me and yet I'm scared of
what will happen when he does.

I cross the path, watching out for a hint of the nightwatchman's
lantern and sprint up the steep slope, though I know that this path
ends in a cul-de-sac. My body hits the wooden fence at the end. I
try to climb the fence, knowing that the older man will easily catch
me. He is stronger, able to turn me around in his arms. I feel his
stubble as he presses his lips against mine, forcing me to open my

mouth. I can't breathe now. It is like he is consuming me, trying to place a hangman's black sack over my face. I feel terror and yet giddy excitement. Distantly I can hear Geraldine calling me. The man's hands are pushing me down onto my knees. I am choking in this blackness. I raise my hands to my face and the skin crinkles like thick brown paper. My breathing is slowing down. The side of my face hurts. I move my hand and realise that my face is covered by a paper bag. Geraldine takes hold of my hand and slowly removes the bag from over my head.

'It's okay,' she says, 'Sean, you're okay; you've stopped hyperventilating. You've had another panic attack. When you start to breathe quickly it over-oxygenises the brain. I had to make you breathe into a paper bag, so you could breathe without getting any fresh oxygen. Take a few slow breaths now, Sean, you had me terrified. It was like you were here with us and yet somewhere else.'

I am lying on the carpet. The light seems blinding overhead. There is blood inside my mouth.

'You banged your head against the wall with all the thrashing,' she says. 'This can't go on, Sean.'

I look towards the bedroom doorway. Benedict stands there, too terrified to cry.

'Go back to bed, son,' I say. 'I just had a bad dream.' He goes away and I look at Geraldine. 'I've lived before. I had another name, a different life.'

'What do you mean, Sean?'

What do I mean? That this face haunting me since the accident is actually my own face from a previous existence? Maybe with such a blank canvas for a past my mind is concocting a fantasy to fill this need to know who I am. How can I explain to Geraldine this new sense of having lived in a past life, when I have never been able to tell her the truth about my present life? How can I say that I have been lying to her for years, that she doesn't truly know who I am because I don't truly know?

'Promise me you'll see someone,' Geraldine whispers, 'a counsellor or a therapist. It's like you left here on the morning of that crash and you've never really come back to us.'

Chapter Five

My childhood career as a thief was short-lived. After my second heist the woman from the shop came running out behind us. The other boys scattered as she chased with unerring instinct after me. I careered between the cars on the main road, almost getting killed before I managed to lose her. She never went to the headmaster, but within hours the whole school knew. I was too scared to try to rob anything ever again but it no longer mattered. Within my primary school I now had the reputation for being dangerous. I clashed with teachers, getting blamed for trouble whether I caused it or not. I welcomed my new reputation because if people were talking about me as a troublemaker it might stop me simply being known for being adopted. But I wasn't going to shed my identity so easily. People always found ways to bring up my past. Corcoran, the oldest teacher there, whose yellowing toupee clashed with the grey remnants of his hair, patrolled the yard using his loud voice as a weapon. His standard roared threat, 'I will speak to your mother about you', would frighten any boy. But when I disobeyed an order, every boy understood his subtle insult when he shouted at me: 'I will speak to Mrs Blake about you.'

Older boys, confident that they were strong enough to beat me in a fight, followed his lead. 'What sandwiches did Mrs Blake give you for lunch?' they would ask. 'Jam? I bet she would have given you ham if you were her real son.' They would lean against the shed wall, defying me to throw the first punch.

The way they emphasised how I was different scared me, but also gave me an odd sense of power and detachment. But after I had passed the entrance exam to secondary school, my father's sister, Aunt Cissie, persuaded my parents to let me leave primary school two months early. 'Leave him there any longer,' she said, 'and he'll be expelled with a blot on his record.'

During chats in her kitchen, around the corner from our own house, Aunt Cissie convinced my father to exaggerate my age and get me a summer job as a van boy, working with him under a bogus name. What did they expect those three months of work to do for me? Straighten me out? Cure my disruptive streak which had me in trouble every week? I wonder if his wife or his sister knew that my father's personality changed when he passed the gates of Pezzani's Postcard Company every morning, that he become someone different, donning the bright waistcoat he kept on a coat-hanger in his van.

'Wait outside here for five minutes,' he said at the gates on my first morning. 'I don't want people seeing us arrive together. Mr Pezzani doesn't allow us to employ relations. From now on you're not my son; you're just a van boy I've taken on.'

If I was not his son, he most certainly didn't seem like my father as he joked with the other salesmen in the yard. We had barely left the premises when he stopped around the corner, so that a workman from the factory could sneak through the gap in the wire fence and smuggle us out a box of rejected postcards. I spent the morning in the back of the speeding van, carefully replacing one good postcard from each packet of twelve with a faulty card, to make up extra sets for him to sell for cash using a bogus invoice book.

Our relationship began to change in the new masculine world of work. I had been hurt when he insisted on me pretending not to be his son, thinking he might be ashamed of the fact that I was adopted, but I discovered that in places like Drogheda and Bettystown he wasn't even married.

'It's well for you two bachelors,' the women behind the counter would say and wink at me. 'If you listen to this driver long enough, you'll break every girl's heart in Ireland.'

Soon I realised that I was seeing my father as he had been before he married. Real life ceased to exist for him when he climbed into his van. Instead he entered a world of illusion and salesmanship. With elderly shopkeepers in Skerries he was a devout Catholic, talking about his work in the Legion of Mary. In Balbriggan he stamped his fist on the counter along with a young bearded shopkeeper and swore that the 1970s would be socialist red with Labour. The Beatles were after breaking up that summer; the New Seekers singing 'Say goodbye, my own true lover'. Every day my father wound down his window to sing 'Happy Days are Here Again' to pensioners queuing for early dinners in Butlins' Holiday Camp. They invariably scowled at him as we drove past.

Fiddling the books seemed like a religion to every van driver who worked that route along the necklace of villages and holiday resorts that hugged the North Dublin coastline. We were a race apart, meeting at lay-bys to compare notes on which shopkeepers were the sharpest to deal with and to swap contraband: soft drinks, crisps, ice cream, plastic sunglasses, fish fingers, postcards, and, on one occasion, two goldfish in a plastic bag which my father and I left tied to a bush outside a school. I discovered that my father filled his day with a succession of small bets on horses. Between three cross doubles, lucky fifteens, accumulators, trebles and yankees I learned more about maths by running bets for him than I had learned at school. My father and I called at chemist shops to collect holiday films to be developed and at hotels and shops to sell racks of postcards.

Outside every shop his question was the same, 'Did you count

McHenry's postcards?' McHenry was his obsession: a salesman for a rival company, with a pioneer pin to proclaim his pious status as a teetotaller. My father claimed that McHenry was so cute he turned the windscreen wipers off passing under bridges to save money.

After focusing so hard on not calling my father 'Da' at work, it was hard to remember not to call him Eddie at home. Whenever I did, it upset my mother. The money I was earning made me flippant. I sometimes tried to keep up our camaraderie when we were back at home and use the language we used on the road. But my father was different there, shrunk back into the quiet man I had always known. Once, after my mother left the room, upset at some remark of mine, I suddenly found myself sprawled on the floor. My neck hurt where he had clattered me: the only time he ever did so. 'That was some man-to-man advice,' he said softly. 'Behave yourself.'

That summer the world was flocking to the seaside resorts of Laytown and Bettystown. Caravan parks were materialising in fields where sheep had been grazing a month before. In one of them, a corrugated iron hut normally used to store fodder was pressed into service as a shop. On our second visit there my father found his old racks of postcards taken down and replaced by a revolving plastic stand supplied by McHenry.

'They're lovely new postcards,' the farmer-turned-shopkeeper explained. 'Mr McHenry had two new cards of Laytown especially taken up there on the sand dunes. They're going down a bomb, especially with the Northern shower. No disrespect, but the postcards of Laytown you're flogging were taken donkey's years ago.'

My father silently crumpled up one of McHenry's new postcard in his hand. Two barefoot thirteen-year-old girls were crossing the grass for ice cream. They brushed past me, in bathing suits that didn't quite cover their buttocks. Sensing me staring at them, they giggled. Mortified, I picked up our rejected postcard rack and followed my father back to the van.

'This is war,' he said grimly, 'and I'm not losing it.'

Although I had been working with my father for six weeks, I had yet to speak directly to his boss – the dreaded Mr Pezzani. Pezzani had come to Ireland thirty years ago to haul his own makeshift circus around small Irish towns, an enterprise that unfortunately coincided with Ireland's wettest summer in half a century. When the circus collapsed in a quagmire of mud, leaking tents and bad debts, Pezzani turned to his second great love – photography – and quickly made his reputation in the postcard business by adding in incendiary and virtually hallucinogenic quantities of chemicals when developing his images, so that postcards of drab Irish beaches and one-horse towns became saturated with such dazzling colours that it was as if African sunsets were superimposed on to damp Irish skies. My father always claimed that they were Pezzani's revenge upon the Irish weather that had capsized his travelling circus.

I had only seen Pezzani once, when my father's van broke down and I was sent to work for a few hours in the processing lab where the hundreds of rolls of films, collected from chemists across Dublin every day, were developed. Indelicate shots were edited out and not returned, though few girls who had their pictures taken on visits to Europe's first topless beaches knew that these private snaps usually ended up pinned to the walls in Pezzani's factory. A few mornings after the incident in Laytown we were about to leave the yard when Pezzani suddenly appeared and opened the passenger door of my father's van.

'All right,' he said to my father. 'Today I give you your wish: I shoot new cards of Bettystown and Laytown especially for you. But if you value your balls they had better sell.'

He then stared closely at me and put one hand out to softly touch my face.

'How come you never introduce me to your van boy? He is very Irish looking. I like his freckles. Today you work on your own and the boy works with me.'

His hand brushed softly against my cheek again.

'What freckles, eh? You sure this boy is old enough to be working?'

My father nodded. I felt that Pezzani could sense his unease. I felt pure terror. Pezzani was the fattest man I had ever seen. With my father, work was an adventure. Now suddenly I longed for the safe anonymity of a classroom. My father had no option but to shrug and, with a warning glance to me, drive off alone.

Pezzani's van was tiny. There was a curtain cordoning off the back where something heavy was stored. The steering wheel was almost between his knees. He drove with the window open, refusing to give way to anyone.

'Thirty years ago when I come to Ireland first all the postcards were black and white,' he said as we sped towards Swords. 'So I introduce colour. At first my boss will not print them. Then I give him a good Italian grandson. When he finds out this he gives me his daughter's hand: a bit late, I already have the rest of her. Now we partners, I say, and no more black and white. It's colour, colour, colour. I learn the secret of what the Irish love in their postcards. They love red and red does not work in black and white. Do you like pictures, boy? Today I show you the secret of how to take great pictures.'

Not only did I like pictures, I informed him, but I intended to be a professional photographer one day.

'Like me,' he said.

'No,' I said, with the naive arrogance of a child, 'much better.'

As he put his head back to laugh, the uneasy thought came to me, as it often did when I came into contact with any strange man, that he could possibly be my real father and I would not even know. Often with tramps in the street I found myself searching their features for any reflection of my own. It was the most powerless feeling.

'Everybody thinks they can be the great photographer,' Pezzani was saying. 'Even the man you drive with. At one time he was a good photographer, but I stop him taking photographs when I find out he is a much better salesman. So tell me, Boy Genius, what do you think of the postcards you sell?'

I actually liked many of Pezzani's postcards: they were far more seductive than actual reality. But it felt unsophisticated to say so and also he had insulted my father. Therefore I worked myself up into a passion as I dismissed his most famous images, describing them as clichéd and detailing how I would handle such pictures, using technical terms to try and impress him. Finally I stopped talking because Pezzani was laughing so much that his van kept swaying across the road.

'So you want to show real life, Boy Genius. Well, tough shit, because nobody in Ireland wants to see it. They want mountains and lakes and a splash of red to hide anything unpleasant. They want to feel good about themselves and most especially they want to cover up bad things. The postcards you hate are the ones that sell in thousands. Do you know what sort of photographer you will be, Boy Genius? A starving one! Show Irish people the truth and they will run away screaming.' He swung onto a smaller road. 'Now here we are: Bettystown. I take the photograph and you watch and learn.'

We pulled off the road onto the dunes. The van seemed about to stick in the sand but Pezzani powered it on, defying it to stall. We got out. There was a crowded beach below us. Pezzani knelt on top of a dune and beckoned me beside him.

'We need to wait for the sun to come out from the clouds and catch the water. That will be the moment. The view is nice up here: it will be nicer when I am finished. McHenry is only an amateur: we will bury him. Only one thing is missing and that thing is red.'

He tossed me the keys of his van.

'Go fetch.'

'Fetch what?'

Pezzani waved me impatiently towards the back of the van and busied himself in removing the camera bag from his shoulder. I opened the rear doors of the van. Amid various objects covered in oilcloths and mail sacks there was a large fuchsia bush in a heavy clay pot tied down with ropes. I undid the ropes and lifted it out, staggering under the weight. Pezzani was kneeling on the next dune.

'Now carry the bush down to that spot.' He pointed and watched me struggle down the slope. 'Wait,' he said, 'bring it a few feet more to the left. Perfect. Now scram before we lose the shot.'

The sun briefly emerged from behind a whorl of cloud and I heard a series of clicks. It went in again. Pezzani changed position and waved for me to haul the bush more to my left. I lifted the heavy pot, staggering as I tried to keep my footing in the sand.

'Fuchsia bushes don't grow in sand dunes,' I called back up at him.

'Neither does money. You just move the bush, Boy Genius. Everybody loves the red.'

'It isn't even red,' I argued, 'it's purple.'

'Only in real life,' he snorted dismissively. 'When I print it, it will be red.'

Then it came to me. On almost every postcard we sold a red bush popped up somewhere in the foreground; framing mountain passes in the Ring of Kerry, sunsets over Galway Bay or views of Dublin from the Wicklow mountains. I was hauling around the most famous bush in Ireland.

'Have you a name for this blasted thing?' I said, struggling back up the slope.

'I call it Lire.' he clicked happily. 'My beautiful little red Lire.'

I put the bush down between the tufts of coarse grass. Two girls with candy floss smearing their faces came up to watch us. Their dog barked excitedly and ran over to cock his leg against the clay pot. I kicked out and he retreated, staring back with hurt eyes.

'They're all fakes,' I said. 'Every one of your cards is a forgery.'

Pezzani changed lens and laughed.

'What do you want me to photograph?' he asked. 'Bored children sitting in their caravans in the rain listening to parents fighting? Most people's holidays are miserable, but I give them happy memories. They look at my postcards when they get home and they see these shitty little beaches the way they would like to remember them. I invent soothing lies and they are grateful because it saves them dealing with the truth. What is so wrong with making people happy? Maybe you should give up your dreams of being a photographer and just stick to trying to rob me blind, you and your driver.'

'I… we… never…'

I imagined my father being sacked, though it was my mother's face I saw in my mind: the shame she would feel. I knew that I was not smart enough to be able to give Pezzani the right answers. He laughed at the obvious terror on my face.

'Do you think I'm stupid? All you Irish love to fiddle. I let it happen because your driver makes me a fortune, selling out of his skin, so he can fiddle a pittance on the side.'

'I don't know what you're talking about,' I stammered.

He screwed the cover back on the lens, enjoying my discomfort.

'It will be our secret. If you do as you are told we can pretend we never had this conversation and you can go home a pound richer. Now stick the bush back in the van.'

The girls had disappeared. The sun retreated behind the clouds. It felt cold. I climbed into the van to tie the ropes around the clay pot. When I turned around Pezzani was standing at the door, watching me.

'Now take off those clothes,' he said.

I froze. This was his purpose all along, I thought. Pezzani had trapped me into acknowledging that we had been on the fiddle and now my father could lose his job. I was unable to stop trembling.

'The light will be gone,' he said. 'Hurry up, boy.'

I pulled the jumper slowly over my head. As I undid my shirt

61

buttons I heard him approach. I swallowed hard as I felt something being placed over my head. What if Mrs Lacey found out? Could the agency demand to take me back? I put up my hand. It was a plastic bowl.

'Please…' I said.

Then I felt it, a cold scissors cutting my hair along the rim of the bowl. He lifted the bowl off. My neck felt cold.

'Now we truly see those Irish freckles,' he bellowed cheerfully, climbing out of the van to shout down at somebody on the beach. 'You'll find clothes in that mail sack,' he called back casually; 'they should fit you, more or less.'

Then he was gone. The air felt cold on my legs. I opened the sack. There was a pair of old knee-length breeches and an old-fashioned boy's jacket from the West of Ireland. I put them on, feeling ridiculous as I stepped from the van. Pezzani was coming back up through the dunes, followed by a man who had been giving donkey rides on the beach.

'Beautiful,' Pezzani said. 'But why do you put your shoes and socks back on? The bare feet are lovely. This was my favourite postcard but you say you did not like it. So, especially for you, I make a brand-new one.'

He climbed into the van and began to root underneath the oilcloths. He emerged with an old wicker creel that he placed on the donkey's back. He handed me the reins and we started down towards the beach. Young men playing soccer stopped to wolfwhistle after me. The Rolling Stones blared on the radio. A straggle of children followed us. I kept my face down, furious with myself for blushing. Pezzani and the donkey owner began to haggle over money. We reached the water's edge and Pezzani pushed me forward until I was standing up to my ankles in the waves with the donkey beside me.

'Now gather seaweed,' he said.

'You are not serious,' I said, 'you're taking the piss.'

Pezzani raised his camera.

'You Irish,' he replied, 'almost as much as red bushes you love freckled, barefoot boys with donkeys.'

I looked at him defiantly, refusing to move. He spread out his arms.

'What is it? Are you still calling me a fake? The donkey is as real as you and me. You want to be famous photographer, Boy Genius? Not a hope. But at least I make you into famous photograph. When you are on holidays with your grandchildren you can tell them this is you on the postcard they are buying – Aran Island Boy Gathering Seaweed.'

Chapter Six

Aunt Cissie had trouble walking by now, but her front garden was still immaculately kept. The window frames were painted the same cream colour as they were when I was young: her front door had the same dark varnish. On summer evenings she still hung a tattered striped awning over it, to protect the paintwork from the sun.

It was early March, the first time I had driven a car since the crash. I needed to get behind a wheel again. I told Geraldine not to fuss, that I was only driving two miles to see my aunt, but I was nervous starting the ignition. The Botanic Gardens were not on my route, but I deliberately drove past the gates to make myself confront the crash site. My father's sister put her arms around me when she answered the door, unable to disguise her joy. A scent of baking filled the house. Her hands were coated in flour.

'I heard you were speeding, wee scut. You weren't speeding to see your old aunt, anyway.'

I smiled ruefully. This doorstep was where I had always ended up when in trouble.

'Is there any tea in the pot, Aunt Cissie?'

'Is that wife not feeding you, Sean? You'd better come in so.'

Her hallway looked small and dark. The original wooden light switches had survived several rewirings.

'You have the house looking great, Aunt Cissie. It hasn't changed a bit.'

'It's not worth changing now when I'll hardly see another Christmas.'

'You've been singing that hymn since I was twelve.'

She slapped me playfully on the arm and pushed me into the living room. I could hear the heavy kettle being filled in the kitchen and the whoosh of the gas. When she entered the living room with a tray she had tried to put on lipstick without a mirror and it was smudged. There were traces of flour in her hair where she had run her hands through it. A blessing from Pope Pius XII hung above the television. As a child I remembered trying to decipher the Latin inscription. She produced the best china, and as soon as I took a sup of tea she held the teapot out to refill my cup, almost pouring through my fingers when I indicated that I had enough. I knew she was disappointed I had not called an hour later when the bread in the oven would be ready. Her eyes followed mine to the faded photo of John F. Kennedy on the wall.

'If we'd only known the truth,' she said, wry humour replacing the religious tones with which she used to speak about Kennedy. 'That man could fairly make the bed shake.'

'Have you the piped television now?' I asked.

'The best company in the world,' she said, 'after the women in bingo. You can keep your soap operas; give me the American wrestling to watch. Did I tell you what I've won at the bingo since I saw you last?'

'Not even the price of the bus fare,' I said.

'How did you guess? It's a good thing I have the free travel.'

We laughed. For as long as Aunt Cissie had been saying she would not live to see another Christmas she had been claiming not to have even won the price of the bus fare at bingo. She stopped talking, a familiar smile on her lips as she waited for me to speak. I smiled back, suddenly embarrassed.

Dermot Bolger

'You've never called to see me in your life without a reason, Sean. So say what's on your mind.'

I put down my cup and tried to think of how to begin.

'Do you know that I was clinically dead after the crash?' I asked.

Aunt Cissie nodded gravely.

'I crashed directly outside the Botanic Gardens. Lately I've been thinking that we only lived a mile away from those gardens, yet I can't remember my mother ever setting foot in them. It was like she was scared of the place.'

Cissie poured herself more tea. A butterfly had flown in through the window and kept flapping about in the folds of the lace curtains.

'Your mother could get strange notions,' Aunt Cissie began. 'She was… ashamed isn't the right word… she was uneasy about not being your real mother. All of us other mothers soon forgot you were adopted. You were just another little terror running around the street. But it played on your mother's mind; she'd spend hours when you were a baby comparing how you reacted to her with how our babies reacted to us. She had a notion that you didn't respond to her like a child would respond to his birth mother. She could blow the smallest thing out of proportion. It's hard for any woman with a first child, but for someone as insecure as your mother…' Aunt Cissie paused. 'How old is your son?' she asked.

'Just turned three,' I said.

'Three is a magical age: you can't tell a three-year-old what's real and what's not. God knows, it doesn't seem long since you were three. Do you remember the times I used to mind you here?'

'You minded every child in the neighbourhood.'

'You were more fun than all of them put together: blathering away with a serious face, hands darting in all directions: everything said as solemnly as if you were announcing the end of the world. Your idea of paradise was having the kitchen to yourself, every pot and pan out on the floor and you so serious about pretending to bake that I half expected to see cakes appear in the pans you arranged under the kitchen table. I never met a child with such a vivid imagination.' She paused. It was hard to imagine myself as that intense child or equate this elderly woman with the strong figure I remembered from back then. 'Why do you ask about the Botanic Gardens?'

'I don't know. It's all part of a jigsaw I'm trying to piece together.'

Aunt Cissie's husband had been among the kaleidoscope of dead faces I saw after my heart was stopped. He was a bus conductor who died of a heart attack while digging the garden one Sunday, leaving her with three children who all emigrated in the 1970s to find work. I knew that I could never tell her about seeing his face.

'I used to ask you who the pretend cakes were for,' Cissie said. 'You'd say, "Mamma, Dada, Auntie Cissie, Baba Sean and the old man who lives in the shed." One time for a laugh I told you to run down and ask the old man if he wanted a jam or an apple tart. You raced down the garden as if somebody actually lived in my shed and ran back panting. "A jam tart," you said. "The bits of apple stick in his false teeth." Three-year-old boys don't invent that type of remark. You must have heard someone say it somewhere, but you frightened the wits out of me that day.'

'I don't remember that,' I said. 'The first memory I have is of sitting on a ridge of grass and watching a worm slither in my hand, but I don't know was it in your back garden or my father's.'

'All children invent things,' Cissie said. 'But your imagination was frightening. When you were three your mother brought you to visit her brother's grave, your Uncle Frank. He fought in the British Army in the war, in the Desert Rats, had half his face blown off. I don't know how they patched him up or how he lived so long afterwards. You stared down at the grave and she thought you were examining the flowers she brought when you said: "That man has no ear." She grabbed you and ran all the way home from the cemetery.'

'I must have heard them talk about him,' I said. 'Maybe I expected to be able to see a man lying in the earth.'

The sun went in behind a cloud and it was dark in the room. Suddenly I wished I hadn't come here. Yesterday I had passed workmen restoring the wooden locks at Binn's Bridge on the Royal Canal. I wished I had gone there instead with Benedict, to share his excitement at watching the huge planks being lifted into place.

'I told your mother the same; you probably heard about his injuries and invented the rest. But your mother was from a staunch republican family: Frank's war exploits were not the stuff of conversation. Still, Sean, you were just a child. The cartoons seemed as real to you as people. Don't dwell on these things.'

'Maybe I feel like I survived the crash for a reason,' I said, 'to make amends for something.'

'For years I was expecting a visit like this,' Cissie said, 'but I always thought it would be to ask about your birth mother.'

'I'm thinking about her a lot,' I said. 'I've thought about her more in the last two months than in the past twenty years.'

'Your mother thought about her every day,' Aunt Cissie said. 'She haunted your mother and your mother probably haunted her. It was a different world back then, Sean. We were not brought up to question authority. Things were the way they were and that was that. Your birth mother must have come from poor folk.'

'Why?'

'The nuns were careful to match poor with poor and rich with rich. No rich couple wanted to feel they had a labourer's child in their family. Your parents got a call to go in to the agency. They had been waiting over a year for a child: forms, interviews, inspections of the house. Everything was done through Mrs Lacey, but there was a nun up in the agency from some convent that day, a Sister Theresa. She terrified your mother; God knows what she must have seemed like to the unfortunate girls in her charge. You were six weeks old in a blue outfit. Your mother couldn't wait to take you home, but the nun started to interfere. She kept looking down at you. "A grand healthy child," she said, "but you'll get that from a girl of nineteen." It was obvious Mrs Lacey wanted her to leave, but nuns had such power that nobody could say boo to them. You see, there was meant to be no information given about your birth mother.'

Aunt Cissie's tea was cold, but she took a sip from the cup.

'Just to fill the awkward silence, your father asked if you had your birth mother's eyes. The nun smiled. "No," she replied. "He has lovely blue eyes, thank God, with no trace of that slut at all." Every Christmas morning when your father had a whiskey here, just us two alone, he would curse that nun for being an ignorant bitch.'

It felt like I had only to turn my head to see him here on Christmas mornings: a log fire blazing in the hearth and him sitting there with a whiskey in his hand when I raced in with my mother after Mass to open my present from Aunt Cissie.

'How did they know she was from Laois?'

'Your father never told you?' she asked.

I shook my head. 'Dad and I were never good at discussing things. As I remember it, he generally left anything difficult for you to sort out.'

'Are you your father's son?' Her eyes had a sudden glint.

'I don't know what you mean.'

'You know well what I mean.'

We were silent for a moment. I think the ghosts of my parents had become very tangible for us both.

'What did Geraldine say when you told her you were adopted?' she asked.

'You know well that I've never told her.'

'I don't know whose eyes you inherited,' she said, 'but you inherited my sister-in-law's sense of shame. The Ireland she lived in was infected with a terrible virus called respectability. God got mentioned a lot, but it was not about loving your neighbours or eternal damnation: life was all about what your neighbours thought of you, about keeping secrets, avoiding scandal, giving no one the chance to look down on you. Your mother blamed herself for not being able to have children. It made her feel worthless because this was what a woman was meant to do in those days. There were no careers for us: we just got married and churned out soldiers for Christ. But I'm convinced your father was to blame – though, God knows, blame is the wrong word. There was a history of men firing blanks in our family – two of my uncles had childless marriages too. Your father never talked to her about this – he let her blame her own body in your head. He loved her and looked after her, but he wasn't capable of saying the things he needed to say.'

'I seem to have inherited her guilt and his tongue-tied reticence,' I said. 'But maybe it's time I found out whose eyes I have. I think I want to find my birth mother, yet I'm scared of what I might find. What do I do?'

She reached for her cigarettes on the sideboard and lit one.

'Your mother changed your clothes the moment she brought you home.' Aunt Cissie said. 'But she couldn't bring herself to throw out the blue outfit you arrived in. One night she looked at the stitching inside the leg. The seam was crooked, doubled over and stitched back up. She undid the stitching. There was the tiniest scrap of paper folded inside it, with a girl's name and address.'

I wondered what my mother must have felt, holding that folded slip in her hand, knowing she would open it even though she dreaded its contents.

'What was the girl's name?'

'I don't know, Sean.'

'I don't believe you,' I said. I was rattled. 'They always told you everything.'

Cissie looked down at the table where her cigarette ash had fallen.

'You had years to ask your father.'

'I know. I left it too late.'

'Your mother had already washed the outfit twice, because she was convinced she could smell the convent off it, the smell of... I don't know... poverty, disgrace. There was a name on the paper and maybe it was your birth mother's name or maybe it wasn't, but either way it wasn't legible anymore. All I could make out was that it started with either an L or an I, and that the words, Co Laois, were in the address. It was indistinct but it couldn't be anywhere else. I figured it wasn't a town address either, because there was no street number: just one word like a village or a townland. And no message, though, God knows, there would have been barely room for a message. It was as if the child – at nineteen that's all she was – just needed to leave her name, some proof that she existed, that she counted for something.'

'And that's the truth?' I asked quietly. 'You're holding nothing back?'

She looked at me and I immediately regretted the remark.

'I'm too old to tell lies, Sean, and so are you. Remember that when you go home to your wife tonight.'

'I deserve that rebuke,' I said.

'Maybe there is a way to find out these things,' she said. 'It won't be easy, because the nuns guard their files like dragons, but if you really want to find her you'll find some way to start. Only two people ever met both of your mothers – that nun and Mrs Lacey. Mrs Lacey was a formidable woman – your mother was terrified of her – but she was a fair woman. Find her and you may be halfway to finding your birth mother.'

She stood up and turned on the light. I rose to go.

'I'll bring the kids over to see you soon,' I promised.

'If I had a shilling for all of your promises...' She smiled. 'Just be sure to bring them down this side of Christmas. I'll hardly see another one out.'

I kissed her and squeezed her shoulder.

'You'll outlive us all,' I said. 'I bet you need to hire a truck to bring home your winnings from bingo. I bet your wardrobe is full of shirts taken off the backs of every bingo-playing pensioner in Dublin.'

She cackled and pushed me playfully into the hall.

'Curse of God on you,' she said. 'Can you not smell that bread burning?'

She disappeared briefly into the kitchen while I opened the front door. She came back out. Her bones had shrunk in recent years, yet I suddenly felt small as I loomed over her.

'You never got to tell me about the Botanic Gardens,' I said.

She put her hand up to the wooden light switch beside the door. We were suddenly framed in the lit doorway. I would have photographed us like this from a long way off.

'You remember nothing about those gardens at all?' she asked.

'Not till I went there myself with a camera when I was eleven.'

'Your mother was a born walker. She wheeled you through every park in North Dublin. I remember the first time she brought you to the Botanic Gardens. You were two years old and my youngest, Patrick, was seven. You had been cranky, but once we entered the Botanics your mood changed. You were staring up, delighted with yourself, like a different baby. After that, your mother started taking you for walks there every second day. It's where you learned to walk properly. You loved the grassy slope down to the pond. Soon you knew your way around better than we did, toddling in front of us, watching the men cutting the grass with their tractor. "The tractor loves Sean", you would say, "the trees love Sean". The only place you didn't like was the yew-tree walk; you'd cry if we went near it. The place your mother didn't like was the rose garden, because you would keep pointing at the bushes in the corner near the wall of the Tolka House pub and saying, "My house is gone: bold men steal my home."'

I could picture the Rose Garden in my mind, a small strip of land separated from the main gardens by the river that cut it off on two sides, so that it was only accessible by a narrow bridge.

'You became very possessive about the rose garden, upset if anyone else dared cross the bridge to walk around it. It was your own fantasy world, like when you were pretending to cook cakes in my kitchen. You'd come out with nonsense: "Mammy Peg washes clothes in the river; Mammy Peg hangs them in the glasshouse to dry. So cold sleeping in the hay." If a tractor came along, you forgot all about this make-believe world. But this constant babbling every day was starting to get to your mother.'

Aunt Cissie reached into her pocket for her cigarettes and lit one; smoke trailing from her hand as she imitated my childish gestures.

I was there with your mother one day, and when we went to leave the Rose Garden you wouldn't come. "Stay home," you kept crying. An old gardener was working on a flowerbed and I asked him how long the Rose Garden had been there. "Two hundred years," he said. "Ever since the gardens were founded. I remember as a boy how the scent of roses would suffocate you. Though of course the roses were on the other side of the bridge back then. We only shifted the Rose Garden across here after we knocked down old Davitt's cottage in the 1940s." I asked him who the Davitts were and he called them the best family to ever work in the gardens: three generations with a hundred and fifty years service between them. Then he pointed to the corner that you used to always point to. "For years we had a great supply of bricks for odd jobs from their cottage that used to back onto the wall of the pub there."'

Aunt Cissie looked at me. 'Your mother got such a fright that she picked you up and ran across the bridge. She never set foot in the Botanic Gardens again and never wanted you to.'

What Aunt Cissie said made no sense. Yet she could see how unnerved I was by it.

'Children believe in silly notions,' she said. 'But you're not a child any more. Whatever fantasy you invented when you were small is not real, but the scared nineteen-year-old girl who wrote her name on that slip of paper is. I hope you find her, Sean, I'd like to meet her one day.'

'How do I know that she would like to meet me?'

'You'll never know, not until you find her.'

She pushed two ten-pound notes into my pocket, one for each of the children. She would have to scrimp on her beloved cigarettes for a fortnight to make up the money. I tried to argue but it was useless. She stood in the lit doorway, waving. I knew she would stay standing there alone, long after I drove out of sight.

Chapter Seven

Something was always going to lure me back to work for the paper. When I turned on my radio one morning in mid-March to hear that a Volkswagen hatchback had been dredged from the River Shannon at Killaloe in County Clare, with a man in the driver's seat and a ten-month-old girl strapped into a baby chair beside him, I knew immediately that it was Frank Conroy. No names were given and the newsreader quickly moved on to details of an IRA bomb the previous day, but already I was waiting for Gerry's phone call.

Two years ago I had spent a night in Frank Conroy's house and later sent him photographs of him and his wife in the kitchen of the bungalow they had just finished building near Killaloe. I was there because a photographer turns up in all kinds of strange places and, with fifty of his neighbours about to lose their jobs with the closure of the nearby tiny Mullabeg coalmine, Frank had taken unpaid leave from his job in Limerick to publicise their plight, when they asked him to serve as press officer for the miners' action committee. We had stayed in touch – although his recent terse postcards had been unable to conceal the agony of discovering that his wife had been diagnosed with terminal cancer soon after they discovered she was pregnant.

Geraldine followed me upstairs after she had persuaded Benedict to eat his breakfast. I had my father's old camera bag on the bed and was packing clothes for a possible overnight stay.

'What's happening?' she asked.

'Police divers have just recovered the bodies of a man and a baby from a blue Volkswagen hatchback driven into the river at Killaloe. I'd say that few men around there drive a blue Volkswagen hatchback and fewer still are trying to raise an eight-month-old baby on their own. I'm sure it's Frank Conroy. They're bound to send Gerry to cover it. He knows I knew Frank and he knows it's time I started working again. I may be away overnight.'

'Are you sure you're able for the drive, love?'

'I need to get back behind a wheel properly at some stage. This is how I make my living.'

But she could see that I was nervous. So far I had only done short trips around town. Benedict was climbing the stairs to see what we were doing. He never liked to be separated from us for more than a few moments.

'I'll be careful,' I said softly. 'I'll phone as soon as I get there.'

'Do more than phone,' she said. 'Think of us every time you're tempted to overtake someone. You always drive too fast. I almost lost you once, Sean, make sure I don't lose you again.'

Benedict entered the bedroom and tugged at her jumper, perturbed by the tense atmosphere. Geraldine picked him up. He put out his arms for me to join in the hug, bringing all three of us together. Last night when I went upstairs to check on Sinéad, I had knelt beside her cot, straining in the darkness to hear her breathing. For a moment I could hear no sound. Every other worry or thought had been utterly eclipsed as I pressed my ear against the cot bars, trying not to panic. Then the child stirred with a loud exhalation of air and I had been flooded with joy. It made me realise how desperately I wanted to be alive to witness every stage of her life until one day she too would kneel in a bedroom to feel the same exhilaration at hearing her child breathe. I entered Benedict's room to fix the blanket he had kicked off. He had stirred and looked up, still asleep, murmuring my name before his eyelids closed again.

At that same time I now realised that Frank Conroy's eyes had been staring blankly into the black waters of the Shannon while his hand cradled his daughter's tiny fingers. I closed my eyes as Benedict lifted his head from the cuddle.

'Silly old Dada,' I heard him say to Geraldine. 'Silly old Dada is crying.'

*

At ten o'clock Gerry phoned. There was no pressure on me to cover the story, he said, but the editor felt that it might interest me. We agreed to meet at the Railway Hotel in Killaloe at three o'clock that afternoon. I packed the car and drove off with a great show of confidence, aware of Geraldine and Benedict waving from the doorway, but inside I was shaking. I was an experienced driver and had previously never given long journeys a second thought, but that crash had changed everything. Now it was impossible to get behind a wheel without reliving the horror of that accident. I wiped the sweat from my palms as I faced into heavy traffic on the Dublin quays. I tried to focus on our money worries, on bank balances and mortgage payments, and forget about the hours of driving that lay head.

Down in Killaloe the cabin cruisers would be tied up on the Shannon, waiting for an influx of German and Italian accents to herald the start of the tourist season. Cars would be stopping beside the river, local people silently watching Frank Conroy's car being hauled from the water. Former miners from Mullabeg would be on the quayside, men I had photographed two years ago when Frank Conroy was elected in his absence onto the local committee to save the coalmine.

If a Japanese factory had not closed in Galway that same week, the media might never have reported the closure of the tiny coalmine. But job losses were suddenly a big news story and so those fifty miners had found themselves the centre of a nation's attention for one weekend. It was the last surviving coal mine in Ireland, producing such low-grade ore that its sole customer, the ESB, had claimed it was no longer economically viable to use it to generate electricity. The Mullabeg miners knew they had no hope of reversing the owner's decision. But they had also known that – apart from the men young enough to emigrate – few of them were likely to ever work again.

The press interviews had been fairly standard two years ago, but by the time the miners' spokesman reached Gerry I could see his nerves start to fray.

'You journalists come down on safari from Dublin,' he said, 'but you haven't got a bull's notion of what life is like in rural Ireland. If you want to know desperation, spent a day down that mine with us. Because there isn't a miner who hasn't cursed it as a crumbling black hellhole that probably should have been closed years ago. All hand work: every tool twenty years out of date. But the fact is that we'd sooner crawl through a black hell underground than walk around above ground in the living hell of unemployment. I see your editor every week singing the praises of rich gangsters in dicky bows: developers, tax cheats, a new bloody aristocracy. So don't pretend your paper gives a shite about us. They're just dying to run another colour spread on the Orphan McHugh and his new country club down the road. Because we all know who'll get his hands on this site when our jobs are gone. McHugh will build another eighteen-hole course so the Germans and the Yanks can hit golf balls over our graves.'

It was Frank Conroy who stepped forward to deflect the spokesman's anger back towards the government for refusing to increase their subsidy to the ESB to use the coal. But the miner was right. Gerry's article was a once-off feature. The lavish country club that the property developer Peter McHugh was building nearby featured on the gossip pages every week. McHugh was one of Ireland's top businessmen, with a string of tightly run hotels and other businesses. He was rumoured to have made a second fortune on shares in Anglo-Irish Bank, the tiny but burgeoning private bank that funded most of his developments. Half of Ireland seemed in awe of McHugh, but the miners had grinned when their spokesman used his local nickname, as if it cut him down to size.

When Gerry finished the interview I had slipped him the roll of film and asked him to have somebody on the picture-desk develop it. I waited until the last of the media was gone. The mine owner had come down in his car. The mine had been in his family for a hundred years, but the low-grade coal would be worthless once the ESB contract expired. The miners had a grudging respect for him.

'He hung on for as long as he could,' the spokesman said to no one in particular when the owner drove off. 'He had no choice but to do a deal with McHugh. But McHugh will screw him like McHugh screws everybody: once a bastard, always a bastard, eh.'

The gathering was breaking up, men heading back to their homes in Ballynahinch and Birdhill and Newport. There was a tiny grotto to the Blessed Virgin over the entrance to the mineshaft. The light around her head glowed with a faint electric hum. Frank Conroy walked across to stand beside me.

'Tell him I'll take up his offer,' I said, nodding towards the spokesman who had removed his helmet and overalls and looked far older in ordinary clothes. 'I've taken the pictures the paper wants. Tomorrow I'd like to take my own. If his offer is still open, I'll go down the mine in the morning.'

'That shaft gets fierce narrow,' the spokesman said. 'You'd be crawling on your stomach at times. You'll meet bigger rats than in Dáil Éireann.'

It took me ten minutes to persuade the men, who were convinced that I would not have the courage to show up the next morning.

Frank Conroy offered me a bed. We sat up talking till four o'clock. I can still remember him in his kitchen with a cat on his knee while his wife teased him about getting coerced onto every committee in Clare: the Tidy Towns, Meals on Wheels, Tourism Taskforce, Community Watch for older people. And I can still see Frank grinning sheepishly back at her, totally in love.

The Mullabeg mine shots are my favourite photographs. At the entrance I had used an old Nikkormat FTN, with a 135mm lens, which my father had left me. In the low winter dawn light I had shot the silhouettes of men who seemed like ghosts, dwarfed against the broken asphalt. But once we entered the mine their attitude changed, as I briefly became a part of their underground world. Their problems seemed temporarily forgotten in the bond that existed down there. Harsh light and utter blackness existed simultaneously in the tunnels, figures shifting in and out of darkness. They worked hard that day, aware perhaps that soon only my images would remain as proof that they once existed as a body of men.

I had used infrared film, which made the black and white images of their faces curiously pale, and spent weeks afterwards in my darkroom bleaching and toning sections of the prints before I was satisfied with them. By the time I first displayed those shots, the mine was closed, the miners living off their smallholdings and the dole. Peter McHugh bought the site. It was rumoured that he planned to use the mine for survival games in an adventure playground designed to encourage corporate workers to bond.

*

Leaving Dublin my nerves steadied. I moved out from the slow lane on the Naas dual carriageway and picked up speed, testing myself. I kept thinking about Frank Conroy's car speeding along the quayside. What had been the point of no return for him: twenty yards away or ten yards? There were no witnesses to say if he tried to brake or had held the steering wheel tight in those weightless seconds when the car soared in mid air, making contact with the water. I could try to understand and forgive his own death. Here was a man who found himself a father and a widower within a few months, who simply could not cope with his world being turned upside-down. But the thought of the dead child filled me with horror. I would kill for my children. I would scavenge and forage for them. I could never contemplate harming them. I knew that Frank had loved his daughter too. This was the question that tormented me as I drove: why did he do it?

Beyond Portlaoise I began to drive more slowly. I was approaching Mountrath; Killaloe was another fifty miles further on. This trip was taking me through the heart of County Laois: another reason why I had accepted the job. I reached the edge of Mountrath and got caught up in a long line of traffic because there was a market on in the town. The Slieve Bloom Mountains were to my left. I had the option of taking the high road up into those hills that would drop me down into Kinnitty and then Birr. If Aunt Cissie was correct about the address stitched into those baby clothes, then the nameless stranger who was my birth mother might have often walked that road as a girl. Maybe she had never left Laois and still travelled that road every day in whatever new life she now led.

I wasn't ready to take that road yet, because just driving it felt too much like a commitment. I had no idea what to look for or where to start looking. Did I even really want to find her? Did I need to have the complications of another life grafted onto mine? I followed the flow of traffic into Mountrath, the drivers impatient to push on towards Roscrea. There was another delay while a woman reversed out of a parking spot on the bustling main street and, before I had time to think about it, I pulled into the vacant spot.

The street market was in full flow: Wellington boots and overcoats for sale alongside plastercast statues of Saint Jude; Guns N' Roses tee-shirts on a stall that was also selling old bootleg tapes of U2 playing in Tullamore. I left the car and walked among the horse-boxes and stalls, studying each face as neighbours chatted or leaned across the trestle tables to purchase goods. That old farmer might be my uncle; the woman with the child in a buggy could be a cousin of mine. My real mother might have run around the stalls here as a child. The odd person glanced at me. If Aunt Cissie was right then I had come home: for the first time I was standing among my own people. I felt short of breath. I wanted to shout; does anybody here know my face? Can anyone tell me who I really am?

My birth mother might only be a few yards away from me now; with her youthful indiscretion long banished. My inconvenient existence written out of the narrative of this place as effectively as if I had been smothered at birth and buried in a shallow grave. Even if I found her here now, what were the chances that she would deny my existence; that I would be made to feel like a beggar, a threat to her proper children? Suddenly I felt an angry surge of helplessness at not knowing where I stood and who I was. I wanted to kick over these trestle tables, these stalls with their tacky coloured bulbs. I got back into my car. The noise of the engine revving made people turn around.

'Fuck you all,' I mouthed through the closed windows. 'I exist too: I'm part of this place, whether you like it or not.'

*

Beyond Roscrea I pulled in again. I had been recklessly overtaking, trying to expel an unexpected rage buried inside me. Maybe it had been there since I was eleven years old and found my identity stolen from me. I took a deep breath. I was late. Gerry would be waiting for me in Killaloe. I knew that Geraldine would start to worry if I did not phone her soon. I started the engine again. My father's old camera bag was on the passenger seat. I touched it, like a good-luck charm.

*

The Mullabeg mines closed down within a month of Gerry's article appearing. There had been talk of a government jobs taskforce for the area, but there is always such talk until the story moves elsewhere. I had kept in touch with Frank Conroy because he was my only contact address for any of those miners when an Italian photographic magazine ran twelve of the Mullabeg shots. I had even called to see Frank and his wife last year, when Peter McHugh's golf and country club officially opened and I was sent down to do a portrait of McHugh for the weekend supplement. I remember how their hands kept touching across the table as they shared their two bits of news with me: that she had cancer and she was pregnant. These two facts were inextricably linked, with the hospital saying that it was against their Catholic ethos to provide any intensive chemotherapy that might endanger the equal right to life of her child in the womb. I still don't know whether his wife would have declined such chemotherapy anyway, whether she explored the option of going to another hospital or whether she simply decided to put her trust in fate or God, deciding that their long-awaited child was too precious to be put at risk. I don't know what was going on in her mind or what pressures she was put under. I just know that she died within a few weeks of the child being born. Nobody knew how she lived for so long or found the strength to give birth.

As I drove into Killaloe I remembered the last postcard Frank had sent me: 'Christenings and funerals don't really mix. I would like to say that the baby is keeping me so busy I haven't time to feel alone, but Rosemary always said I was a bad liar.' Gerry was waiting for me in the bar of the Railway Hotel.

'The dead arose,' he said. 'I hope you kept your hands on the steering wheel this time.'

He turned to catch the barman's attention. I smiled, looking at his bald patch, at the same tweed jacket he had been wearing since I first met him. That tattered jacket had occupied the corner of many of my photographs: Gerry interviewing spokespeople after EC summits, talking to relief workers among starving children in Africa, blending into crowds of political hacks at by-election counts around the country, always with the same quizzical expression, his look of innocent exasperation that provoked people into saying more than they meant to. It always amused me to watch Gerry studiously ignoring the PR flunkies who sometimes hovered around him at gala functions, trying to persuade him into a dinner jacket. He turned towards me now, holding out a drink.

'It wasn't much fun for Geraldine,' he said. 'She only had forty seconds to spend the insurance money before you changed your mind and came back.'

When we went outside, the quayside was deserted except for the odd onlooker who stared into the water and then walked past us without speaking. The town was silent. Flowers had been left on the stones. A note with one bunch had obviously read 'In loving memory of Frank and Baby Emma', but somebody else had crossed out Frank's name. His car had already been dredged from the river. There was nothing to see.

'The stupid bastard,' I said. 'I know he was grieving, but why bring the child with him?'

I pointed the lens towards the water where Frank Conroy and his child had died. In my mind's eye I could see Frank travel back up through the freezing water towards a beckoning cone of light. Had his child journeyed with him, or had Frank known a different journey: hissing faces pushing him further down into the black waters and away from the light towards which his child floated, lost to him forever? I lowered the camera, too overcome to frame anything.

'If the child wasn't in that car you and I wouldn't be here,' Gerry said quietly. 'Suicides are two a penny in Ireland: people just don't want to talk about them. They're scared that even a mention in the paper will provoke ten copycat deaths. It's a silent epidemic. In every generation there's something we're afraid to talk about. Maybe

Frank just couldn't cope. Forty years ago he wouldn't have been expected to cope. There was no stigma about giving up your child then: the nuns and Christian Brothers turned it into an industry, with the government paying them a premium for every child. Back then a parent could knock at a convent and hand over a baby with no questions asked, no neighbour thinking badly of them. Indeed if a father was left alone with a baby the nuns were on top of him, anxious to grab the child. Rich Americans might not have actually paid for the children they found it so easy to adopt from Irish convents, but they always left a significant donation. It was how the world worked back then, before children became the centre of the universe. Can you imagine a father giving up his child now; how his neighbours and his family would judge him? There are no safety valves anymore, no convent doors to knock on or kids quietly being given to relations to be raised. Frank's wife gave up her life so he would have a child. That's a big weight for a man to carry. What do you do when you find that you can't cope with the child or with the shame of giving up your child for some social worker to put her into care?'

I raised the camera, focusing on the sheen of sunlight on the water. I pressed the shutter. 'What are you,' I asked, 'an amateur psychologist?'

'I'm just a bald man in a crumpled jacket being ignored by everyone in Killaloe for fear that they might have to criticise a neighbour.'

*

Back in the hotel I phoned Geraldine to say I would be home at lunchtime the following day. She put Benedict on the line. He was missing me badly and said nothing, but I could imagine his mouth almost biting into the receiver as he listened to my voice. After a few moments I made a second phone call. I needed to soft-soap my way past receptionists and secretaries, but I knew that if I persisted Peter

McHugh would eventually speak to me.

'Well if it isn't the "fuck them all" photographer,' he said when he came on the line. 'What can I do you for?'

'I'm in Killaloe,' I said. 'Is there any chance I could see you in the morning?'

'No can do,' he said. 'Nothing personal: the press are a necessary evil, but you're an evil I don't actually need for anything just now.'

'This is personal,' I said. 'I want to borrow a shovel.'

'What the fuck do you want a shovel for?'

'I want to check if I have blue blood inside me.'

Chapter Eight

Next morning, as I drove from Killaloe to meet McHugh, I remembered the first time we met. I rarely worked with Valerie, the paper's society columnist, but there was serious advertising revenue built around the glossy supplement being published to mark the opening of McHugh's Country Club and I had been drafted in. Valerie had two articles planned: a bland, flattering interview for the supplement and a mocking piece for a bitchy column she wrote under a nom de plume in a fashion magazine.

Within minutes of them meeting I knew that McHugh had Valerie figured out. His initial watchful charm settled into something harder as he registered the condescension behind some of her questions. Flatter him, the editor had instructed her, and make sure to get some good quotes about growing up in the orphanage.

'You're not a Mullingar girl, no?' McHugh had asked after a few moments.

'No. I'm from Glenageary in South Dublin, why?'

'Oh, just the fine way you're built.' His eyes flickered past her to observe me waiting with my camera. 'Beef to the heel like a Mullingar heifer.'

The only time McHugh opened up was when he was discussing business. The restaurant on the golf course and even the running of the country club were all franchised out, as was the health studio and the nightclub being built on the grounds. This was the method McHugh used to build up his chain of twelve hotels. He had arranged for two golf buggies so that Valerie and I could attend an onsite meeting with the golf architect who was still working on the course being built behind the hotel. We stood on a small hill beside the proposed tee for a short par three.

'You've two choices,' the architect said. 'If you tee off from up here you get a nice elevated view but the lake doesn't come into play. However, if we have the tee-box down in the hollow it will be a less impressive view but a more challenging shot directly over the water. I suggest we move the tee.'

McHugh had stared at the trucks unloading tonnes of sand for the fairways as workmen remodelled the landscape.

'I like the view up here,' he said. 'Let's move the lake instead.'

Valerie began to laugh. He looked at her.

'My office is at that big window over there,' he said. 'If the tee is in the hollow I won't be able to see the nice folk from Glenageary losing their nerve and then losing their balls.'

McHugh had achieved his success by ignoring Dublin. For years after the national papers had proclaimed that the Irish showband scene was dead he had still packed crowds into his ballrooms in Clare and Limerick. The music artistes he managed rarely played Dublin and their songs were never played on national radio, although occasionally skits about them were performed by alternative Dublin comedians on television programmes that nobody watched. The artistes themselves were too busy playing in packed hotel lounges around the country. Twice a year McHugh travelled to Nashville to book major country acts, which Dublin promoters felt were too big a financial risk. The local radio station which he owned boasted that he had never lost money on an act.

He was tolerating Valerie because this interview was one of the commitments which, as a businessman, he needed to fulfil. He knew that Valerie would mock everything about him and that her attitude was shared by many who read her society column. They looked down on him, yet he also knew that Dublin 4 readers were fascinated by the money he made and convinced that he must be bribing politicians and twisting by-laws to achieve this success. They saw him as a redneck bogman in pin-striped Wellingtons and were puzzled by his refusal to reinvent himself like most of Ireland's new aristocrats had done. He had earned his money and now he could earn respectability if his wife would only host a fundraising charity ball on Bloomsday or if he bought himself an honorary doctorate and let it be known that he wished to be referred to as 'Doctor'. If he was only willing to meet people's expectations he could have been lauded in Valerie's social column every week. But – although happy for them to pay his overpriced green fees – McHugh had no interest in appealing to Valerie's readers. Every remark seemed intended to infuriate her target audience and amuse local people in Clare.

I had paid little attention to the interview until Valerie probed him about his childhood, spent in an industrial school in the midlands. His replies were sardonic and vague. But there was no humour in his eyes. They had grown watchful and darted about the room. Our eyes made contact, his gaze hostile.

'But seriously,' Valerie persisted, 'you must have seen great cruelty there?'

'No.' His voice was emotionless.

'But the reports now emerging about those institutions say that boys were savagely beaten and starved, that they were essentially slave-labour camps.'

'It was tough, but so is life.'

'But was sexual abuse not common? Is it not true that Christian Brothers who abused children in good parishes were sent to such institutions because there would be no chance of scandal, no way for boys who were locked away there to complain, with nobody caring whether they were alive or dead? Are you saying there were no paedophiles there?'

'I saying the industrial school was tough, but so is life.' He stared coldly at Valerie, bringing the interview to an end. 'There's a press pack about the country club outside. The pleasure has been all mine.'

After Valerie conceded defeat and left it was my turn to try and pose him for the colour shot to adorn the cover of the weekend supplement. He watched me open my camera bag.

'You're the sly boy, eh? Sitting in the corner the whole time, never opening your gob.'

'A good photographer is neither seen nor heard,' I said, adjusting the lens.

'Really? You had five minutes,' he said sourly. 'You now have four minutes and forty seconds.'

McHugh reluctantly lifted his head in various poses when I asked him to, but no matter how I tried to frame it, the photograph would not work. Before the camera he was ill at ease. His eyes were belligerent, as if refusing to engage with Valerie and her readers. His hostility was a defensive mechanism, killing the photograph. Finally I lowered the camera to put in a new roll of film.

'Listen,' I said. 'Valerie's feature will be three pages long. Most people are only going to skim the whole thing. Valerie likes to think that readers hang on to her every word, but people are busy on a Sunday. Every person who picks up the newspaper is going to stare at this photograph however. Valerie can twist your words any way she wants, but the photograph is yours to use. So forget Valerie, think of everyone you've met who will find themselves staring into your eyes next Sunday. Why not stare back into their eyes: the envious motherfuckers.'

'I don't get sweet-talked into doing things by smart-arsed Dublin fuckers,' he said.

'I'm not a Dublin fucker.'

'Where are you from so?'

'I'm a bit like you, McHugh: the nuns have the records locked away and I haven't got a fucking clue.'

He looked at me; his head to one side and snorted. I clicked. The shot felt alive.

'What do you want?' he said. 'A hand-out? Violins?'

'Do people always want something from you?'

'You bet your life they do. Everyone wants something. Is this your sob story at dinner parties?'

'Even my wife doesn't know.' I had shocked myself by breaking the habit of a lifetime and telling him. But being behind a camera seemed to insulate me from the words.

'Are you ashamed or something?'

'I've just never wanted to let it define me.'

His eyes narrowed, his gaze watchful. I clicked again.

'Am I'm supposed to feel flattered?'

'I'm making conversation. Did anyone ever tell you, you can be a contrary bollix, McHugh?'

He threw his head back and laughed. The shot was perfect, his eyes alive.

'Not to my face this long time past. Staff tiptoe round me, especially the senior managers: I keep them on their toes. But they call me worse things in the village.'

'The Orphan McHugh.' My accent was wrong, but I got the sneer into my word. 'I heard it from the miners at Mullabeg before the mine closed down.'

'"The Orphan is a Bollix". Somebody painted it in big letters outside the country club gates after I bought the mine. There were assistant managers on their knees at dawn scrubbing it out in case I saw it. I went out the next night and painted it back, just to see the suits out with their scrubbing brushes again the next morning.'

'Nobody ever called me an orphan, mind you,' I said, changing the lens. 'I had loving adoptive parents. You must have been as ugly as sin if they could find nobody to keep you.'

'Don't push your luck, boy!' His anger was unguarded. I had his face tight in my viewfinder and managed to get three shots. I knew he had been adopted by a family in America who sent him back after six months. 'My time is money,' he added. 'So maybe it's time you fucked off?'

'It's easy to tell me to fuck off,' I said, beginning to click again. 'But how about all the mini-Hitlers in that industrial school; all the farmers who hired you to out as slave labour; the locals who looked down their noses at the line of boys being marched through the village with short trousers and welts on their legs? Think about the laugh they had at the thought of you trying to hire your first show-band; the smirk of bank tellers after each bank turned you down for a loan? You were meant to disappear to England and be grateful for some menial job. They all wanted you to fail, because you were an upstart who didn't know your place. They'll be sick as dogs when they see your mug staring out at them in the paper again. They're all trapped inside this lens, McHugh, forced to look at you. So forget me, forget Valerie: you just stare back at them.'

I clicked rapidly as I spoke. I had only seven shots left on the new roll. But I knew I had the perfect picture by the way he gazed, as if transfixed, not into the lens but right through it. Even when I ran out of film I held the camera steady until he lowered his eyes.

'You're one sly bastard,' he said. 'Still, I suppose it takes a bastard to know one.' He pressed a button on his desk and a secretary's voice answered. 'Barbara, bring in a bottle of that rare 1927 Bushmills.'

'How many glasses, sir?'

'I don't know.' He looked at me. 'I haven't decided whether to pour this photographer a drink or smash the bottle over his skull.'

*

Now, eighteen months later, I was driving in through the gates of that country club again. The golf course was deserted. Even with reduced morning rates, few local people could afford to play it. Delivery vans were unloading in the hotel car park. I walked into reception. In the past I had done commissions for hotel owners who wanted their picture mounted behind reception desks. McHugh had no such interest in ego: there were no pictures of him here, just a few anaemic contemporary artworks that deliberately said nothing. However he had broken the habit of a lifetime and allowed one of my images to be used as his official Christmas card. 'They made a mistake,' he had written on the copy he sent to me. 'They printed "Seasonal Greetings from Peter McHugh", when I could have sworn I told them to print, "Fuck you, you envious sons of bitches".'

Eighteen months ago, after I accepted his offer of dinner, that bottle of vintage Bushmills had died a slow death between us. Sitting in his office, with just a soft desk lamp on, and the shapes of moonlit trees and huge dunes of sand and clay visible on the half-built golf course through the window, he gave me the interview he would never give to Valerie or any other journalist. Perhaps it amused him that I would never use a word of it, but I think it was that, despite our different childhood experiences, we felt a kinship.

McHugh had traced his birth mother through a private detective. A timid Donegal woman, she had been terrified by his sudden appearance. But he claimed to have had no real interest in her: it was his father's name he was after. He extracted it from her and used his contacts to track his father down to a building site in Birmingham. McHugh hired a Rolls Royce to drive him there from Birmingham airport. The navvies had stopped work as the chauffeur opened the door of the Rolls Royce and McHugh emerged. When he barked out a name the foreman pointed to an old man standing up to his knees in muck in a trench. McHugh picked up a shovel from the bank of earth. 'Hello, Daddy,' he said to the old man and then calmly split open a gash in his skull.

'What did you do that for?' the foreman screamed at him.

McHugh dipped his finger in the blood on the rim of the shovel.

'I wanted to check if I have blue blood in me,' he said and turned to let the chauffeur whisk him away.

I remembered this story as the lift doors opened and McHugh came down into reception.

'Do you know how many business appointments I had to cancel this morning to see you?' he asked.

'It will add to your mystique.'

He looked at me. 'You left your camera behind.'

'It's in the car.'

'You're just afraid of getting blue blood splattered all over it.'

*

I am not sure what advice I expected from Peter McHugh. I had been surprised he had even agreed to see me. I was constantly thinking about my birth mother now, but maybe there had never been a time in my life when I wasn't thinking about her – even the act of trying to banish her from my mind had involved being acutely aware of her. I expected a hard man's sneer from McHugh; for him to tell me to focus on my life now. He had only once tracked down his mother and never even bothered to speak to the woman again. He was the ultimate self-made man, living in the present. He would set me straight. But instead he confronted me, like I had confronted him when taking his photograph.

'One part of me is desperate to find out who I really am,' I told him. 'Another part of me keeps saying that the person I really am is Sean Blake: a photographer with a wife and children who love him. Shouldn't that be enough for anyone?'

'If it was enough for you, you wouldn't be sitting here, with suppliers sulking outside in their Mercs because they can't see me.'

'I'm scared that if I find her I won't know what to say. It was different for you; you were put through orphanages, industrial schools. You didn't want answers, you wanted revenge. You found your father; you settled old scores and you moved on.'

Peter McHugh eyed me coldly. 'Cop yourself on, Sean. Do you think I really settled anything; that I don't have regrets? I regret that I never went back and visited my mother again. She was scared witless, but if I had persisted, if I had given her time, she might have felt different. I was a young man in a hurry. She told me that she smoked a hundred cigarettes a day. Anyone who smokes that much is holding more than smoke inside her. She coughed herself to an early death in Letterkenny Hospital. I regret that I didn't make an effort to get to know her.'

'And your father?'

'I regret that I only hit the bollix once for what he did to her, and that I didn't hit him hard enough. How many regrets do you want to carry through life?'

'These past months it has been gnawing away inside me,' I said. 'I won't know any peace until I find her.'

'Good,' he said. 'At least you're being honest. Unfortunately you can fuck the church and the stage agencies for a start. They have all the facts but they hide behind the law. They won't give you the steam off their piss. You're invisible and they want you to remain invisible because that was how their system worked and they're not going to admit there was ever anything wrong with it. You're on your own and they will oppose you at every turn, so the first rule is to grasp at any straw.' He stood up. 'Come on; let's bring some terror to the kitchens. Let's pretend to the chef that you're a health inspector.'

I followed him down a succession of corridors until we entered the kitchens. Conversation died, staff bent earnestly at their tasks, two trainee managers looking up nervously as he glowered at them. We passed through double doors into a secluded dining area off the main restaurant. A table was set there with ten places for a private dinner that evening. He asked me to wait and when he returned he was accompanied by two of the women who worked as cleaners. Watching McHugh find them chairs, I was seeing a different man. It felt as if the three of them were part of an invisible circle. He introduced them by their first names only and said that both of them had secret children in the 1950s. One of their husbands still did not know this. They had agreed to talk to me because he had assured them that nothing said in this room would ever be repeated outside of it. The women were uneasy in my presence and yet curious to meet me. As they gazed at me I knew that momentarily they were substituting me for the blank space they carried within them. I found myself doing the same as I gazed back. I wondered how McHugh had got them to open up to him. They looked out of place in this elaborate dining room and yet at ease with him, treating him with an affectionate respect. They listened to the information Aunt Cissie had told me.

'Maybe she was from Laois and maybe she wasn't,' the oldest woman said. 'Don't presume you know because of an address on a piece of paper. The nuns could have changed your clothes after your mother handed you over. You mightn't have been given to your adoptive parents on the same day. There could have been another set of foster parents you know nothing about. Clothes got passed around; everything was second-hand, used over and over. That address could have been sewn in to those clothes by somebody else months beforehand.'

'It's all I have to go on,' I said. 'I have to believe it refers to me.'

'Your baby was also taken by the Catholic Protection Society,' McHugh gently said to the younger of the women. 'Can you remember any girls from Laois in the convent where you were?'

The woman looked at me.

'I'd help you if I could,' she said. 'There were lots of us. We were young and scared. We were encouraged not to use our real names, to tell each other as little as possible. We were shamed and made to feel ashamed. I still feel guilty. I have four other children and yet I'll die feeling guilty. You can try going back to the agency. It may take years of badgering before they tell you anything, but who knows? The law might change. At least you – as the child – have some chance. We, the mothers, have none. We signed the form in the brown envelope, we handed our babies over and they closed the door in our faces.'

'On the day I was handed over,' I said, 'my father asked a nun if I had my mother's eyes. "He has lovely blue eyes, thank God, with no trace of that slut at all," she said. If I went near that agency I wouldn't just be looking for my mother, I would be looking for the nun and I know what I'd say to her.'

The women were silent. A trainee manager walked into the room and McHugh snapped at him that we were not to be disturbed.

'She might still be in whatever convent she had you,' the older woman said, 'Some women never left: they didn't know they had the right to leave or maybe they were made to feel so ashamed that they lost the willpower. In the laundry where I had my baby one woman had been there for thirty-four years. A priest brought her in when she was sixteen. She never had a baby: but her parents had died and she was alone in a house of brothers. She was regarded as being too much of a temptation. She used to work twelve-hour days in the laundry for the nuns: slave labour because they never paid her a penny. She kept thanking the nuns because she was terrified they would put her out. She was grateful for the slightest bit of affection. I've never forgotten her face; I never will.'

We were silent then: the distant sounds from the kitchen becoming clearly audible.

'I once met a woman living in Kildorrery,' the younger women said quietly. 'I was in a church in Limerick at Our Lady's altar. I was praying for Brendan… my child… I don't know what name they gave him. A woman was kneeling beside me; she had lit a candle. We looked at each other and we both knew at once that we were praying for the same thing.

'When I left the church she was waiting outside. She walked on a few paces and looked back. I could see she was begging me to follow her. She stopped in the furthest corner of the car park, behind the grotto where no one could see. And as soon as I touched her shoulder she began to cry. She had never told a living soul before. She was from Laois. She had been brought to a convent in Sligo by her father and then sent on to a bigger laundry in Cork because the nuns needed more workers there. She gave birth in Cork. She said there were no trained midwives, just other girls helping out. When her waters broke she started to scream and an ignorant heifer of a girl from Waterford slapped her face and told her the pain was no one's fault but her own. Some years ago, when her husband thought she was off on a pilgrimage to Lough Derg, she went back to that convent. There were girls still there from her time, working as skivvies because after they gave up their children they had nowhere else to go.'

The woman stopped talking and looked around.

'What a thing to be telling a stranger in a church car park in Limerick. She wouldn't go for a cup of tea in case we would be overheard. She had never told a soul and so I suppose she had to tell someone. After she told me she couldn't wait to get away. I shouldn't be telling a soul either, because it's not my business, but I'm telling you.' The woman looked at me. 'She said her name was Byrne. She said she lived in Kildorrery.'

'Did she have a boy or a girl?' I asked. 'It's really important that I know.'

The anguish in the woman's voice was replaced by a kind of pity.

'There were dozens of us from Laois, dozens from everywhere. Don't expect to find her so easy. The woman from Kildorrery had a girl.'

*

Three hours later McHugh was driving me to Kildorrery along the small roads beyond Ballyneety and Bruff. Many people we passed recognised the car and gave an affectionate half-salute. With every mile I grew more nervous. I had promised to call Geraldine before I left Killaloe, but had not expected to get caught up with McHugh

like this. It was half one in the afternoon when we reached Kildorrery. McHugh stopped for a quiet word in a shop and then drove
for a mile back out into the countryside until he reached the house
the shopkeeper had described.

'You might be wise to stay out here for now,' he said. 'I want to
see if she is alone and if she is willing to talk.'

'What makes you think she will talk to you?'

He opened the car door. 'When you're Peter McHugh, people
often do.'

It was a whitewashed two-storey labourer's house; the windows
painted a flaking purple. A cat stared at me from the window ledge.
The mobile phone began to ring as it had incessantly during our
journey. I ignored it as McHugh had done. Now that I was on my
own, I wished I had never agreed to come here with him. It felt as if
the most private part of my life was being thrust beyond my control
into public view, like I was being forced to sift through a mesh of
secret lives without any certainty that I would ever glimpse the one
I sought. I waited for the door to open and a woman to appear, but
when McHugh came out he was alone.

'She wouldn't talk, so,' I said as he climbed into the car.

'She didn't talk much, but she did talk.' He started the engine.
'She didn't want to have to see you. She has a daughter somewhere
who is seven weeks younger than you. She wasn't going to cry when
I was there, but if you want to see a woman cry now then walk up
to that window.'

'We shouldn't have landed on top of her. She must have been
terrified.'

McHugh released the hand brake and hit the accelerator hard.
The gravel scattered beneath us.

'If you want something,' he said, and his voice was grim, like his
thoughts were elsewhere, 'then let nothing get in your way.'

We drove in silence. Passing the bridge at the hamlet of Bruff, his
car phone rang again. McHugh ignored it.

'Our friend in Kildorrery remembers that there was a girl from Laois in the Sligo convent she was first sent to, a girl from somewhere remote in the Slieve Blooms who was due to birth give six weeks before her. She remembers because the girl's mother died and the nuns decided she didn't look pregnant enough to be prevented from going home to the funeral. They took her back to Laois, but the girl's father would not have her in the church. They let her visit the grave at twilight when the churchyard was deserted, then brought her back to Sligo.'

'Did the girl have a name?'

'If she had, our friend in Kildorrery wasn't telling.'

Something in McHugh's voice warned me not to continue the conversation. His story about finding his father was one of bravado, but that bravado was forged out of childhood experiences that he never talked about. After being sent back from America as a child, the nuns had regarded him as damaged goods, unsuitable to be given to anyone else for adoption. He had spent the next fourteen years in a virtual gulag, never knowing what it felt like to drink from a glass, being beaten or hired out as cheap labour to farmers. When I had asked him to stare into my camera lens I could only guess at what ghosts he saw there.

I had met other survivors of industrial schools. You recognised them from how they lived alone in bedsits, unable to form close bonds with anyone. You met them in menial jobs or in pubs looking for fights at closing time: men who had never known what it meant to trust another human being. How had McHugh achieved his success? What rage had propelled him to where he was now, starting with nothing except his bare hands and a shovel and a mind sharp enough to learn how to undercut the slave driver he first worked for on some building site? Behind the expensive suits and the growing property portfolio, what dreams haunted him at night? Was this why the woman in Kildorrery talked to him? The phone rang. He glanced down at it, back in businessman mode. Before picking it up he glanced across at me.

'You're on your own from here, Sean.'

*

There was heavy rain as I left McHugh's Country Club and started back towards Dublin. But I wasn't going directly home. I kept going over the details of the story told by the woman from Kildorrery. At Roscrea I took the side road to Kinnitty. There was no one in the sacristy there, but an old man directed me to the priest's house. The aproned housekeeper who guarded his privacy reluctantly produced a set of keys and accompanied me back to the church where all the parish records were kept.

After inspecting them, I drove up into the Slieve Blooms, stopping at every church I encountered on that crumbling mountain road where the tarmac had been corroded by winter ice. In Killinure I was unable to find a single living person. Except for the flowers on the altar, nothing suggested that a person had entered the church there in days. From there I made my way across twisting boreens to inspect the records at Ballyfin Church, before crossing the mountain again to reach Dunross.

I hadn't phoned Geraldine yet: I didn't know how to explain where I was. For years I never spoke to anyone about being adopted. Now, for a whole morning, it had been the central fact about me for everybody I encountered. Any success I had achieved in life seemed stripped away. Instead it felt like I was one of thousands of lost children from a time I could not comprehend: all of us linked by having slept in lines of cots in some convent, all connected through the stigma of invisibility.

How could I tell Geraldine what I was doing up here in these mountains, when I had never told her about my past during our courtship? With each year it seemed increasingly difficult to break that silence, when I knew how hurt she would be by the fact that I had kept the truth from her. I didn't want to lie to her now, so I kept putting off finding a call box, even though I knew how anxious she would become as the day went on.

I reached Dunross at half five in the evening and tracked down the sacristan who lived near the church. We entered the sacristy and he closed over the heavy wooden doors and blocked out the light. It brought back memories of being sent down by my mother to our local church with a note about arranging for a mass to be said, listening to the sounds of disrobing and the clink of brass before the priest came out. The sacristan lifted down the heavy register of births, deaths and marriages.

'You say you work for the newspaper,' he said. 'What exactly are you looking for?'

He held the book open on the table, his fingers idly turning over the neat handwritten pages.

'An article about life and death in the 1950s,' I lied. 'We want to take a couple of months at random, April and May 1956, and see who died in a typical parish at that time.'

It took him several minutes to find the right page. The other parishes had yielded nothing: although the priest's housekeeper in Kinnitty had stopped halfway down the list of names, suddenly animated as she recalled a schoolfriend who had been buried in May 1956 – the last person in the parish to die from TB – and recalled how none of the girl's sisters even found a husband afterwards, because of the stigma which the disease still carried. In Ballyfin the records had showed that an infant died in April of 1956, two girls were born, and an old unmarried farmer had been found dead. I felt foolish dredging through these records. If I really wanted to find my mother I should begin with the adoption agency. I would meet a stone wall there, but at least I would have made a proper start to my search. But I knew that I would never set foot in that agency because I would feel humiliated at putting myself back at their mercy. This was why I was here, playing at being the detective but keeping this business at a safe remove from my real life. But I knew that unless I could rule myself out of the story that Peter McHugh had been told, it would keep playing on my mind. Watching the sacristan search through the register now in Dunross I wanted to draw a blank here also, for the pistol barrel to have spun and clicked empty against my cheek, allowing me to return to my life in Dublin, with a false lead having been extinguished.

'There wasn't a single death in April or May of that year,' the sacristan said, scanning the page. 'Two births in late April, if they're of any interest.'

'No,' I said, turning away and searching my pocket for the car keys, 'Thanks for your help anyway.'

'Now that I remember it,' he said, 'there wasn't a death in the parish for months back then. I was an altar boy. It sounds callous but we loved funerals, because you always got a good tip for serving at funerals. The records show that there wasn't a death that year until the second of June when Mary Sweeney died.'

I stopped.

'How old was she?'

He glanced down at the columns. 'Forty-nine. She was young to go.'

'Had she any daughters?'

'Three… no, I tell a lie… four. Two sons as well, one of them a priest. They were a nice family, from a small farm about a mile and a half down the road. I remember serving at her funeral.'

'Has she any family still living in Dunross?'

'What sort of story are you after again?' His curiosity became tinted with suspicion. 'Your face is familiar if I could place it.'

'You've seen it in the newspaper,' I said.

'Have I? The Sweeney farm was bought by a neighbour years ago. He has a herd of deer down there: venison for export and to supply some of the big hotels. It's funny, seeing them in the fields. Most of the land is idle though: he gets a grant from Brussels to keep it that way. A spy satellite in the sky making sure it stays fallow. The wonders of technology, eh?'

I fingered the car keys in my hand. It would be so simple just to drive away. The women in McHugh's office were right: that scrap of paper could have been sewn into those baby clothes months before I was born. Even now Geraldine and I regularly swapped baby clothes with friends because children grew out of them so fast. In whatever convent I was born in there would have been nothing new: a cot where other babies had lain, sheets that had been washed a thousand times, faded clothes that a dozen babies had worn. Even thinking about this made me feel unclean. Yet surely if that outfit had been rewashed so often, the writing would have been totally illegible.

'Can you remember if all of Mary Sweeney's children were at her funeral?'

The sacristan looked up. I knew that he no longer believed my story but his hostility was gone.

'That would have been thirty-five – ' He looked into my face as if assessing my age. '– no, thirty-six years ago. I just remember a clatter of clerical students arriving and getting a half-crown pressed into my palm.'

He waited for my next question.

'You must have known the daughters?'

'I didn't know them all. There was a big age gap between them, Sorry; what did you say your name was again?'

'I didn't say my name.'

'No, you didn't, did you?' He glanced down at the book. When he looked up there seemed a hint of pity in his eyes.

'There were four daughters. One is married to a chemist in Cork. Never comes back here. The eldest girl went to the States before I was born. She is a matron of some hospital over there: a bit of a dragon by all accounts. The youngest two have been away in England for years. Ellen comes home every summer. She's getting on in age, but there's great gas in her, good company, you know.'

'And the fourth daughter?'

'The baby of the family? I wouldn't know about her.'

'Why not?'

He shrugged, as if this silent gesture should be sufficient explanation. 'I was just a child,' he said. 'One day the girl was there, a bit dreamy but no harm in her. Then one day she was simply gone.'

'What happened to her?'

'If a girl vanished back then… well I suppose the adults talked about it, but as a child, if you asked a question you got a clatter. They were a good family, the Sweeneys, the only family from here ever to raise a priest. They were well respected.'

'What was the girl's name?'

He made a clicking noise with his tongue as he pondered the question and then shook his head.

'Like I say, I was just a child. She was never really mentioned much by anyone afterwards.'

'What do you think happened to her?' I asked.

He closed over the register and placed it up on the shelf. He opened the door. The late evening light seemed sharp after the gloom of the sacristy.

'We're not children now, are we? It's a changed world. I remember when *The Late Late Show* started on television in the 1960s and there was a fierce row for weeks, the whole country scandalised after a bishop complained that a woman on the show mentioned how she wore no nightie on her wedding night. I was watching it last Friday night and Gay Byrne had Bishop Casey's mistress on, talking about bringing up the bishop's child without a scrap of help from him. It's changed times all right, and to think that back then they wouldn't even let the poor Sweeney girl attend her own mother's funeral.'

*

I drove away from Dunross church and turned left onto a side road. It was after six o'clock. Geraldine would be frantic with worry by now. How long would it take the sacristan to lock up? I pulled in at the gate to a field. A mile further down this road the woman who might be my mother had once lived. She would have walked past this spot a thousand times. The hedges needed to be trimmed; there was a riot of weeds and spring flowers in the ditch. I picked a dandelion clock from the bank and closed my eyes to gently blow the seeds apart: one o'clock, two o'clock… I was trying to envisage her as a young girl, pausing here in the late evening sunshine to pick such a dandelion and blow the seeds away, saying with each puff 'he loves me, he loves me not'. I imagined her father walking ahead, driving a small herd of cattle who lurched against each other. I could almost hear his voice telling her to hurry on. I could see the scene so clearly that it frightened me. I opened my eyes and looked down at the car keys in my hand. I pressed the button and the car bleeped repeatedly when I locked and unlocked the doors, as if that electronic noise could banish ghosts.

When I thought the sacristan would be gone I drove back to the church. There was a stile in the stone wall of the graveyard. I climbed over it and began to walk among the headstones. A woman passing on a bicycle watched me with open curiosity. I turned away, leaving the gravel path, moving through the ranks of graves. The largest headstone was a memorial to two local youths 'Brutally done to death by British forces, July 1921'. The more recent ones had oval photographs built into the black marble: the same family names being repeated over and over. Six times I came across gravestones with the name Sweeney on the back, but each time the names and the dates were wrong. It was seven o'clock. I was still two hours' drive away from Dublin, but I couldn't bring myself to leave. Several times I almost lost my footing in the half-light, yet still I began another circuit through the headstones.

I located the headstone at the very top of the graveyard. *In loving memory, Mary Sweeney, d. June 2nd, 1956. Also her husband, Michael Sweeney, d. March 20th, 1965.* It was in granite, the lettering weathered. There were withered flowers in a vase filled with rancid black water. I put out my hand to touch the stone and looked across at the lights of farms across that valley. Then the certain realisation came to me that I had been here before. I felt no doubt: this was the grave of my grandparents. At this same time of evening, I had been here at this spot as a five-and-a-half-month embryo in the womb of a woman whose first name I did not yet know. The graveyard had been as empty then as it was now, another car waiting at the gate. But there had been no family waiting for my mother at the end of her journey. There had been a driver and a nun and long miles of silence on the journey back to some convent.

I reached in for the small Pentax I always carried in my inside pocket and raised it to my eye. The view was framed, within my control. For a moment I was eleven years of age again in the Botanic Gardens, with the same sense of the forbidden as I clicked. I lowered the camera and raised my head. I did not know if she had cried that night, granted her few moments alone by her mother's grave when all the neighbours were safely gone, but I cried, like I have not cried in decades; for her and for me, the pair of us alone on that June evening in 1956 when we were the one flesh, and I cried too for the ache of the years that we had been apart.

It was a quarter past ten when I finally reached home. Geraldine was standing in the lit doorway, Benedict asleep in her arms, in his pyjamas with a coat thrown over him. Her face was lined. She looked exhausted.

'You're all right,' she said, 'you're safe. Thank God. I kept thinking that maybe you'd crashed. Then I started thinking about what Frank Conroy did…' Her voice changed. 'You never phoned. All day I was waiting for your call, you stupid, selfish bastard.'

Chapter Nine

March was always the month that Elizabeth loved best: when the garden in Coventry became a true refuge for her. The lengthening evenings when she would clear out the forget-me-nots and other early flowering biennials starting to droop in the flower-bed and transfer the hardy annuals coming into bloom. When she looked back, a decade of Aprils merged in her mind. Evenings spent listening to her daughters' voices squabbling cheerfully over their homework in the kitchen while she knelt to lift bulbs from the soil or cut back the fuchsia or tend to the barberry that was about to burst forth in a mass of yellow flowers. Twilights when the garden was illuminated only by the light spilling from the open door of Jack's shed and she would call him in for his supper before the girls got ready for bed. Every March she had sworn that this was the year when she would try to forget about Francis.

Elizabeth placed her hand against the windowpane and looked out at the wilderness of her garden. She remembered the March evening in 1965 when the woman next door came in to tell her that her sister Ellen was on the phone. *'Daddy's dead, Lizzy. Come back to Ireland with me for the funeral. We'll face them together. It's been nine years. Nobody can keep you from your rightful place at the grave this time.'* Come back to Ireland. After nine years she thought that she had learned to control the urge inside her. She pretended to Jack that she was going over for the funeral; pretended to Ellen that she would meet her outside the Gresham Hotel in O'Connell Street in Dublin; pretended to herself that she would not go missing again.

The open deck of the cattle boat; a scarf round her hair as she let the sea spray drench her. How could she have been so stupid as to let her old fantasy take hold of her mind: the fantasy about finding Francis and the pair of them running away for the day, fleeing down some laneway near his school before anyone missed him. Taking the rickety St Kevin's bus up into the Wicklow Mountains to sit in a café near Glendalough that served fancy ice creams, with dance music playing on the wireless. And what a perfect little gentleman Francis had turned into, solemnly telling her the details of his new life, patiently understanding how she loved him despite the things she had been forced to do.

His shining hair and his smile when she said: *'You're the only man in my life, you always will be.'* He would be too shy to ask for a second ice cream, but she would know with a mother's instinct and the shop-owner in his apron would smile as he carried the banana boat down to their table. *'Will you come to visit me again?' 'I promise I will, Francis, but it has to be our secret, just you and me.'* Then it would be time to bring him back to Dublin before school ended, the bus taking them down towards that cursed city where they would have to part. No, she would keep him, they would run away together, anywhere she could find work. She would leave the girls, leave Jack... make sacrifices just to mind him. She could see them in that café in the mountains, his bewildered angry voice asking: *'Why did you sign me away? I want to go home. Why are you trying to steal me, you mad woman?'*

Elizabeth had screamed on the cattle boat to block out his imaginary words. She had screamed until some returning navvy up on the deck took her shoulders and gently steered her away from the rails, asking no questions, just guiding her into the safety of the warm, crowded bar, with the echo of her scream left to fade out among the seabirds and the swell of the dark waves.

On that March morning in 1965 when the boat docked in Dublin, she had thought of Ellen who had travelled over a day early and was waiting for her on the steps outside the Gresham, where the doorman in his top hat would be summoning taxis from the rank. How long would Ellen wait for her? She knew that her sister would wait until the very last minute before running to the ugly new bus station to catch a bus that would get her to their father's funeral on time.

Even when walking among the crowds of passengers up the Dublin quays Lizzy kept up the pretence that she would join her sister. She would travel to Dunross and confront them all. Then she thought about how Francis would be waking up somewhere in this city; his bare feet touching cold lino as some woman called him for his breakfast. What name would she be calling him? Who was this woman who had stolen her child and was she cruel to him? Elizabeth prayed that she was a kind woman, that Francis had a home where he was happy. Soon he would be walking to school. If she only knew which school it was it would be enough simply to stand at the gate and see him pass. It was nine years since she had seen him, but what type of mother would not know her own child's face?

She had no fantasies now about illicit afternoons in Glendalough. She would give ten years of her life just to glimpse him amid a bunch of children and know that he was well. She was haunted by the thought that if he died nobody would bother to tell her. She could not stop visualising a small grave with a tiny headstone she would never read. *Oh Sweet Jesus,* Lizzy prayed, *allow me one sign that he is well. Strike me down; let me die the most terrible of deaths, but just spare my son any suffering.*

People on O'Connell Bridge were looking at her like she was demented. She realised that she had been talking aloud. She needed to get away from them. There were buses pulling out along the quays. She ran towards one and jumped onto the open platform at the rear. *I'm in your hands now, Jesus,* she prayed. *If it is Your will that You forgive me my sins then I will find my son because You will lead me to him.* She stared out at the passing streets, waiting for Christ to show her a sign. There was a Christian Brothers' school just across the road from the last stop. She fought against a rush of joyful tears. *Sweet Jesus, I know that you have led me here and I am forgiven.*

She stood outside the gate. A handful of boys were already inside the yard, using schoolbags as goalposts and shouting as they chased a ball. A car drove in, a teacher who glanced across at her. More boys passed, one of them sniggering at the state of her. Her lower lip was sore from biting it. She found that she could no longer pray. Her head fell dizzy. She could just say one word: *Jesus.* She could not pray to the Blessed Virgin, who conceived without sin. Only Jesus, being a son, could understand. There was a brooch in her handbag, she took it out. *I offer you up this pain, Jesus, for just one glimpse of my son.* She inhaled deeply as the brooch pin ripped into her palm. Her teeth were clenched. *I offer up this suffering.* Boys were flooding past in a blur of faces. *Jesus, grant this sinner a sign.* A Christian Brother was coming out, menacing, authoritarian: she began to back away. He followed her, suspicious. She stood on the far pavement, glaring at him. If he tried to move her further away she would sink this brooch pin into his heart.

*

Elizabeth's daughter Sharon entered the kitchen and watched her mother's palms press against the window. She seemed like a moth trapped behind the glass. Sharon would have to pack for her and there was so little space in those hospital lockers. They should never have let her try to continue living an independent life in this bungalow for so long. It had been cruel to leave her here, even with a nurse coming in, but she had refused to move in with any of them. Once the garden started to grow neglected they should have recognised the signs. Even though her mother was weak with pain, every room in this bungalow still shone as if she was terrified that someone would find fault with it, but Sharon knew that the garden had been her mother's real home, just like the shed had been her father's refuge.

It was two years since her father had died. The heart attack had been unexpected but maybe he had experienced warning signs because in the weeks beforehand he had twice mentioned to her husband – who sometimes went along to games to keep him company – how he would love to have his ashes scattered behind the goalposts before a Coventry City match. On the night of his death, after they had all made their way back here from the hospital, they had wanted to discuss this with Elizabeth. But when Sharon went into Elizabeth's bedroom she had found her mother taking off her good clothes and putting on her favourite tattered old coat.

'Where are you going, Mummy? We're all here to keep you company. You can't just go walking around the streets like Daddy said you were always doing.'

It was only when Sharon broke down that Elizabeth had stopped and sat on the bed to take Sharon's head in her lap like she did when Sharon was a child.

'Mummy, it's like we're losing you, like you're in a world of your own where nothing else matters. Daddy's just died and you haven't even shed a tear.'

Her mother had stroked her hair.

'I've no tears left. I cried more tears in this house than anyone ever saw. I need to go out for a walk, Sharon. I feel that I'll go mad if I don't go out. Maybe I'm going mad anyway: everything feels odd these days. He was a good man, your father, a good man.'

'Steve says that he wanted to be cremated, but I always thought you and he would be buried together.'

'Your father and I didn't have much in common. If that's what he wanted then he should be cremated.'

'But what about you, Mummy, when your time comes?'

'Don't bury me over here. I want someone to bring me home.'

'We'll bring you home.'

'You're good girls… but you can't bring me home.'

'What do you want, Mummy? What can we do for you?'

'I want to go for a walk on my own.'

*

At least on the visit to Dublin after her father's death she had not gone back to the Catholic Protection Agency. The first time she ran away, two years earlier, she had stood across the street from it to watch a girl arrive with a baby in her arms. The girl was already climbing the steps before Elizabeth found the courage to move.

'Don't…!' She ran across the road. The girl looked back at her in terror and then ran into the building. Elizabeth sat on the steps, gathering the strength to push open the door. The same nondescript paint was on the walls in reception, the same thin strip of carpet across the tiled floor, the same heavy wooden crucifix above the desk as the receptionist demanded to know why she wanted to see Mrs Lacey. Mrs Lacey was busy; she had no time to be seeing the likes of her. The receptionist refused to allow Elizabeth to wait in the hall and threatened to call the police if she loitered on the steps outside. The woman grew increasingly angry.

'What are you coming back here for? We took you in and sent you back out that door without a stain on your character. You walked out of here as good as a virgin.'

Cowed, Elizabeth retreated to stand out on the pavement, knowing that she was being watched from a window upstairs. Two passing women steered around her and glanced back, whispering. Elizabeth retreated further to the railings on the other side of the street. An old tramp sat there, tobacco stains on his grey beard.

'You stay away from that place, Mrs,' he said. 'Pray to God that he'll eventually give you a child of your own instead. You don't want to be stuck with the leftovers of every whore slipping up from the bog to leave their bastards on that doorstep.'

Elizabeth stood at the railings for five hours before Mrs Lacey came down. The windows of the building were lit up in the dusk, the open door framed by light when she appeared. The woman slowly crossed the street. Elizabeth eyed her cautiously. She wanted to run, but kept her fingers tightly pressed for support against the bars of the railings.

'Any talking we have to do can be done out here,' Mrs Lacey said quietly but firmly, 'and then you really should go on your way.'

'I want him back,' Elizabeth said.

'Don't be daft, girl. Talk sense. The child is happy in a good Catholic home. What right have you to come here demanding anything?'

'Francis is my child.'

'There is no child of that name now and you know that the boy was never truly yours. You had no real right to the child, even before you signed him away. Signing him away was just a legal formality. Do you understand? He was always God's child. You have no right to try and contaminate him further with your sin.'

'Then please, just give me a first name for him or a photograph… something of his… even just a piece of clothing. You could arrange it, you know where he is. If you wanted to tell me you could.'

A car swung into the parking space beside them, the driver in a black coat beeping for them to move. Mrs Lacey lowered her voice.

'You're inadequate, do you realise that? It's not natural for you to want him back. Every child has the right to a proper home. What sort of evilness lies within you that you deny him a second life? I see a wedding ring on your hand. What would your husband say if he knew about this? He'd beat you black and blue and you would deserve a good hiding. He'd turn you out on the street if he had an ounce of self-respect. You would never have hooked a man if we hadn't given you this chance to restart your life. Are you trying to deny an innocent child the same chance? You're selfish, do you hear me? If you had any natural feelings you would never show your face here. Now I know about your tricks in the past, Little Miss Needlework. I know…'

Mrs Lacey stopped then as if she had said too much. Information was power: this was something Elizabeth had learned from dealing with such people. She tried to contain the surge of hope: somebody must have found her name and address stitched into those clothes. Was it his adoptive parents or had it been intercepted before Francis was handed over? She wanted to ask but knew that Mrs Lacey would not tell her.

'Your husband could have had you committed to an asylum for turning up like this. I know a dozen doctors who would sign the committal papers. Don't think you're safe just because you now live in a pagan country. If you were sent to prison for a crime, prison is a terrible place but you would know your length of sentence. But when you're committed to an asylum you're committed for life, girl, and I don't think too many of your family would come running with a key. Now please, for your own sake, forget this nonsense and go home.'

Mrs Lacey started to walk back across the road. Elizabeth followed at a distance, too scared to approach and yet unable to let go. There was a car coming in the dusk. She stopped and stood in its path, hoping it would plough into her and end this. She was unnatural, selfish, evil. The driver beeped in annoyance and then swerved and was gone. The woman stopped on the steps and beckoned Elizabeth towards her. Mrs Lacey produced a handkerchief and handed it to Elizabeth to wipe her eyes. She shook her head when Elizabeth tried to give it back.

'Keep it,' the woman said kindly. 'Have a good cry: I often need a good cry too at times. Then go back to your husband where you belong. Don't waste the second life we've given you. Have children of your own, children who will belong to you. I'm only thinking of your own good and the child's good. In years to come you'll be grateful to me. And remember, God in his mercy can forgive anything.'

'Then please tell me one little detail about him,' Elizabeth said softly. 'Is he well? Just give me something of him to take home.'

The kindness was gone. Elizabeth felt like a dog about to be beaten.

'You will never find him. But we can find your husband if you keep making a nuisance of yourself. You're no spring chicken anymore. No man likes to discover that he bought used goods. Think about everything you could lose. You've disgraced your child enough. Now try to live with at least a bit of dignity for his sake.'

Elizabeth stood there with nowhere to go after the woman closed the door.

*

Sharon emerged from the bedroom with Elizabeth's packed bag. Her mother was rooting at the bin. How could she have known so quickly that her old coat had been put in there?

'I have your good coat packed,' Sharon said. 'That old coat is ancient; please, Mummy, just leave it back in the bin.'

'I have to wear it.'

'Mummy, you look like a tramp in it.'

'This is the coat he'll find me in.'

'Mummy, Daddy can't find you. You have premature Alzheimer's and cancer. Daddy's dead, he had a heart attack. I'm trying to mind you. Just for once, Mummy, could you focus on me, please?'

Sharon held her mother's gaze and after a moment her eyes grew clearer.

'I'm sorry,' Elizabeth said, 'sorry for everything. Sorry I wasn't a better mother. You see I'm unnatural... evil... selfish... that's what a woman told me once.'

'What woman? Who would say those awful things? We're going to the hospital, Mummy, do you understand? You were a good mother. You just always judged yourself too harshly. I have your bag packed, Mummy. Are you ready to go?'

Chapter Ten

In the week after my return from Killaloe the atmosphere was tense between Geraldine and me. The evenings were getting brighter and I built Benedict a bird table I had promised him, while he pretended to help me, babbling away about fixing a tractor on an imaginary farm owned by his new invisible friend, Gary the Goat, who, he claimed, lived in his pocket. Benedict's incessant talking filled out the growing silence between his parents.

I went back into the newspaper offices as if trying in infiltrate my former life. Gerry was working on the feature on Frank Conroy. He had spent another day in Killaloe while I went to see Peter McHugh. Some locals had told him that Conroy's was a copycat suicide, inspired by a former Mullabeg miner who deliberately parked his car onto a level crossing near Birdhill. Others claimed that Conroy was drunk and unaware of what he was doing or that he even had the child with him in the car.

'I hate covering suicide stories,' he said. 'We can't ignore something that is happening more and more, but I don't know if anything I print will result in three or four more copycat deaths. It's the domino effect: the more we talk about it the more dominos we get. At one time we were happy to kill ourselves slowly with whiskey, now, like everything else, we're in a mad rush to do it. A father kills his child because he cannot cope. I want to understand him, but no matter what tragedy he's endured, I'm still not in the business of putting excuses in his mouth.'

The domino effect. The porch of the church in Killaloe had been plastered with posters advertising helplines for girls who found themselves pregnant. One in every fourth baby in the state was born to a single parent. Illegitimacy could now be talked about, people like me acknowledged. But whereas every parish once had some girl who was made to disappear at night, the unmentionable disappearances were now occurring in sheds and under bridges, with suicides hushed up.

'Geraldine panicked on the morning you left Killaloe and didn't phone her,' Gerry added. 'She called me. Unlike you, I carry a mobile phone. I think she's been worried that since you came out of hospital you might try and pull a similar stunt yourself.'

'What did you tell her?'

'I said there wasn't a chance. If you meant to drive your car into a river you'd have left your dad's old camera with me for safe keeping. There's no way you'd get that camera wet.'

'Very droll, Gerry.'

'If your dad was here, Sean, he'd tell you that it's time you got yourself back in harness; time you stopped licking your wounds and got back to being yourself.'

I left the Killaloe photographs on his desk.

'Maybe that's harder to do,' I said, 'when you're not rightly sure who are you are anymore.'

*

My dreams were becoming increasingly disturbed. I was back sleeping in the same bed as Geraldine and often woke abruptly as if somebody had called me. I would listen to her breathing in the silence that was broken most nights by Benedict waking from one of his night terrors. One night I dreamed that an awards ceremony for press photographers was being held in Dunross graveyard. Smart women in pink dresses and men in dinner jackets wandered aimlessly through the headstones, wondering why the location had been chosen. I stood on the path, trying to block off the corner of the graveyard that contained my grandparents' headstone.

But when I turned around I found myself standing on a slope leading down to the Tolka River. Two huge pits were being dug into the sparsely wooded slope and a line of saplings waited to be planted. Men laboured at these pits, while others worked with long saws on tree trunks that must have been felled by a storm because their roots were upended. A man, stripped to the waist, grinned at me as he lifted a heavy wheelbarrow and began to push it up the low hill. I knew his face from somewhere. I looked down to find that my clothes were ragged. I had an old-fashioned spade in my hand. My arms seemed younger, covered in hair. I was whistling though I know that I cannot whistle.

There was a man-made pond, planted with water lilies, below the slope. Beyond this was the river, with cows grazing in a sloping field on the far bank. Behind me there was a crackle of burning twigs and the tang of smoke. A toothless old man crouched among the few remaining mature trees, boiling up a billycan. A horse-drawn cart approached, laden with rich, brown earth. The driver cursed at me cheerfully to get back to work. I walked to the cart and began to shovel the soil down into the pit. The man with the wheelbarrow stopped beside me. The barrow was wooden and rudimentary. His naked shoulder deliberately brushed against mine. I knew his face now; I could remember the sound of his breath as he chased me beneath moonlit yew trees. He grinned conspiratorially and I found myself grinning back, whistling as I plunged my spade into the soil on the back of the cart. When I looked into the pit I saw the half-buried remains of Frank Conroy and his child.

I woke beside Geraldine, trying to restrain my breathing. Sinéad was sleeping in her cot in the corner of the room. My vest clung to me with sweat. I recognised that spot in my dream, although it had changed. There was now a bridge over that pond in the Botanic Gardens. The saplings that were about to be planted were a hundred years old. I had photographed that spot as an eleven-year-old boy. Snatches of the whistled tune lingered in my head, but when I tried to piece it together they were gone.

*

If there had been anyone to take the children off our hands for even one night, it might have given Geraldine and I the chance to repair the new strains in our relationship. But my parents were dead, Geraldine's father lived alone in Athlone and her two sisters had migrated to America and New Zealand. Sinéad kept waking at night with teething pains. Often it was simpler to just take her into our bed, where she would suck her thumb for comfort and sit up to play her favourite game of softly slapping our faces. Eventually Geraldine would abandon hopes of trying to get her back asleep and hand her a hairbrush. The baby found a soothing comfort in clumsily trying to brush Geraldine's hair. I would drift in and out of sleep, hearing Geraldine wince whenever the hairbrush hurt her.

Soothers were threatening to damage the shape of Benedict's mouth, yet he clung to one at night for comfort. Finally we pricked his favourite soother with a pin so the suck would grow less powerful and he might tire of it. But he regularly woke in the night, crying for me to drive to a chemist and buy him a new one.

At dawn we were both generally wrecked from a lack of sleep. It was better not to speak at breakfast, we were so exhausted that even a casual remark sounded like an accusation. Geraldine was facing another day of Benedict blocking the baby's path whenever Sinéad tried to crawl and of Sinéad breaking up the jigsaws that Benedict tried to make. I tried to help out; changing nappies and feeding them their breakfasts. But Geraldine and I often wound up quarrelling about silly things and I would storm off, with Geraldine left holding Sinéad and Benedict who always cried when they saw me put on my coat.

The irony was that I generally had nowhere to rush to. Certainly there were a few small commissions to attend to, but I had lost the compulsive urge to work that once propelled me. The photographs from Dunross graveyard lined my studio wall, each shot spliced to merge into the next so that it looked like the Pentax had taken a wide-angle three-hundred-and-sixty-degree shot. I had also blown up the negatives of the black-and-white shots taken by the river in the Botanic Gardens when I was eleven. They were blurred and criss-crossed with marks, but I arranged them on my wall as well. These two sets of shots – taken a quarter century apart – confronted me each morning, like a puzzle I needed to solve. This seemed the only way that I could make sense of my past: by sifting through images and rearranging them as if my life was one of Benedict's jigsaws that would eventually make sense if I could get the pieces in the right order.

One morning in late March I decided to visit my parents' grave. When I was small they had surely discussed the possibility of me wanting to find my birth mother. They were both dead now, while there was a strong chance she was still alive. So why did I feel that I was somehow betraying their memory by starting to look for her?

I was eighteen when my mother died and thirty-one when my father followed her. During his fifteen years as a widower he faithfully visited her grave once a week, with a small bottle of water and flowers from the garden she once carefully tended. Occasionally I had accompanied him to stand beside the grave in Glasnevin cemetery. He never blessed himself and it was impossible to know whether he prayed or talked to her directly in his head. Our only conversations there were about the condition of the grave and where to dump the withered flowers from last week. Apart from trips to the pub, his only other outings in those final years were to see Shelbourne play in whatever hired ground they managed to base themselves in. Shelbourne's glory days were long over by then; the crowd at games tiny. It was hard to know which weekly excursion he found the loneliest.

For four years after my mother's death I lived awkwardly in the same house as him, with our lives – and our ideas about life – splintering apart. He wanted me to find a steady job after I left school, even cutting out advertisements for positions as prison officers and leaving them on the kitchen table. But I hadn't wanted to be a prison officer or a civil servant or a clerk in an insurance company. My only interest was in photography: something that should have brought us together but drove us farther apart. In his eyes there was no money in photographs: you started out by wanting to capture images so powerful that they stopped time and you wound up, if you were lucky, doing first communions and hating the job that had once been your passion.

At the age of twenty I was doing unpaid work on an underground magazine when I first met Gerry, who was also cutting his teeth there. We photo-documented protest meetings against plans for a nuclear power plant in Wexford; PAYE mass-action marches by workers in Dublin; pirate radio stations which broadcast from cellars under snooker halls; squatters occupying listed buildings which developers had bribed councillors to rezone for destruction. Sometimes my father came up into my makeshift darkroom in the attic and scanned the prints drying there. He'd shake his head.

'Can you not take one shot without some weirdo protesting about something in the background?'

'We can't all block reality out with a fuchsia bush,' I'd snap back, waiting with my hands immersed in chemicals until he left.

Aunt Cissie once scolded me for making him feel like a peasant. He had his wife's death to cope with and deserved to be allowed do so without my smug and totally untested superior notions about life. And he was right partly about the photographs I took for the magazine. More and more people drifted into the editorial collective, people who seemed destructively opposed to everything – including creativity. Meetings became an endless scrutinising of submissions to flush out latent examples of sexism and racism. A flour-bombing raid was made on the Photographers' Gallery for showing an exhibition of Jérôme Ducrot's crushed nudes: a raid that Gerry and I opted out of, seeking refuge in a pub.

My breaking point came when the magazine refused to print a small ad by an unemployed couple who had been evicted from their flat. They turned up at the magazine's office with one child in a pram and a baby wrapped in a blanket. Gerry and I took their handwritten ad and promised not only would it be printed, but it would be printed for free. These were the sort of people this magazine was set up to represent, but the collective editorial board was swollen with art students with axes to grind and we were denounced for accepting the ad which read '*Married couple; husband a good handyman, can turn his hand to anything, wife a good cook and organiser, desperately need caretaking or any position.*' The board demanded to know how we could expect them to print an ad with offensive terms like handyman, husband or wife. One faction suggested rewriting the ad in an acceptable fashion to read '*two people co-habiting, one handyperson, one cook*', while another faction wanted to invite the couple to come in and be educated about how they were demeaning themselves. The atmosphere at the meeting suggested that the couple had brought their poverty on themselves through their own grammatical ignorance.

Gerry and I cleared our desks and left. I knew my father would be in the local pub, drinking alone at the counter. He was surprised when I joined him. After several pints I told him what happened and he laughed and cursed them viciously. Then, as if opening himself up to me, he began to curse others too: people he had spent years defending against my charges – Irish politicians, the church, even Pezzani's poxy fuchsia bush. In the pub we were on neutral ground. I was getting a glimpse into the mindset of his generation who felt forced to justify causes and beliefs they had long grown to despise among themselves.

Three years after my mother's death Pezzani's postcard business was bought over by an Australian company. Pezzani's laboratory for developing holiday snaps was closed down in the rationalisation. By the time I moved in with Geraldine, my father had been forced into early retirement. Pezzani's postcards were now printed in Hong Kong. Considered too surreally old-fashioned to be passed off as reality, they were now rebranded for the nostalgia market, and art professors, eyeing up an untapped niche, started to describe Pezzani as an iconic master of irony.

My relationship with my father was improving but it was Geraldine who bonded us together. She was the first decision in my life he fully approved of. 'An Athlone Town fan,' he had chuckled on the evening they first met, 'don't mention John Minnock's penalty!' When she laughed he was delighted that she'd understood the reference. It became their running joke. Twice a week we brought him for a drink. In his favourite corner of the local pub he became the old-fashioned charmer I remembered from my summer working on his van. All that was missing was the waistcoat. When he died I found a photograph of Geraldine in his wallet along with one of his wife. His will was simple. *'To my son, Sean, who chose a career that will never support a family, I leave my entire estate with the greatest regret that it is not enough to be much help to them.'*

I had not expected to be so devastated by his death. My work was starting to become known; I'd had a Dublin solo show and signed a contract for a book of photographs. The public recognition was nice, but after he died I realised that the impetus driving my work had always been an attempt to make him proud of his adopted son. He left £9,000 in a post-office savings book. I was infuriated, imagining all the small luxuries that he could have bought during the last few years when he stretched out his pension, denied himself cigarettes and that last drink in the pub before going home to an empty house. He had been determined to leave me a cash sum in addition to his house. With the house deeds in an envelope in the wardrobe, there were old contact sheets, wonderfully candid shots of Dublin street life in the 1950s. Photography had been his passion and he was a better photographer than me. But at some moment in his life he stopped photographing what he actually saw and settled for shooting what Pezzani wanted him to see. I had been the catalyst for this: he had needed to buckle down and show the adoption agency that he could be a responsible and conservative parent. The dates on the contact sheets ended the year they brought me home, when he accepted the responsibilities of being a family man, under the watchful eye of Mrs Lacey of the Catholic Protection Agency.

Among his papers there was an agreement with Pezzani, made in the year that my father went to work for him – a contract to take shots for postcards on a tiny percentage royalty. I remembered asking him once if Pezzani ever paid him for his images used on the postcards, and my father had laughed at the idea of Pezzani parting with cash. Maybe this was why my father always kept up a small fiddle on the side, to feel he was getting something back. My father was a meticulous man; his life's earnings were neatly detailed in notebooks along with tax certificates. They showed that he had been paid just his wages and a small commission as a salesman.

I traced down Pezzani to an old people's home outside Bray. He sat out on a balcony, staring at the Wicklow Hills. His mind seemed muddled at first, then his eyes became clear. He readily admitted to having cheated my father, chuckling as he remembered their occasional confrontations on the subject.

'I had him by the balls because if he lost his job he was frightened he might lose you. But you are chasing the wrong man: the Australians bought out my entire business; liabilities, creditors, everything. I know your face now. You're the boy genius, the Aran boy with the donkey. Go forth and do what Aran boys always do with donkeys… screw them good.'

This was the only piece of Pezzani's advice I ever took. The parent company in Sydney ignored the first letters from my solicitor. I knew it would be impossible to calculate a sum for back royalties and make them admit liability, but because there had been a breach of contract I demanded to have the copyright and original negatives of my father's work returned to me. Almost nothing of his work remained in print. But the few shots of his still in use were intractably part of sets of bestselling posters and table mats of vanished Georgian Dublin doorways and public houses, sets that the company could not afford to scrap. Bad planning had ensured that my father's photographs could never be replaced because the buildings were gone.

On the day before the case was due in court, the Australians made an offer to settle. For me the sum was enormous, for them it was no more than the legal fees of a week in court. My team had taken the case on a no-foal-no-fee basis. After I paid off my senior and junior counsels I still had enough from my father's estate for Geraldine and myself to live on for several years. My solicitor declined his fee and settled instead for a framed copy of his favourite photograph of mine: a shot of Dublin's most notorious gangster dropping his trousers when leaving the Four Courts to reveal a pair of Mickey Mouse boxer shorts.

I remember leaving the solicitor's office and walking down the quays. It was a summer's evening. I visited shop after shop until I found one of my father's images among the postcards hanging on a rack outside a newsagent. How often had I mocked those pictures as an adolescent? I would have given every penny of that settlement for him to be alive for one second and get to hold the cheque nestling in my wallet. It was Pezzani who cheated him, but I had inherited my father's affection for the Italian. I didn't know if he would still be alive, but I drove to the nursing home. He sat in the same chair, still looking out at the Wicklow Hills.

'He won't know you,' the nurse said. 'He knows no one, but if we lift him away from that view he gets angry and cries out.'

I leaned down. His eyes stared ahead, not acknowledging my presence. The nurse thought I was crazy, but I persuaded her to let me leave the fuchsia bush I had brought with me against the balcony railings so that it formed a foreground to frame his vision of the hills. Perhaps I only imagined it but there seemed to be the flicker of a smile. I left the postcard on his lap, the address side up. Across it in black marker were the words, 'The Aran Boy did as instructed: I screwed them good.'

*

My parents were buried beyond the Republican plot in Glasnevin Cemetery, near the locked side gate for De Courcy Square. As a youth I often drank in Kavanagh's pub there, which had a hatch in the wall where gravediggers once knocked at for porter on hot afternoons. I arranged the flowers I had brought on my parents' grave and then stood beside it, unsure of what to say to them in my mind.

A hundred yards beyond their grave, the eerie wilderness that constituted the oldest part of the graveyard began. Ancient capsized headstones were arrayed around family vaults with stone angels that had been untouched for a century. These were the tombs of the rich. Elsewhere there was just the stump of wooden crosses or nothing remaining beyond some hint in the shape of the earth to suggest that bodies lay there. Beyond this silent expanse there were ivy-clad railings, and through these railings I could glimpse people strolling in the Botanic Gardens.

It was mid-morning. A man with a wheelbarrow of cuttings walked through green gates, behind which smoke rose from a bonfire. A young girl was kneeling among the sample beds of vegetables. I felt like a voyeur from a city of the dead as I watched her. I felt that even if she turned and stared directly towards me I would still be invisible, standing amid the slumped headstones. I raised the Pentax and kept clicking until I heard the finished film rewind itself.

These moments of feeling at a loss among the living occurred less frequently now. But whenever I went for a check-up the doctors advised therapy. Everybody who underwent a near-death experience suffered some sense of loss, they said. With professional counselling I could overcome this malaise. But it was not that simple for me, because there were things I felt that I should be able to remember, things I had blocked out, memories I needed to confront before I could move on.

I went back to my car and drove around to the entrance of the Botanic Gardens. I stopped opposite the spot where the crash had occurred. A hired limousine decked out with ribbons was parked outside the gates, the chauffeur enjoying a cigarette while the photographers arranged a bride and groom in poses among the flower beds inside the entrance. Construction work was in progress on rebuilding the old Victorian glasshouses. I walked down steps towards the river, passing the sluice gates of the mill race, the hanging willows and rhododendrons, and reached the small bridge leading to the rose garden.

I stopped, suddenly and irrationally scared as I remembered Aunt Cissie's remarks. Could I have really caused my mother anxiety in this rose garden by talking about imaginary people in the same way as Benedict now babbled on about sharing an illusory world with Gary the Goat? I crossed the bridge. A sundial stood on a raised plinth in the centre of the small area. There was a high wall in front of me. Beyond it, up on the road, I could see the top of a girl's head as she waited at the bus stop. The river cut off two other sides of the rose garden and the fourth side was blocked off by the gable end of the Tolka House pub. I pushed aside the screen of bushes that grew against this wall and stepped into the undergrowth. Broken brickwork protruding from the pub wall betrayed the outline of where the roof and walls of a cottage had once been built up against it. This was the corner that Aunt Cissie claimed I always pointed towards as a child, saying 'My house is gone: bold men steal my home.' Maybe the bushes had not been so high back then; maybe this outline of a wall was visible. Otherwise how could I have known that a cottage once stood here? I glanced behind me, half expecting to see that young man from my dreams watching me with his mocking grin.

*

A gardener with an armband and a walkie-talkie was leaning against a huge bloated tree on the slope above the pond. The branches spread out above his head in a canopy of lime-green leaves which darkened to a rusty plum colour where they were exposed to the sun. A red-beaked bird moved among the clusters of reeds on the pond. I approached the man, uncertain if Aunt Cissie had remembered the family name correctly.

'Excuse me,' I began, 'do you mind me asking if the name Davitt means anything to you – here in the gardens?

'Is it someone who worked here?' The man shook his head. 'It doesn't ring a bell, but maybe Eddie who is patrolling in the arboretum might know. He remembers back to when they used horses here. Is this Davitt chap related to you?'

I shook my head, as he spoke into the walkie-talkie. There was a crackly reply that I could not decipher. The gardener looked up.

'I know the guy you're after now,' he said. 'There's a photograph of him in the front lodge, taken with five other gardeners just after the war. The Grand Old Men of the Gardens it's called: they had three hundred years of service between them.' He pointed. 'Head up towards the Chain Tent. Eddie says that he'll be glad to talk to any relation of Austin Davitt.'

I followed a steep path up towards a circular wooden hut with a cast-iron bench inside it. The grass was allowed to grow high among the trees here so that wild flowers could thrive. A squirrel watched me for a moment and then bobbed out of sight. The second gardener was near retirement age and sat on the bench waiting for me.

'I'm not related to Austin Davitt,' I said. 'I'm just curious about something. Did he live in a cottage where the rose garden is now?'

'That's right.' He nodded. 'Davitt was born there. Both his father and grandfather were gardeners here before him, as far as I know.'

'Would many other people have lived in the gardens, back in the nineteenth century for example?'

'Just how old do you think I am?' he asked, amused. 'I haven't a clue, to be honest. I do know that all the apprentices had to live in, they were actually locked in at night. God knows what they got up to, though of course it was all lads back then. Their terms and conditions are displayed in an old poster up in the offices. You were paid four shillings a week and had to bring your own bed linen and cutlery. But I tell you one thing, you'd put up with being locked in if some of the girls working here now were serving their time with you. You see, it's written in black and white that you were legally entitled to "the share of a bed with another person".'

He laughed, but I wanted to get away because I was flooded with that perfect recollection of running at night up through the yew walk, being chased by another man in the dark. We were locked in, I thought, we were dodging the nightwatchman; knowing that we would lose our jobs if we were caught. There was no logical way in which I could remember such a moment and yet the memory was absolutely clear, bookmarked on either side by oblivion. The gardener stopped laughing and glanced at me.

'Are you all right?' he asked.

'I'm fine,' I said. 'Just one last question. Was there ever a pit or mass grave dug on the slope leading down to the pond, maybe during the famine or some cholera epidemic?'

'Not that I know of.' He shook his head. 'The last time any digging was done there was after the destruction caused by the Night of the Big Wind in 1839. Every second house in Glasnevin was damaged and almost every tree flattened on that slope. You see the original soil on that slope was too shallow for an arboretum, the roots couldn't take hold. Before they planted new trees they needed to dig deep trenches and bring in good soil from elsewhere.'

Chapter Eleven

During our courting days there was a game Geraldine and I loved to play. Dismounting our bicycles we would sit on a bench and recall moments from the past that we discovered we had shared. We always laughed about two that occurred in 1973 and 1975.

Our shared memory of 1973 was of Dalymount Park in Dublin, when – before the penalty shoot-out rule was introduced – Shamrock Rovers battled it out with Athlone Town in the FAI Cup in a tie that went to three replays. Seven and a half hours of football was spread out over four floodlit nights, by the end of which most of the supporters – and none of the players – were on speaking terms. I am not sure why I kept attending the replays, but somehow I felt compelled to keep returning until the tie was finally settled. It turned out that Geraldine had only been forty yards away from me on those nights, hoisted onto the shoulders of her oldest brother, her fourteen-year-old voice shouting for Athlone Town. Geraldine claimed that marriages resulted from those nightly trips up and down from the midlands; babies conceived whose births were notable for the protracted length of their mothers' labours.

Two years later in 1975 I was on my knees praying in front of the radio, while Geraldine was among the crowd packed into St Mel's

Park when – after a freak draw in the UEFA Cup – the mighty aristocrats of AC Milan descended onto the narrow streets of Athlone. Geraldine's father was on the management committee that year. He needed to run to a local chip-shop and persuade the Italian proprietor to abandon his bemused queue of customers and act as a translator when, moments after the draw was made, the chairman of AC Milan telephoned the tiny Irish club.

During the match, whenever the Milan stars went to take a throw in they found themselves shaking hands with local people who spilled out through the wire fencing to sit on the touchline. Midway through the first half, twelve thousand breaths were collectively held when Athlone Town was awarded a penalty. John Minnock, otherwise enjoying a superb game, stubbed a weak shot harmlessly at the keeper. A draw was a miraculous achievement, yet Minnock's missed penalty soured the day. Geraldine maintained that a dark cloud settled over the town as his foot stubbed the ball and it had never lifted since.

On the first night that we lay in bed together we discovered these links in our past. It was in a friend's borrowed bedsit in Rathmines, with yellowing wallpaper and an Ian Dury album cover stuck to the ceiling. I remember the smell of the joint he had left neatly rolled for us and the hot ports I made, as well as the scent of the mince pies that Geraldine had cooked. We were so caught up in each other that we forgot about them heating in the oven, until thick smoke alerted us. Geraldine always claimed that I looked like Tarzan that night, standing up on the table in my underpants, to hold the smouldering oven tray out the small window and let the smoke dissipate. I remember smiling back at her while across the road signs flashed on and off for kebab shops and late-night supermarkets on Rathmines Road.

We found it hard to leave the haven of that bedsit and mount our bicycles which we'd chained together in the hallway, when we could use my friend's eight-iron to flick the repeat switch on his record player and make love again on the small mattress, despite the fact that the nuns always locked the door of Geraldine's hostel at midnight.

Finally, at half eleven, we cycled quickly across the canal and down a line of streets with emptying pubs: Wexford Street, Aungier Street, George's Street. We sped down cobbled lanes onto the quays to reach Henrietta Street before the nuns turned the key in the hostel door. At five to twelve our bicycles slowed as we freewheeled up Bolton Street. The bicycles halted on the hill up to the hostel. It was a new phase of our relationship, both of us unsure of what to do next. I knew she was the one for me and I knew there was so little I could offer her. My voice didn't sound like my voice: 'I take photographs, that's all I know how to do, all I've ever wanted to do. I will never be rich, do you understand? If you stick with me you'll never have anything. My worldly possessions consist of two cameras, ten thousand negatives, this bicycle and whatever condoms we have left.'

*

The queue outside the Register of Births, Deaths & Marriages stretched halfway down Lombard Street. But after the doors opened, most people crowded into the ground floor in search of birth certificates and I was able to reach the upstairs research room. Here the ledgers stretched back into the last century, arranged in a loose order on old shelving. The room was quickly filling up with visitors – professional researchers, geologists, elderly Americans. There were four volumes for 1956. I took down the last one, with R–Z on the spine. It contained thousands of entries, giving the surname and first name of each child, the date of birth and the district where the birth was registered.

I ran my finger slowly through the list of Sweeneys. This was a moment of truth. Until now I had been able to convince myself that the story of the woman from Kildorrery could be invented or incorrectly remembered. The address sown into those baby clothes could be a case of mistaken identity. There was nothing definite to link me to Dunross except for my own, possibly imaginary, feelings in that graveside.

I already had a name and a life, so why did I need to superimpose a second life onto it? Now that I was here, I couldn't decide if I wanted to find a Sweeney listed under my date of birth. I reached the end of a line of names and paused before turning the page. I suddenly longed for there to be no Sweeney with my date of birth. I would then be free of this new obsession about disturbing the past, having no other clues to search with. I would have to focus on my present life and nothing else.

As I turned the page, I found myself praying for the first time in decades: *Lord, let me not find myself here.* Four lines from the end of the second page the list of Sweeneys ran out. There was no child listed under my date of birth. I felt a sense of release. Some child other than me had been in their mother's womb in Dunross graveyard, standing at that grave like an outcast. I was anonymous again.

But then as I stood up the cold realisation struck me. What had I been thinking of? I took down the first ledger for 1956 and midway down a page, I found myself: Blake, Sean, with my date of birth and with the names of parents who had not even known that I existed on the day I was born. Months after my birth my details had been falsified and back-dated into the official records. How could I be so stupid as to think that any trace of my first life would be allowed to stain the official version of who I was? There was no Sweeney under my date of birth because no Sweeney child had ever officially existed. An elderly American woman sitting beside me looked up. Her eyes seemed about to brim over.

'I've found my grandmother,' she said. 'She was born in Leitrim in 1873 and slaved as a maid all her life in Boston. I'm so pleased she's here.'

'I'm delighted for you,' I said.

She noticed how my hands were trembling and reached across to lightly touch my fingers for a second.

'Isn't it funny that something as simple as a row of names in copperplate writing can hold so much pain?'

*

'What sort of project are you working on, Mr Blake?' The official from the Botanic Gardens turned the key in the curved oak door at the top of the stairs. We stood in gloom for a moment before the door opened. Two high windows looked down over the bend on the road where I had crashed. A curtain of ivy was encroaching across the upper panes. The room had the pervasive melancholy of old Dublin pubs on winter afternoons. The bookcases were ancient, the leather bindings dating from the nineteenth century. The man waited for an answer to his question. The rain was loud against the panes of glass. I stared out at cars slowing on the bend.

'I'm looking for a ghost,' I said.

I turned to see his reaction. He was impassive; no trace of humour or anxiety in his gaze.

'Sometimes we bring our ghosts to places with us,' he said.

'Do you believe in ghosts?'

He looked around at the shelves of bound records and files of photographic plates. 'We call this Bluebeard's room,' he said. 'The cleaners don't like being in here by themselves at night. None have ever seen Bluebeard, none will admit to believing in him, but if they're in here at night and the door closes, he's suddenly more real to them than anyone outside.'

'What about you?' I asked again. He looked at me closely. Both of us were trying to place each other's face.

'I just need to believe that you're a bona fide researcher doing something for your newspaper so I can enter your name in the day book. After that you're on your own. I'm downstairs if you need me.'

He closed the door as he left. I was alone with Bluebeard. I wondered how the cleaners imagined this ghost. As a phantom with a cutlass and a blank eye socket materialising through the shelves? If there was a ghost here it was probably an earlier version of one of them, one of the anonymous women who gave Washerwoman's Hill its name, stooped for eternity on her knees with a scrubbing brush.

I sat down with no idea of what to look for here. How could you start to look for a nameless young man, when you weren't even sure that he had ever existed? All I had was fragments of dreams.

When not dreaming about his face I regularly dreamed about being in a public place with Geraldine and the children. I might be walking just behind them when suddenly confronted by a wall of glass that I would press my palms against, calling out to them although they could not hear me as they walked on, with Geraldine bending down to laugh with Benedict, oblivious to me because I had died in a car crash. I would wake and long for Geraldine to wake too and hold me in her arms. I took these dreams as a sign that I was coming to value the miracle of having survived. Every morning my feeling of relief was tangible. I'm alive, I would keep repeating like a mantra in my mind, longing for Benedict to wake to the sound of the milk truck and sleepily run, demanding a hug. Then, in the midst of my happiness, that young man's face would enter my head, as if he was demanding that I find him, as if drawing me back into this malady of unease.

This library in the Botanic Gardens seemed a good place to start. There were hand-coloured maps from The Royal Dublin Society; coloured glass plates of perennial herbs; engravings from the *Illustrated London News* recording the visit of the Queen and her Prince Consort in 1849 while famine raged at a discreet distance beyond the gates; ledgers that I could barely decipher; and, finally, sets of old photographs.

I worked my way through the photographs with an odd terror.

Time ceased to exist. The rain grew in intensity and the room became dark. I switched on the light. In the windowpane I could make myself out, sitting at that Victorian desk with my image superimposed on the cars passing outside. My hands shook as I lifted each photograph. Three men prepared to blast a tree stump in winter. Their top hats and collars seemed comical as they posed in the snow with Nobel's newly invented dynamite. A nameless group of workmen posed in 1913, the older men with over-sized moustaches. A child in a pinafore knelt beside a sapling at the turn of the century. I recognised the tree from the position of the glasshouse in the background. It was still there, towering over its surroundings, while the child must now be dead.

I turned over an old photograph of the pond in summer. The name 'W.D. Hemphill' was stamped on the back with the date 1897. There were notes about marsh plants growing at the pond's edge and the aquatic plants crowding the stagnant water. This was the landscape of my dream; young trees clearly visible on the slope where I had dreamed of working at a deep pit. I held the photograph close in the light, peering at it with a haunted intensity. My hands shook; I put the photograph down and took a deep breath, trying to calm myself. What time was it? What if the door was locked, the official having forgotten that I was trapped in here with the ghost of Bluebeard? I stood up and placed the ledgers back on their shelves. I tried not to look panicked as I went down the stairs. I just wanted to be out in the evening air, among the umbrellas and sodden overcoats, going home to my family like any mortal man.

*

Throughout my childhood there was a fuss made over the two callers who came to the house to see my mother: the Avon Lady, who discreetly sold cosmetics, and Mrs Lacey, who was referred to as 'Mammy's friend from Cork'. My main memory of her visits was of being summoned into the musty living room which was never used for any other purpose. Before the age of eleven I often felt on inspection, without knowing why. A smiling Mrs Lacey would ask me questions and I sensed how important it was to my mother that I smiled back as I answered, before being sent out to the back garden to play, while my mother and Mrs Lacey whispered behind the closed sitting-room door. My mother only seemed happy when her friend was gone. She would wave at the doorway until Mrs Lacey was out of sight, then lean against the closed door with her eyes closed. This was the only part of Mrs Lacey's visits that I enjoyed, when I could stuff myself with the freshly baked scones in the kitchen, covered by a spotless dishcloth, and my mother – as giddy with relief as a schoolgirl – would sing to herself before shooing me upstairs to take off my Sunday clothes.

But after my eleven birthday my own anxiety became worse than my mother's. I would stutter when Mrs Lacey asked me questions, frightened – even into my early teens – that she had the power to whisk me away from my home. However, neither my fears nor my mother's fears could ever be spoken about. On the one occasion I made a spiteful remark about Mrs Lacey, my mother lifted the milk jug and flung its contents across the table into my face.

I drove through the entrance of the private nursing home off the Malahide Road: a large Edwardian house with a modern extension built onto it. Two nurses' aides were cycling past the row of trees that bordered the driveway, white uniforms flashing beneath their coats. I parked and rang the bell in the porch. Three old women stared out from the bay window of the large front room: observing me with a sort of vacant interest. There was the noise of a large iron key turning, before I was ushered into the hallway that smelt of wax and disinfectant. It was Gerry who had tracked down Mrs Lacey for me. He did not inquire who she was and I did not ask what contacts he had used to trace her. Like a good journalist he always knew somebody who knew somebody who knew everything.

'You're not family?' the matron asked. Her office was small, almost a cubbyhole under the stairs. There was the thump of feet above us.

'No.'

'Mrs Lacey's sons don't visit anymore. You might think that's cruel but they looked after her for as long as they could. Alzheimer's is a wasting-away of the brain. Relatives do come but after a while the patients don't know who they are. Sometimes people can't bear to see it. Mrs Lacey won't know you, whoever you are.'

'I'd still like to see her, please. She was...' I paused. 'She was my mother's special friend.'

The hospital grew shabbier as we ascended the stairs. She had been my mother's friend, a good and concerned, if somewhat bossy, woman. She had also been one of only two people ever to meet both of my mothers. One woman from the agency always oversaw each handover. My birth mother would have placed me into Mrs Lacey's arms. The only mother I ever knew would have taken me from them. I had no idea what length of time passed between those events; if there was a period when she was my sole protector, when I looked up at her with bewildered, unfocused eyes.

The matron opened a door and we entered the day room. None of the women sitting there looked up at our arrival: too engrossed in their own worlds. Two nurses were transferring a woman onto a commode. Mrs Lacey sat in a chair near the window. Her hair was grey, her face blotched and wrinkled, but I recognised my mother's special friend and hated myself for the stab of satisfaction I felt. She had never meant me harm. For all I knew my birth mother might have tossed me into a ditch without her. I remembered an assignment one winter, crossing a bog with Gerry to photograph the shallow grave where an anonymous infant had been found. My adoptive parents had shown me nothing but unqualified love. How could I possibly feel any thrill of revenge?

The matron started talking to the nurses, allowing me the space to approach the woman. Her hands were agitated, her speech slurred. I knelt beside her and tried to decipher the words. 'Dinner, get dinner, get dinner.' It was like an incantation which brought her no comfort. She leaned forward, staring at the floor, moving her head as if she had dropped something but couldn't see where it had rolled. I spoke her name softly, but she never looked up.

'Boys home soon, get dinner, get dinner.'

I spoke my own name, but got no response. A nurse approached me.

'You can see the way she is,' she said.

'Can I sit with her for a while?'

The nurse nodded. I found a chair and brought it over beside her. The woman across from us had her head thrown back, repeating the words 'Nurse, please' in an expressionless, singsong voice every few seconds. Listening to her was like a form of torture. Mrs Lacey's indifference to my presence allowed me to stare at her. Despite the illness, something about her profile reflected how formidable she had once been. She stopped raving suddenly, as if aware there was somebody with her. We were silent, reunited. There must have been moments when we were all alone, thirty-five years ago. If she had put her hand out I would have taken it in mine and cried like a lost son. I knew that this might be as close to my real mother as I would ever come.

'Margaret Blake.' I kept repeating my mother's name. Mrs Lacey began to stare at me.

'Get dinner, dinner, dinner.' Her voice grew weaker with every repetition, like a record trailing away.

'Sweeney, Sweeney. Dunross. Sweeney. Laois. Sweeney. Margaret Blake.'

Her hands began to pluck at something, her knuckles white with effort. I repeated the names and her hand movements continued to grow in agitation until it seemed that she was trying to pull the skin off her fingers.

'Tell him and you'll lose him. Tell him and you'll lose.'

The whisper was so intense it took me several moments to decipher it. Her hand motions suddenly made sense. She was plucking at a baby's clothes, tearing open the seams. The nurse came back.

'Every day the same, worrying about dinner for her sons coming home from school,' she said. 'You are not one of them, are you? I often think she's the loneliest woman in this ward.'

*

Outside the hospital, rush-hour traffic had crawled to a halt. Geraldine would have dinner ready, back in my real life where I was late again. This was her most difficult hour – the baby screaming to be fed in her high chair, Benedict blabbering about tractors. She would have been alone all day, coping with them. Benedict was increasingly jealous of Sinéad now that she could crawl. He would purposely plant toys in her way to try and block her behind a chair, insisting that Geraldine place her back in her tummy. 'Daddy's home from his adventure,' he would cry every evening when my key turned in the lock, with Sinéad putting out her arms to be lifted up, reciting her two words, 'Dada' and 'Yeah'.

I owed it to Geraldine to go home and help her. I wanted to do so, but instead I drove across the toll bridge until I reached the Pigeon House wall. I walked out along that long pier of crumbling rocks with the sea pounding on both sides. There was a deserted red tower at the end. Before we were married, Geraldine and I once walked for miles in winter to reach here; Geraldine convincing herself that the tower was a coffee shop. The huge twin chimneys of the Poolbeg Power Station split the sky. There were Travellers' caravans parked near it, smoke from a bonfire, children playing in the rain on a leather sofa with the stuffing pulled from it. Even the men who usually fished here were gone home.

'Tell him and you'll lose him.' It had been Mrs Lacey's job to ensure that no clue remained to my past. Had my mother asked her about the slip of paper at once or spent years losing courage before she blurted it out? And if my birth mother had wished to sever all contact, why leave her name in the hope that it might be found? I stared out at a tanker entering Dublin Bay, tasting salt on my lips from the waves splashing against the rocks. How often as a child on holidays in Courtown had I thrown a message in a lemonade bottle out into the waves, my name and address stuck in the neck? I used to imagine some distant white beach where one day the bottle would be washed up. *Find me, son.* That was her message. All of my life she had been waiting, never sure if her message had sunk beneath the waves or if someone had prised open her message, for it to be discarded or treasured.

Chapter Twelve

'You're back,' the official in the Botanic Gardens said. It was lunchtime on a Friday. How often during the previous week had I slowed down outside those gates and then sped on again. 'You seemed in a fierce hurry leaving last time.'

'It was Bluebeard,' I joked. 'I didn't mind him being a ghost, but you never told me he had BO.'

The man took the keys from the shelf behind his desk. I followed him up the varnished stairs again. He bent to insert the key and, looking at the back of his head, I knew where I had seen him before.

'I don't think Bluebeard is the ghost you were looking for,' he said, opening the door. 'Do you want to be more specific?'

'I don't know how I can be,' I replied. 'This is a rather strange personal matter.'

'The last time you were here I knew your face from somewhere,' he said, 'It was Charlie at the front gate who figured it out. You're the guy the paramedics pulled from the car that crashed outside here at Christmas.'

I stared out the window at that spot on the busy road.

'I saw you too,' I said, after a moment. 'I recognise your bald patch. You were standing with another man just outside the gates.'

'Sure you were in a coma? You looked dead to the world.'

'I was clinically dead. I saw you from a great height. Can you believe that?'

I turned to face him. The doctors had wanted me to go to professional counsellors, yet I had not even been capable of discussing this with Geraldine. This stranger was the first person I felt able to talk to. He reminded me of the sort of quiet men my father used to drink with. He nodded slowly.

'Maybe I do,' he said, 'or maybe I just want to believe you. My missus died eight years ago. She mumbled a lot at the end... the names of dead people, like they were crowding into the ward to greet her.'

'What if I told you that I saw those same types of faces?' I said. 'Faces I knew, faces that might have some reason to greet me? There was one face I didn't know, but I knew he was connected to me. That face has haunted me since that crash. I don't know who he is; just that he won't leave me alone. I also know he's connected in some way to these gardens. I told you it made no sense.'

'Life rarely does,' the official said.

'How long did it take you to get over your wife's death?'

He took a packet of cigarettes from his jacket, lit one and then held out the packet. I shook my head.

'You don't get over grief,' he said. 'You learn degrees of forgetfulness. It still hits you, all of a slap, at unexpected moments, years later.'

'What if you had momentarily died yourself?' I asked. 'How would you focus your mind back on to everyday things?'

'The same as we all do.' His tone had the quiet resoluteness that my father would have used. 'At some stage we all lose loved ones. It knocks the stuffing out of us; we just want to curl up in a corner and die. But we pick up the pieces and get on with life. Now you've been through a crash but what have you actually lost?'

His accusation made me think.

'I know what I could lose,' I said; 'a wife and kids who love me.'

'If you're a father your job is to get on with working for your kids. Anything good or bad that's happened to you doesn't change your priorities.'

He looked away, as if embarrassed by his outburst. I thought of Frank Conroy and how those words could have applied to him. What had been his last thoughts, staring out into those freezing waters?

'Listen… thanks.'

'You wouldn't want to mind what I say,' he replied, embarrassed. 'But tell me one thing; will it help if you find this ghost of yours?'

'I want to nail him,' I said. 'I want to discover who he is and what he wants from me.' I looked around at the bookshelves. 'I want to find him here and leave him here. That probably makes no sense to you.'

He reached out his foot and gently pushed the door shut, then took the keys for the glass doors of the top shelves from his pocket.

'Any old fool can have sense,' he said. 'The name is George, by the way. I know nothing about these things, but I know every ledger in this room and I'm in no hurry.'

*

We worked together through the early afternoon, George bringing up coffee at three o'clock. He had made no comment on the few scraps of dreams I could tell him about. He just kept opening drawers and producing more photographs. I had no idea what I was looking for or looking at. Could the long-dead woman with gloves and an apron, in a photograph he was showing me, have been my mother in a previous life? Could the man holding a pony harnessed up to the grass mower have been me, or my father, or someone I had known? The image from the Yew Walk came back vividly, the feel of a man closing in on me, the strange thrill of knowing I was about to be caught.

My eye stopped at a Victorian family posed on a donkey cart outside the Keeper's residence, the son smartly turned out in a sailor suit. I could at least be sure that I had never been him, because my memories – if they were memories – all had the taint of poverty. But perhaps I had stood in bare feet to watch this donkey cart pass, having been taught to bow and call the boy sir. If so then surely I had watched the cart pass with hatred, because the face that haunted my sleep held no room for servility.

'Let's start again at the beginning,' George finally said. 'You say you had a dream about labouring down by the pond and that may have been after the Night of the Big Wind. Let's put a date on that.'

There were day books undisturbed for decades. We needed to wipe the dust from our fingers before turning the yellowing pages. The cottage by the river was listed as being in the tenancy of one Jeremiah Davitt. A gentleman's copperplate handwriting approved his continued employment after his ninetieth birthday; 'Noted for his generosity, he could mow before my grandfather first opened his eyes, yet is still able to cut better than any man in the gardens.'

A less-educated hand recorded that in January 1839 the Aurora Borealis had been being clearly visible during that ferocious storm, when workmen from the gardens struggled to rescue a constable trapped under a fallen wall. There was a list of local residents given permission to shelter in the cellars of the keeper's house after the roofs of their own cabins were blown away. The corpse of a goat was found in the gardens, having been lifted by the wind from a field near Glasnevin Village. Various hands noted the location of numerous trees felled by the storm. The meteorological readings recorded how the wind was dying in ferocity and also the depth of fallen snow.

There were entries in the following weeks about repairing the storm damage and complaints about the poor state of paths after the fallen trees had been hauled away. The arrival of four hundred tons of gravel for resurfacing was recorded, at a cost of sixty pounds.

George and I were searching for half an hour before we unearthed the first references to work being done on the slope above the pond. Notice was given that the heavily depleted arboretum was to be extended, with new trees planted according to their needs for light and space and not in their botanical order. There was a list of workmen assigned to prepare deep pits that would be filled with good loam, replacing the existing shallow soil.

Rain clouds had gathered throughout the afternoon, with neither of us noticing how dark the room had become. I looked up, suddenly wanting the place flooded with light. George read out the detachment of workmen: In charge: *P. McArdle, outdoor foreman. Workers assigned to him: F. Goggins, P. McGovern, A. Drumgoole, E. McKenna, J. Davitt, A. Morgan.* I touched the names inscribed in the ledger, wondering if I could have once answered to one of those names in a previous life.

I closed my eyes and had a clear image of Jeremiah Davitt as the toothless old man, boiling up a billycan as he crouched among the trees in my dream. I knew it was him, yet I also felt that his face was a memory from my own childhood. I could remember playing in the dusk at five years of age and running into my mother in the kitchen, crying out that an old man was staring at me from the hedge at the end of the garden: a figure with a puckered, wizened face concocted out of twigs and briars.

F. Goggins, P. McGovern, A. Drumgoole, E. McKenna, A. Morgan. There was no other Davitt listed here, apart from the old man. But if I had not been a Davitt, then how could I have babbled to my mother and Aunt Cissie about Davitt's demolished cottage once being my home? George was staring at me quizzically.

'This must feel strange,' he said, 'trying names out for size.'

It was something I had been perpetually doing since my eleventh birthday, taking down the phone book and flicking through the pages, wondering which surname I had been born with. In my early teens I used to let the phone book drop onto the floor and tell myself that if it opened on the same page three times in a row then the name printed on top of the page was mine. Often on buses and trains I had found myself staring at strangers, as if something in their faces would tell me if they were my real father or mother.

'Where do we go from here?' I asked him.

'It's nearly six o'clock,' he replied. 'Should you not go home to your family?'

I should phone Geraldine and tell her I was okay. But how could I explain where I was? I closed my eyes. That young man's face materialised, watching me. Fuck you, I thought, I'm going to track you down and put a stake through your heart. I'll dispatch you back to hell. The image dissolved, out of reach again. I opened my eyes.

'I told my wife I'd be late,' I lied. 'But I'm delaying you?'

'Delaying me from what?' he replied. 'I sold the house after the missus died: I was only rattling around inside it. I've a one-bedroom apartment now at River Gardens: as nice and impersonal as a hotel. I'm in no hurry anywhere.'

Below us, the main gates were locked, the gardens deserted. Across the road, the Addison Lodge pub was busy as people stopped for an after-work drink. We worked on, as the rush-hour traffic slackened and the road grew quiet. I kept examining the names in the Victorian daybooks where staff had signed themselves in and out, obeying the strict rule that, after half ten, the gates were locked for the night, with workers confined inside this private world.

Had I once stood behind those gates at night, watching revellers enter the alehouse where the Addison Lodge now stood? Farmers returning to Finglas and St Margaret's, pausing here beyond the city's limits? Had I spied shop boys and kitchen maids on twilit walks, or horse-drawn carts heading for Finglas Bridge to turn left for Drogheda?

George had climbed the stepladder to take down more ancient ledgers. He blew away the dust on one. It drifted across the room in a slowly dissipating cloud.

'Here's Frederick Goggins,' he said, finally tracking down a reference to one of that party of workmen. 'It's a notice of his death in 1843, in his sixty-second year. He sounds a bit old for you – if you ever existed.'

'I'm not making this up, George.'

'I'm not saying you are.'

'Maybe you should tell me to cop myself on. Maybe the whole business is nonsense.'

'We all need to believe in our own bit of nonsense,' George said. 'When I was a boy in Cork we lived at the top of an old house. The sort of place the wind rattled through, stairs creaking, pipes banging in winter. I used to lie awake, terrified of ghosts. When you lose someone you love you're overcome by a new type of fear: a fear that there's no ghosts, no mysteries; there's just oblivion and you'll never see any trace of them again.'

'Is that why you're helping me?' I asked.

He blew a layer of dust from another leather-bound cover and shrugged.

'I suppose I want to believe – or try to believe – that something more exists of the woman I loved than just bones in a coffin.'

Neither of us spoke for a moment. Then, in silence, we resumed working our way blindly through the old records.

*

An hour later, when my eyes were aching and it was nearly nine o'clock, we found another reference to the Davitt family. It was an entry for 1859, a reprimand for Charles Davitt, Jeremiah's son, who had allowed an inmate of The Richmond Asylum to be buried in his father's grave. It was regarded as unseemly and he was warned as to future behaviour.

The entry noted that: *Although a number of years have passed since this inmate was dismissed from his duties as a labourer in the Gardens, the instructions that all staff were to avoid contact with him on pain of instant dismissal, and that gatekeepers should contact the constabulary if he made attempts to ever re-enter the Gardens, still applied at the time of burial.'*

George watched me as I read the words aloud.

'I keep seeing the name Davitt in my head,' he said. 'But not from these ledgers. Where the hell do I know the name from?'

He climbed the stepladder to take down a bound index of nineteenth-century papers and specimen collections, and searched for several minutes before writing down a box number.

'I have it now,' he said. 'You sometimes get architectural students who ask to see the original Frederick Darley plans for the glass-houses. There's an entry for a Davitt just below him in the index.'

He reached for a high ladder resting against the tallest book case and used the top of it to push open a trap door into the attic.

'Hold this ladder steady, will you,' he said. 'I'm doing this for thirty years and I still hate heights.'

There was a light switch inside the attic. His legs vanished and I was alone for a few moments until I heard his voice say 'Catch!'

I caught the leather-bound volume being tossed down to me, choking as a half century of dust was disturbed on the binding. The pages were stiff and I had no idea of when this album was last opened. The date 1843 was stamped on the first page. George descended the ladder as I read the inscription aloud: *'These preserved herbarium specimens have been collected by Jeremiah Davitt to enliven the final years which the Lord in His mercy has allowed him to enjoy, and with a view to making himself master of that interesting aspect of Botany. It is his wish that we should know each grass which we pass, so that they will afford us ample contemplation and wonder and lead us from Nature unto contemplating the Greatness of Nature's God. Jeremiah Davitt gives thanks to his ward, also of the Botanic Gardens, whose youth and energy was invested in collecting so many of these specimens in the evenings and at night.'*

I turned over the pages carefully. The first half of the bulky volume contained different specimens of grasses, with names and descriptions. The second half held over a hundred specimens of mosses. There were pious remarks inserted by the old man throughout the text, in his own writing. How many evenings had he spent in that cramped cottage by the Tolka working on this collection in poor candlelight? Had he left pages blank, waiting for his ward to come in from walks at night, clutching rare grasses and mosses?

But had this book been his ward's path to nightly freedom, an excuse to be out beneath the stars after curfew, to keep the type of rendezvous that the old man could never have conceived of? The image came to me of a young man walking through woods, whistling as he held a caught rabbit, whose brains he had just splattered with a rock.

I turned to the final page of the manuscript where some gentleman had written in pencil, *'Well done, good and faithful old servant, &c.'*

George was watching me, hoping that the collection might spark some memories. I shook my head as I handed it back.

'It proves that the old man had a ward,' I said, 'some boy he took in, maybe the young man who later caused such scandal that he became the inmate in the Richmond Asylum, with all staff banned from having contact with him. But all I have in my mind is a face and no photographs go back that far.'

'Do you want to stop searching, so?' he asked.

I almost said yes. Maybe it was tiredness or hunger, but the longer I spent in that room the more uneasy I was becoming.

'No,' I said. 'If you don't mind we'll push on. When I leave here I don't want any excuse ever to come back.'

*

It was another two hours before we found the name Davitt again. It was in a complaint in 1844 from a member of the Dublin Society. George read it out, running his finger carefully along the faded handwriting.

'*Can the Curator ascertain the truth of stories that one Mrs Martha Davitt has been running a public laundry from her father-in-law's cottage in the grounds of the gardens, and drying these clothes at night in the Society's hothouses, where her husband is in charge of the coal? And that furthermore Mrs Davitt's endeavours to enrich herself have been at the expense of the cleanliness of the apprentices' lodgings, not only in the basement of the Professor's house, but in a lean-to attached to her father-in-law's cottage, where she sleeps two young men in quite unsuitable conditions.*'

Listening to the words, I felt a sense of suffocating claustrophobia. I felt unclean. I wanted to vomit.

'It stank,' I said. 'That shit-hole of a cottage stank.'

'What are you saying?' George put down the ledger.

I closed my eyes. My chest tightened. I wanted oxygen. I could see Martha Davitt's unwelcoming face leaning over me. I could sense the fear of her which had never left me.

'I remember the stink,' I said, 'a smell of shit and mouldy spuds and damp clothes everywhere. I remember how I was always hungry and she was a mean-mouthed bitch who resented my presence. Don't ask me how, but I remember sleeping on damp straw and freezing at night and wiping myself with leaves after shitting by the river.'

I opened my eyes. George looked startled.

'Where are you getting this from?'

The nausea had passed. I tried to calm myself. 'I don't know,' I said. 'I'm tired; I'm getting things mixed up. I do remember being frightened as a child in a cottage, but I'm sure it was in Wexford. Hand me that phone, will you?'

I wasn't sure if Aunt Cissie would be in bingo at this time on a Friday night. I was about to hang up when I heard a click and then her voice.

'Aunt Cissie.'

'Sean?' She sounded concerned because I rarely phoned her. 'Are you all right?'

'I'm fine,' I said. 'I just wanted to ask you something. Do you remember the holidays we all took together in Wexford when I was a child?'

'At Mrs Butler's guesthouse outside Courtown? I remember the place well.'

I could see throngs of midges under the trees outside that small guesthouse, with Ford Anglias parked on the gravel.

'But there was another place we went to once,' I said, 'when I was very small. A cottage we rented, maybe at Curracloe beach or somewhere like that.'

'Sean, we always went to Mrs Butler's. It was all we could afford.'

I looked across at George and then around at the crammed bookshelves.

'I'm telling you, Aunt Cissie, we went to a cottage one year. I remember standing on the flagstones, with a woman towering over me. Maybe she owned it and was giving us the keys. I remember being frightened by her.'

'Sean, you dreamt it. We went to Mrs Butler's for one week every summer: one room for your family, another for Jack and me and our boys. There was never anywhere else. What is this about? Is Geraldine there with you?'

I put down the phone while she was still talking. I took up my coat, thanked George for his time but said that I was leaving. I walked quickly down the stairs and stepped out into the air. The gardens were in darkness. A night bird was calling from a tree. The front gates were locked. I began to pull at them, not caring how much noise I made. The watchman came out of the green doorway.

'What's your hurry?' he asked. 'Would you not think of ringing the bell?'

'Just open the gate,' I said. 'Let me the hell out of here.'

Chapter Thirteen

It was eleven o'clock when I left the Botanic Gardens, but I still could not bring myself to go home. I was too spooked. I headed towards town, winding down the windows, playing loud music on the radio, trying to focus on this life and nothing else.

Couples passed in bright clothes. The doors of pubs were open along Dorset Street, music coming from upstairs windows, drinkers spilling out onto the pavements. The expectation of sex hung in the air, bringing back memories of my youth. Back then I had loved to undress girls, taking my time, garment by garment, kiss by kiss. But it was nine years since I had known any other body except Geraldine's.

Gerry and I were sharing a flat at the top of a house in North Great George's Street when I met Geraldine. But from the start I had borrowed friends' flats for our liaisons, not wanting to bring Geraldine there. She was different from the other girls who once shared that bed with me, someone more serious, a new start. Gerry still lived in this flat, even though it was too big for him alone. From time to time different women lived with him, young girls with long hair and eyes that seemed slightly too large, as though bewildered at how they had found themselves there with an older man.

I knew Gerry would be in as I parked in North Great George's

Street, rang the bell and looked up at the bicycle mirror mounted above the top window sill which allowed him a veto on callers. The window opened and a set of keys were tossed down. Gerry was waiting at the top of the last flight of stairs. I could see into my old room, littered with copies of American magazines and rows of books lined up along the floor. A reading lamp in the room behind him lit up his old portable typewriter on the table.

'You never hear of computers?' I said.

He shrugged his shoulders and walked towards the shelf of bottles.

'I'm addicted to Tippex. Shut up and drink this.'

I took the Southern Comfort from him.

'You look dire,' he said. 'Shouldn't you be at home, getting covered in baby vomit?'

'Shouldn't you buy a house, Gerry? You earn a small fortune. What has you still living here?'

'This place suits me. Property-owning is an overrated vice.'

The view from the window had changed. Previously there had been a gap at the end of the row of Georgian houses across the street, an unapproved car park where lock-hard men with peaked caps plied their trade. Now modern replicas of those Georgian houses had been built to replace the old houses demolished two decade before. Every point on the skyline seemed to have a crane, as if the whole city was starting to rebuild itself.

'It suited what you were,' I said, 'a young Turk, unafraid to poke his nose into anything. Remember those early rezoning stories, the time we were nearly beaten up when a developer found us at the next table in the restaurant to which he'd brought three county councillors.'

Gerry smiled and refilled my glass.

'"Get your child a cowboy outfit for Christmas. Buy him Dublin County Council". It would have been a great headline if we could have found someone to print it.'

'When was the last time you did a good investigative piece?' I asked.

'It is opinions editors want now, colour pieces. We did our stint, like two angry wasps buzzing around. But I'm not twenty-one anymore. There should be young journalists coming up, snapping at my heels, exposing this scandal and that. But they've all had to emigrate. They're writing for *The Irish Echo* in New York or *Time Out* in London. You can only investigate when you've something left to find out. At this stage I know how the country works inside out. After a while you're only going through the motions, pretending to be shocked. Did you notice anything about all the exposés I did? They changed nothing. Irish people prefer their politicians grubby, it allows us to call in favours from them, have the rules bent when it suits. Any TD I ever got expelled from a political party was re-elected as an independent on the first count next time around. Any crooked official simply retired on a full pension. Nobody ever went into their offices and put a gun to their head. The people we exposed are still in power, telling the same lies. What's left to investigate?'

'I need you to investigate something for me. If I gave you a woman's name from thirty-five years ago could you track her down?'

'I couldn't guarantee it: some people disappear without a trace. Who am I looking for?'

'The missing piece in the jigsaw of my childhood?' I drained the Southern Comfort and held out the glass. 'Fill that high, I need Dutch courage.'

There were three rings of the bell: a lover's code. We both looked at the bicycle mirror. She had long red hair and had just dismounted from an old black bicycle. I had not seen her before. I tossed him the keys.

'It's one tough life you lead,' I said.

He opened the window. I heard the keys fall.

'I can cope with getting old,' he replied, 'just don't ask me to do it gracefully.'

We drank in silence, listening to the sound of solitary footsteps and a bicycle banging against the banisters. There was a burst of song from a party of girls passing on the street below.

'What do you need Dutch courage for?' he asked.

'I've never told you the truth, Gerry. I've never told anyone who didn't know me as a child. I simply reinvented myself. I was adopted. I have a name for my birth mother; I need someone to find an address for her.'

'Will you contact her?'

The girl opened the flat door and put down her bicycle. There were flowers and a bottle of gin in the front basket.

'I've been chasing after the dead,' I said, 'haring down cul-de-sacs to avoid facing the fact of having to find her. Maybe she'll turn me away if I find her, but that's the risk I need to take, for her sake and for mine.'

*

On those first evenings when Geraldine and I used to bring my father drinking he would sometimes create openings for me in the conversation until he realised that I seemed incapable of telling Geraldine the truth about my past. Some nights he looked across at me and I held his gaze. We both understood how we had become complicit in a guilty secret, because the truth seemed like a betrayal of his wife, who always hated anyone to know that they were unable to have children. Although we never discussed it, the longer it went on the more we both felt trapped, sensing how Geraldine would be hurt we had not told her before. We were betraying her with our silence to avoid betraying a dead woman.

One night in the pub my father started talking to us about his early years of marriage. It was a Sunday night after Shelbourne had survived relegation again and he had drunk more than usual. At first I thought he was taking the decision out of my hands and was about to tell Geraldine. Perhaps he intended to and lost courage, but I think he was trying to find a way for me to tell her and justify my earlier silence, by explaining how my mother's insecurity still exercised a hold over us.

The world my father evoked was as new to me as to Geraldine, or at least the way in which he described it was. The streetwise young photographer and the shy Mayo country girl setting up home after getting married. The deposit for the house leaving them poor, but – in their childless state – still with enough money for occasional excursions to the city pubs where his bohemian friends drank, and from where, after last orders, they set out in a convoy of cars for bona fide pubs beyond the city limits, where the licensing laws allowed travellers to drink with impunity after closing time.

It did not seem right to him to leave his new wife at home without a baby, but she was shy and claimed that his old friends were peculiar and whispered behind her back, wondering what he was doing with her. Nothing he could say would persuade her that they welcomed all-comers into their company without comment and accepted her as she was. She felt bewildered by their arguments about politics and the church, although he liked how she was different from the other women who drank among the artists and weekend anarchists in McDaid's pub off Grafton Street, women who even consumed pints if publicans were willing to serve them.

He enjoyed having a foot in both these worlds: the new suburban estates where most husbands spent their evenings working amid rows of potato beds in long back gardens, and at city-centre pubs where fierce arguments and ideas flowed. But my mother found unconventional people threatening. She feared that she was the butt of remarks when she overheard men joke to him about barber shops and rubber goods smuggled in from England. He would reply curtly that no priest was going to rush him into anything, embarrassed because he knew that she recognised the veiled reference to them not having children. 'At least they're not like your relations,' he would whisper, 'staring at your stomach every time we visit. My friends think we're being independent.' But still she pondered every remark in her head, constructing the worst possibilities from them.

My mother preferred the company of the other young wives on the street, but soon almost every one of them was pregnant or raising a small child and, as time passed, this became an unspoken barrier to friendship because they were immersed in a world that she had not yet entered. Motherhood was the only role that she had ever considered for herself, because it seemed the one thing that made sense of a woman's life. In visiting those bohemian pubs, my father wanted to retain the right to be different: my mother was desperate for an even more fundamental right – the right to be the same as everyone else.

Soon their weekend trips to bohemian pubs petered out. He took a spade from the shed and, with a quiet melancholy, started to dig the garden on Saturdays like the other men, sensing something slip away without him. They would eat their dinner in silence, with the absence of a child ever present, like an uninvited guest. He would go for walks at night while she lay awake, waiting for him to come in. Always he would pause for one last cigarette, with the city's lights spread out before him. I could imagine him turning for home and thinking of her in that bed, with the light out and the door ajar, her face troubled as she waited for his limbs to eventually slip against hers and try once more for the child who showed no sign of coming. And I could see him lying awake, after she drifted to sleep, staring up, sleepless, torn in two.

I think of how my parents felt on those streets crammed with children: the chants of girls on skipping ropes, singing 'Vote, Vote, Vote for de Valera'; the shouts of boys playing football matches that only ended when it become impossible to discern the shapes of bodies darting about in the dusk. Toys and improvised go-carts and dolls littered every doorstep. What anxieties did they endure before deciding to approach the adoption agency and also during the long wait before their application was approved? Everywhere my mother looked, another woman's swollen stomach mocked her, making her feel inadequate and incomplete, as if she had failed in her primary duty in life.

The barman was shouting for us to go home by the time my father finished talking to us in the pub that night. Geraldine took his hand.

'It must have been hard for the pair of you, adjusting to each other. But then, after all the waiting, along came this fellow.'

My father looked directly at me, challenging me to speak. I knew how difficult it had been for him to talk so openly about his life. Now was the perfect time to tell Geraldine. I nodded at him and glanced towards the door, indicating that I would tell her on our long walk home. I fully intended to after we stopped to buy chips, after we kissed in a damp laneway overhung with dripping bushes. I put it off until we were in bed and then I just kissed her again and again, wanting nothing to exist except the pair of us in that darkened bedroom. I failed to take the chance to explain and there just never seemed to be as good a moment again.

*

It was one o'clock when I got home from Gerry's. I had not expected Geraldine to be up, but she was sitting on the sofa with her legs tucked under her, watching a late-night film. She did not look up. I realised how distant we had grown and how much I had hurt her over the previous three months. Since the crash I was so preoccupied that I had let our marriage slip apart. I sat behind her on the edge of the sofa, unable even to put out a hand and stroke her hair.

'Benedict's been crying out for you in his sleep,' she said without turning her head. 'Since dinner time he's been demanding that I produce you like a rabbit out of a hat. He has me all day, you see, so I'm boring. He wants the excitement of Daddy condescending to visit us.'

The side of her face looked old in the light from the television.

She flicked off the set and sat back, her features hidden by her hair.

'I keep asking myself: was I blinded by love or have you totally changed in the past few months? Sean, there's nobody stopping you from leaving this house if you want to. But you've not properly lived here with us for months. There's just been a ghost walking around. It's like somebody stole the man I married and left a stranger in his body. Tell me I'm wrong, that you haven't changed, that you were always like this.'

'I was always a bastard,' I said quietly.

'Don't be funny, Sean. I'm sitting here tired and cold and I'm not in the mood. You were always a bit too intense and caught up in your work, but you were a good man, a good husband and a good father. The man I married was no bastard.'

'He was,' I said. 'A bastard from birth and when I was young a lot of kids were not shy about reminding me of it. I can't tell you whose bastard I am, though. There are laws against finding out. The adoption agencies have the records stashed away where the likes of me can never access them.'

She was silent for a moment, then turned to stare at me.

'How long have you known?'

'Since my eleventh birthday.'

She lowered her eyes. There was shock there, but also hurt.

'I'm sorry,' I said, 'I didn't think it important.'

'How could it not be important? I've told you everything about my life. It's not important that you're adopted, it's important that you kept a secret from me.'

'I didn't want it to be important or to affect us in any way. I didn't want us touched by the past. I didn't want it to define me like it used to define me in neighbours' eyes when I was a kid. I was sick of always being different. I simply cut all ties with the people I grew up with and never told anyone new. I didn't want to discuss what it felt like to find out at the age of eleven that everything you thought you knew about yourself was actually a lie; to be told you were not truly part of a family but to carry on pretending that you were.'

'Your mother and father loved you.'

'They could not have done more for me and I loved them as much as any son could love his parents. And I loved that you loved my father too and I never wanted you to think less of him.'

'Why would I have thought less of him? This explains so much. I remember when Benedict was born and I had to fill in forms about any history of illness in our families. I couldn't get a word out of you except a no to every question. You got so uptight that night when I pressed you for any information.' She paused, as though the news was only now truly registering. 'Jesus, I can't believe you never trusted me!'

She hugged herself as if she had been slapped. I put out my hand and she shrugged it away.

'I'm sorry,' I said. 'But for years I kept it at arm's length in my mind, not wanting to admit that it was like an aching wound. I hold Sinéad now and I see myself as a baby, being passed from hand to hand and called by a name that I don't even know.'

'Does it hurt?' She looked up. Her teeth bit softly into her lower lip.

'Yes.'

I was shaking.

'What has been happening during these last few months?' she asked.

'I've been searching for my birth mother, or trying to decide if I want to search for her. I'm afraid of what I might find, afraid I would be rejected again. It's been thirty-five years, maybe she has forgotten…'

'No.' Geraldine took my hand. 'No mother ever forgets. Not deep down, not inside. What else have you been doing these last months? You never talk to me anymore.'

'The thing with being adopted,' I said, 'is that you could be anyone. You're always trying out lives for size. I've been trying to track down a ghost and lay him to rest: maybe the ghost of my former self. None of it makes sense, but I have memories that don't seem to belong to me, memories that have come to the surface since that morning when I clinically died.

'Don't say that,' Her voice was scared, 'you were never truly dead.'

'That's what happened to me. Even if only for a few seconds, I was dead and gone from you all. I've never really been able to talk about it because I feel so guilty that I felt no grief at leaving you. I felt utterly serene; it felt like a wrench to be dragged back to life by those paramedics. I came back shaken up, trying to make sense of all of my lives, real and imagined. But I just want to be here with you, Geraldine, that's the most important thing about whoever I am.'

How long had it been since I'd cried? Geraldine knelt on the floor beside me. She put her head on my lap and I lowered my face until it touched hers. I stopped speaking, but continued to cry, silently, while she hugged me. We stayed that way for a long time. Finally I raised my head. My tears had stopped. I stroked her damp hair.

'The first time I brought you down to Athlone to visit my dad,' she said, 'my dad said afterwards, "He's a lovely young man and to think that for years I thought all Shelbourne fans were bastards."'

Her shoulders began to shake. Her eyes were wet but she was unable to contain her laughter. I pushed her gently back onto the floor and fell beside her, both of us laughing hysterically, with fresh tears on our faces. Whenever we stopped, one of us would repeat her father's words. We were still laughing when I undid the buttons on her jeans, removed them and entered her. We were suddenly serious then, neither of us speaking, our bodies bonding together, shutting out the world. We remained lying like that for a long time after I had come, my cheek against her breast where her blouse had been ripped open. We would need to check the floor carefully for buttons, in case Sinéad put them in her mouth. Finally we rose.

Geraldine had gone upstairs when the phone rang. It was half two in the morning.

'Are you still awake?' a man's voice said. 'I think I've found something.'

I recognised the voice: it was George from the Botanic Gardens.

'You're not still in that library, are you?'

'Once you start searching these archives it gets kind of addictive. But there's no doubt in my mind now.' The man's voice was triumphant, almost giddy. 'I have it solved: everything fits.'

'Listen, please just go home and forget about this.' I had sought his help, but now I resented him, as if he was trying to destroy the peace of mind I had achieved after making my confession to Geraldine. 'All that stuff was just my imagination. I've my own life to lead now.'

But George's voice seemed mesmerised, as if during all the hours peering at those ancient ledgers he had slipped into an altered state. I was not even sure if he heard what I was saying.

'It's all in the records if you work back. Jeremiah Davitt found a young boy near Finglas during a cholera outbreak. The boy's parents had either died or abandoned him. There's a letter giving Davitt permission to raise the boy in the cottage he shared with his son and daughter-in-law. Davitt gave you the surname of the man on whose land you were found.'

George's voice went quiet. I could see him, looking out at a taxi passing on the road behind the window, blinking as if the absurdity of what he had just said was dawning on him.

'It wasn't me he found, George,' I said quietly. 'It was someone who lived a hundred and fifty years ago.'

He sounded suddenly tired. 'I know. I'm sorry. I got carried away. It just seemed to fit in with some of the things you said.'

'I know, George. Listen, it's late, go home. Coincidences happen. There must have been thousands of starving boys back then. We both got too caught up in some confused sliver of memory that may at some stage may or may not have been mine. But I now know what is really mine; I know what life I treasure and what is precious within it.'

'You're right,' he said after a moment. 'I get caught up in odd things too, ever since the missus died. You start to search for signs, wanting to believe in other lives. But fair play to Davitt though. He stood his ground when his daughter-in-law wanted nothing to do with the boy. Old Davitt found the boy sitting on a ridge of earth, in a potato field riddled with blight. The account said the child was so famished he was trying to eat a worm.'

I wanted to thank George for his time, or apologise for wasting it, or wish him well in coping with each day with the loneliness of knowing that his life partner was gone. But I could say nothing as George put down the phone. I closed my eyes and vividly remembered the sickening feel of a red worm slipping down my throat. This had happened in my back garden however. I was certain of that. It was my earliest memory, sitting on a ridge of earth after my father had dug a potato bed.

I was conscious of the coldness of the room. I turned out the light and stood in the dark. I was frightened to turn, because I felt that a young face would be waiting there, with an insolent, knowing sneer. I recognised his sneer now. How often had I photographed that expression on men standing in dole queues, on impoverished labourers waiting to be picked at dawn by contractors on the streets of Kilburn, on kids with cropped hair and ragged clothes playing among bonfires of unsold rubbish abandoned after the Ivy Street market? That sneer was a badge of defiance, the last defence for people with nothing else left to fall back on.

It felt as if I had only to stretch back my hand to touch my unknown past. What did that ghost want from me? *Search on.* The whisper came from inside my own skull. I could see his face in my mind, but the sneer was gone and there was a pleading there instead. I had buried myself away, playing at ghost-hunting to avoid the risk of being hurt in my real search. George might not have left the Botanic Gardens yet. If I phoned him back he would tell me the surname of that ghost. I could track down the records of the Richmond Asylum and maybe find the location of whatever pit he was buried in. But this was not what he wanted. *The dead can take care of ourselves,* his voice seemed to be saying, *find the living while you still can.*

Slowly I reached back my hand to touch the empty night air. I felt strong. My search wasn't over; my true search was only beginning.

'Thank you,' I said to the darkness. 'Whoever you are, and whoever I once was.'

Chapter Fourteen

His plane would have landed fifty minutes ago. She had phoned Birmingham International Airport to confirm its arrival, from the only phone still to accept coins on the concourse outside W.H. Smiths. The electronic notice board in Coventry Train Station confirmed that the next train from Birmingham was due in three minutes. She ordered another coffee, although she had drunk two cups already in the hour that she had been here. It was crazy to have come here so early, crazy to phone Dublin Airport to confirm that his plane had taken off safely: even the note she had sent him was crazy.

She began to drink the fresh coffee as soon as it arrived, feeling that the staff in the coffee shop were watching her, that they knew there was something furtive about her trying to pass herself off as an ordinary customer. God Almighty, what was she going to say to him? With Ryanair, there were flights from Ireland into all sorts of English airports, even flights from Knock airport in Mayo. How different things had been on those nights in the late 1950s when everyone was herded onto the Dublin quays. She remembered leaning on the rails of the boat to watch frightened cattle and sheep being loaded into the ship's belly. People didn't talk on planes, she knew that. Not like on those mailboats that used to lurch out past the lights of Dublin Harbour, facing into dark waters and uncertain futures with only the handful of boys staying up on deck to bother looking back.

She drained the coffee cup. It was a cigarette that she needed, but it had been five years since she'd managed to give them up. She would not start smoking again, even for this. She felt uncomfortable standing there with an empty cup so she ordered again. The taste of coffee was making her sick. She saw the girl serving her glance at the tremble in her fingers.

Five more minutes before the train got in: not that there was any guarantee he would be on this one. She could leave a note for him with the girl behind the counter, only she had no idea what he looked like. '*I would send a photograph, but I have none of myself,*' he had written. She longed to cross the busy concourse and walk out the exit. She should have written much more in her reply, certainly not just '*Meet me on Friday week at 3pm in Coventry Station at the coffee shop beside W.H. Smiths. E. Sweeney.*' But what could she have said? A letter did not seem the right place. How would she recognise him? If he didn't show up on this train or the next or the next, would she just continue to sit here, drinking coffee after coffee until she became the butt of jokes among the staff – the lonely woman pretending to have someone to meet?

She had his name written on a piece of cardboard in her bag. Initially she'd planned to stand at the entrance to the platform and hold it up, but she had lost her nerve. It would be too sudden, having to search every man's face, never knowing if one was going to touch her shoulder, or if he would be confronted with the sign bearing his name and decide to walk past. She would not frighten him off; she would wait here patiently and give him time to approach, if and when he was ready. He deserved that. She just didn't know if she would deserve his forgiveness.

The notice board announced that the Birmingham train was in. She turned back to the counter so as not to have to watch the passengers emerge. After a few moments there was the bustle of people entering the open-plan café. A man's voice beside her ordered coffee. Her heartbeat seemed so loud she was afraid of collapsing. Then the man's voice called out to a woman, asking her if she wanted a Danish pastry. It was not him. She would have to turn. He would be expecting her to look out for him. He could not be expected to tap women on the shoulder. Why had she picked such a public place? But it had seemed safe, neutral. Not a place for public displays of anger or grief.

She turned and she knew him at once. He had his grandfather's eyes. But he had not yet seen her. He stood by the square of telephone booths, looking around. He was built like all her family, he had solid Sweeney shoulders. His expression was almost disinterested, like a traveller mildly impatient between connections. But she knew that he was as frightened as she was: the same fear that caused her hand to shake seemed to have turned him to stone. She would have to make the first move. She got down, a little unsteadily, from the stool. She felt that the staff were watching, that she looked like a woman in late-middle age trying to pick up a stranger. The station seemed to have gone silent. There was the muffle of a loudspeaker, but she could not decipher the announcement. He turned as she approached. His expression did not change but he leaned back against the phone booth as if needing support. She knew that he had not slept last night. He regarded her with the naked curiosity of a child. It brought back memories of dancehalls. She swallowed and nodded at his silent question.

'What name was I given?' he said.

'Francis.'

'Francis.' He pronounced the name slowly, like an unfamiliar word in a foreign language. 'My name is Sean now. That's the name my parents… the only parents I knew… gave me. All the way here I've been thinking that I don't know what to call you… Elizabeth, Lizzy, Mother?'

'Francis… your mother is dead. Lizzy died ten weeks ago. I didn't know how to break such news to you in a letter. Sweet child, I'm so sorry. I'm your Aunt Ellen.'

*

Lizzy had been right – that fact made this moment all the more painful. Every day he had indeed been a day nearer. Ellen had never wanted to believe her sister because she was trying to protect her. She had spent years trying to quietly deflate Lizzy's hopes because the four times that Lizzy had disappeared over the years had taught her how dangerous these hopes were. Time was meant to heal grief but her sister's sense of loss had grown in recent years because she had known that time was running out. On the night after the funeral of Lizzy's husband, when Sharon summoned a doctor to prescribe a sedative because Lizzy was crying so much, only Ellen had known that the tears were really for her son.

Ten years ago on a visit to Dublin Ellen had looked up a private detective agency in the phone book. She had expected to meet a man in some shabby office. Instead a woman in her thirties had welcomed her into a bright suite in Fitzwilliam Square. There were people working on computers, like the backdrop on the *News-At-Ten* on television. The detective had shaken her head like a professional counsellor, explaining to Ellen that while the grown child might have some chance of finding his mother, there was no way that a mother, or a relative of a mother, could unearth any facts. The religious institutions kept the details of all adoptions locked away and no political party had the guts to compel them to release any information.

'Have I half brothers or sisters?' Francis – or should she call him Sean – asked. How long had they been walking like this through the streets of Coventry? She didn't want to suggest that they stop somewhere, because he was struggling with such pent-up emotion that she was afraid he would walk away from her.

'You have three half-sisters.'

'Are they nice?'

'They're very nice, they've done well in life. They looked after Lizzy in as much as any of us could. But they're very... well, English, I suppose, in attitude. As they grew older I think that Lizzy saw less and less of herself in them. They became strangers to her and, God knows, she was always a stranger to them.'

'Did she tell them about me?'

'Lizzy kept her life hidden in compartments. I think the nuns ingrained that into her: a sense of shame and secrecy. But if you had turned up she would have told them, she would have told the whole world. Your half-sisters know nothing about the way things were in Ireland. Lizzy never encouraged them to visit Laois. Maybe she was scared of what they might find out, but I think you were the part of her life that was just too precious to talk about.'

'So I just got written out of the story.'

'Your mother was written out of the story by our parents, by my brothers and sisters. She lost her family and lost her self-worth: I think she got a rawer deal than you, Sean.'

Her words sounded sharper than she had intended. For a moment she thought he was going to walk away from her and keep going without looking back. Instead he stopped and observed her coldly.

'You had no right to lead me on in your letter. You could have written that she was dead.'

'I wanted to meet you, for Lizzy's sake, for my own sake. I didn't know if you'd come if I told you the truth.'

'I came here to meet my mother. Do you know how hard it was for me to do that?'

'Lizzy's house is for sale,' Ellen said. 'I found your letter in a pile of junk mail last week when I came up to help her daughters clear out her possessions. I saw the postmark and I knew at once it was you because nobody from Ireland ever wrote to Lizzy. I slipped it into my handbag before her daughter could see it. I went home and my hands were shaking before I opened it. I could have simply not replied, I could have burned it, I could have written you back out of the picture like all my family – all your family – did. Instead I did what I thought was best, what I've always tried to do for Lizzy. I don't see why you're so angry with me.'

This stranger put a hand out to touch her arm. 'I'm not angry with you,' he said, 'I'm angry with myself. I could have found her in time, or at least I could have tried to. But I didn't, because of pride or a fear of getting hurt. I felt I had been rejected once and I didn't know if I could cope with being rejected twice. I didn't know if she wanted me to find her. I still don't know for sure. Tell me the truth, please. Tell me everything you know.'

*

Ellen still remembered the first time she took the boat to England in the autumn of 1961. The talk onboard was all about the new Pope John.

'That man is a breath of spring,' an old labourer said, pausing at the rails beside Ellen. 'In his first week they handed His Holiness a sealed envelope that no Pope had opened since the Middle Ages. "Enough of this nonsense," says Pope John, "we're making some changes here." He opens it and reads it, and his face goes grave with all the cardinals staring at him, white as sheets. "I should never have opened that," says His Holiness, "it was the bill for the Last Supper."'

Watching the labourer move down the deck, looking for someone else to tell his joke to, Ellen wondered how to begin the search for her sister. The only clue she had were rumours that a Ballyfin girl who worked in Coventry had seen a girl who looked like Lizzy wheeling a pram in that city. For a year Ellen had been saving to go to England. She would need to find work in some factory, but before searching for a job she had allowed herself enough money to spend two weeks in cheap digs in Coventry to see if this rumour was true.

Over the next fortnight she walked the streets of Coventry from early morning until dusk, catching buses at random and loitering outside schools and parks. Lizzy was an ache within her, the cause of the civil war that meant her family would never be whole again. Her money was almost gone when she thought that she caught a glimpse of her sister on the side street of a new suburb. She followed at a distance, still not certain that this was her younger sister. This figure looked so much older as she pushed a large black pram with a baby inside it and a three-year-old girl balanced on the edge. A slightly older girl with pony tails walked alongside, holding up a whirling paper windmill. Only when the figure paused at the kerb to look around was Ellen certain that this was her sister.

'Lizzy, Lizzy!'

At first the figure seemed not to have heard but then, as Ellen was about to reach her, she pushed the pram off the kerb and ran across the busy street while cars braked and horns beeped. A driver leaned out of his window to scream 'Stupid bitch!' Lizzy was a hundred yards ahead before Ellen could get across the road. She vanished down a maze of narrow red-bricked streets with the eldest girl screaming in terror as she was dragged on. The windmill lay on the roadway, flattened by tyres. Ellen dodged down side streets, asking people if they had seen a woman running with a pram and occasionally catching a glimpse of her sister in the distance.

The houses ended abruptly. There was a green space, a bombed-out wilderness waiting to be rebuilt. A dirt track had been created by passing feet and halfway up the track a cloud of dust betrayed the moving pram. Ellen began to run. Workmen were building a new estate at the crest of the hill. The streets had no names yet, just arrows pointing towards site numbers. Rubble lay on the edges of the pavements. There was the noise of hammering from unfinished roofs. Ellen had almost run past a small laneway when she stopped

A Second Life

and stared down it. It was Lizzy all right, her eyes as wide as on those times she used to wake up in bed beside Ellen after having a nightmare. She was crouched behind the pram, her face pressed against those of the scared girls. All of them stared at Ellen as if expecting to be beaten. It was hard to know who was shielding who.

'What do you want?' Lizzy whispered as she approached.

'I want you back as my sister.'

'Did they send you?'

'To hell with every one of them.'

'Who is this, Mummy?' the eldest girl asked. 'Why is she chasing us?'

Ellen knelt. 'What's your name?'

'Sharon.'

'I'm your Aunt Ellen, Sharon. Will you show me a place where we can get ice cream with sprinkles on top?'

After the ice creams in the Wimpy bar, she sat with Lizzy on a park bench until dusk while the two eldest girls played and the baby cried with hunger. Finally she persuaded Lizzy to bring her home to meet her husband. The man called out to ask Lizzy where she had been before Lizzy had the front door open, more baffled by the absence of his tea than if it were an international crisis. He went silent when he saw Ellen, cowed by the sudden intrusion of a stranger in this domain. Ellen knew that Lizzy would never have looked at such a man before the nuns took her away. Whatever happened in that convent had crushed her sister's spirit. She sensed how it was this new vulnerability and meekness within Lizzy that had attracted him to her. Jack did not seem like a bad man, just someone who liked the fact that his wife had no past and did what she was told.

'Jack, this is my sister,' Lizzy said nervously.

'I never knew you had a sister.'

'Well, you know now,' Ellen said.

'I'm afraid you can't stay here,' he said defensively. 'There's just no room.'

'I don't intend staying.' She stared him straight in the eye. 'You already have four women in your life. I mean, just how many women can you handle at one time, Jack?'

The man looked away and Ellen felt bad for teasing him and discreetly putting him in his place. Later on she would always feel guilty that her sudden appearance probably robbed him of a peaceful life, because two weeks after Ellen made contact with her sister, Lizzy disappeared for the first time.

*

The hotel was one of the finest in Coventry. An Indian doorman bowed and opened the glass doors for them; a waiter more handsome than a Hollywood actor took their order for coffee. In her first year in England, Ellen had often stood outside such palatial hotels, longing to go in just once and order coffee but lacking the confidence, even with a full pay packet in her handbag. 'You'll never be a lady,' her mother used to say, 'until you learn to drink coffee.'

Francis sat across from her. He had his grandfather's good looks, although it was difficult to reconcile her father's features with his modern haircut.

'There was no day when Lizzy did not think about you,' Ellen said. 'It's important you know that. But what were her choices as a nineteen-year-old girl? It was a different world. Maybe she could have kept you, but what sort of life would you pair have led and where could you have lived it? Certainly not in Ireland, where every door was closed in her face, and probably not over here, with no money and the social services snapping at her heels. I mean the English were still shipping children born out of wedlock off to Australia ten years after you were born. She was so young... how could a girl like her stand up to...'

Ellen stopped. What would Lizzy have wanted him to know and what would she have held back?

'She ran away four times,' Ellen added. 'Her husband Jack would phone me in a panic and I'd spend days tracking her down.'

'How did you know where to look?' Francis asked. Ellen watched the waiter return and take the credit card which Francis left on the table.

'I always knew she'd head for Dublin, Ellen said. 'That was where she gave you away. I'd try the churches first in case she'd be sitting in the back of one. After that it was schools. Do you know how many primary schools there are in Dublin? I grew to hate Dublin from all that tramping around. The first time it took me four days to find her. There were mothers waiting for their children outside a school gate in Clontarf and Lizzy was standing a little way off. I could see them looking at her, knowing she didn't belong. She just stared in through the gates, scanning every child that came out. If she took a step nearer the children I think one of the mothers would have hit her. When all the children were gone I went up and took her arm. She didn't try to run away from me. She never spoke all the way back across on the boat, like everything had been drained from inside her.'

The waiter returned, bearing the credit card on a plate. Her nephew – the phrase sounded strange – left a tip in cash. Ellen fought against the threat of tears. What would Lizzy have given to be here at this moment? During her last weeks in the hospital, with the bones starting to protrude through her skin, Ellen could see the pain Lizzy was suffering. The only thing keeping her alive was willpower, the doctor said. Lizzy rarely spoke but Ellen knew she was only staying alive to give Francis more time to find her.

When her daughters gathered at her bedside, Lizzy barely acknowledged them. They were good girls. She had not been an easy mother, repeatedly disappearing during their childhood and wandering the streets in her last years. They did not deserved to be shut out of her death. Ellen had tried to place her daughters' hands in hers, but Lizzy would close her fingers, using every last bit of strength simply to stay alive. Where had Francis been? Why had he left it so late? She almost felt like shaking him.

Ellen still went to mass in Birmingham in order to meet other Irish women of her age. But religion had long ago ceased to be anything other than a fairy tale for her, a memory of numb knees during the boredom of family rosaries in Laois. Ellen was certain that there was no world beyond this one where her sister might meet her son. Lizzy's chance had died when the life-support machine in the hospital was switched off. Ellen stared at him and had to look away.

'I could have found her before,' he said as if reading her thoughts. 'But it's only in these last few months that I've become obsessed with finding her. It's been tearing me in two ever since I survived a car crash last year.'

Ellen put down her coffee cup.

'Was it just after Christmas?'

Francis sat back. His expression was enough of an answer.

'Lizzy woke up in a panic one morning soon after Christmas,' Ellen said. 'She was beside herself with worry. She claimed she'd been woken by the noise of a crash.'

*

They took a taxi to what was once Lizzy's house. The probate had not yet come through, but already there was an auctioneer's sign erected in the garden. Sharon's husband was sharp in this way – too sharp, Ellen thought, but she knew when to hold her tongue, especially since Lizzy's death when her presence was now superfluous at family gatherings. Ellen still felt that she was of use in the awkward clearing of possessions, but after this she knew that she would have little more to do with the lives of her nieces.

Lizzy's clothes had gone to the local Barnardo's shop, along with most of the household goods. The electrical items were dumped because the charity shop refused to take them. Lizzy's daughters seemed reluctant to take any mementos, though in reality Lizzy had kept few personal things: just a broken watch that Ellen remembered her father giving Lizzy as a girl, a miraculous medal on a broken blue thread and some faded cuttings from Irish papers in the 1950s. The daughters had been perplexed by these last possessions until they thought of the obvious way out – they gave them to Ellen.

The family were uncertain too about what to do with Lizzy's ashes. Lizzy had agreed with Jack that her daughters be raised in the Church of England, but she had remained a Catholic, though they never saw her publicly practise her religion. They could remember her praying when they were sick as children, but she had refused to allow a priest near her in the hospital. As Lizzy's death had loomed the girls had relied on Ellen for guidance. There were always nurses moving around the ward or visitors talking at the other beds, but for Ellen it was the presence of any of the daughters that made the subject of burial impossible to mention. Only once, when she and Lizzy were alone, had they been able to talk openly.

'Lizzy, for the girls' sake have a proper funeral. Give them the chance to grieve with a priest and a mass… Father Tom would come over… he'd visit you this minute if you'd let him. You could patch things up… heal these wounds, for your sake and his sake, for my sake too. It's what you want deep down.'

'I want Francis.' Lizzy's eyes were closed, the words barely audible. Ellen had never heard Lizzy mention their brother Tom's name in all her years in England. 'Coventry is not my home. Don't leave me in a hole in the ground here. Burn me and scatter my ashes.'

Very few people had attended the cremation, where the ceremony – or utter lack of ceremony – was exactly as Lizzy instructed. No speeches, no music, no prayers. She had asked for no flowers, but at the last minute her daughter Sharon drove to this house and made up a small bouquet from Lizzy's flowers from the garden. They lay in a small blaze of colour on the polished wood as the coffin slowly vanished. Ellen felt there was a touch of spite about Lizzy's instructions: this was her way of running away from her family one last time. Afterwards nobody spoke, like the hollow occasion had robbed them of their grief. There was a meal in Sharon's house. Ellen had kissed her nieces, knowing that the cremation had left such wounds that she was unlikely to see them all together again.

Yet she had kept in touch with Sharon in recent weeks. It was Sharon who gave the urn with Lizzy's ashes to Ellen, as if the daughters could think of nothing else to do with it. This had occurred on the day when she had been helping Sharon to sort through this house, the day she discovered Francis's letter among the post in the hall. His letter had seemed like the ultimate black joke. That night in Birmingham, Ellen had placed the envelope on the kitchen table and stared at it with terror. There was a box of matches by the cooker. Twice she almost managed to find the strength to burn it. Her husband came in. 'Won the pools, have you?' She put her hand out to cover the address, then went to the bathroom and locked the door.

I am taking the liberty of writing to you at what I believe was once – and I hope still is – your address. A journalist friend of mine has been trying to track you down, through contacts, old records, a slow process of elimination really. I think I have found you, but if I have the wrong person then I apologise. I apologise also if you do not wish to be found by me. It is possible that by now you will have put me firmly away at the back of your memory, and – should you wish me to remain there – I do not wish in any way to intrude upon your life.

It's funny trying to write this letter because I've probably been writing a letter to you in my head all my life. But if you should wish to know something more of me, and about the two grandchildren whom you do not know you have, then I would be glad to either exchange letters or travel somewhere to meet you. I am now almost twice the age that you were when you gave birth to me. I have been a parent too. I cannot claim to know anything of the experiences you went through, I do know that you have not been home since you left

Dunross, except once for your mother's funeral. And from the date on the headstone, I know that you were carrying me inside you when you stood at her grave. I have stood at that grave too.

If you decide that we should meet, I don't suppose either of us will know what to say. I might have your hair or your eyes, but we will be strangers. I had a good home. You should know that. I was well loved. We were not rich, but I lacked for nothing. But I believe that once you may not have wished to part with me. There was a scrap of paper found like a message in a bottle. This letter, in turn, is my message in a bottle to you thirty-five years later. If it causes you too much pain or the years have erased any feelings for me, then simply cast it away. I would send a photograph, but I have none of myself. But I suspect and I hope that if we ever meet we will recognise each other. Whether you reply or not, you will always be in my heart.

Yours sincerely,
Sean Blake.

It felt so strange now to be talking to Francis in Lizzy's kitchen, where Lizzy had spent so many long afternoons thinking about him.

'Lizzy and I were never that close as girls,' Ellen told him. 'There were four years between us: four years is a lot when you are small. Our brother Tom was the closest to her, just a year older. You couldn't keep them apart. He even slept in the same bed as Lizzy until he was five. The pair of them shared their dinner off the one plate when they were young, refusing to eat off separate ones. Giggling and running wild in the fields. I had to mind them. I was her older sister: my responsibilities hammered home to me. She was everyone's dancing pet. In school I'd own up to things she done just to save her being slapped for them.'

Ellen paused.

'I never worried about myself, I knew how to get by… with boys, with life. My feet were firmly planted from an early age. With

Lizzy it was hard to know what she would do with her life, she was brainy but also too trusting and a bit scattered. With Tom, the future seemed mapped out. It wasn't going to be easy because you didn't just need a vocation to be a priest, you needed hard cash. The lads who went for the priesthood were generally the sons of strong farmers with good land. As unlike Tom as you could get, we had just about enough acres to cling to respectability. Very few sons of labourers made the priesthood. It was all about class; everything in Ireland was about class, and people had a hundred ways to let you know your place.'

The kettle was boiled. The kettle and a few mugs were the only things left in Lizzy's house that had not been given away or thrown out. There was a jar of coffee but no milk. Ellen brought two cups of black coffee over to the table.

'An aunt of my father's helped,' Ellen said. 'His family never liked my mother; they felt he had married beneath him. My mother's great dream was to shut them up by becoming the mother of a priest. She saw Tom's ordination as the making of all of us, the path to marriage into respectable families. She wanted us all to get on in life, that's what any mother wants. I mean she also wanted what was best for Tom, she didn't push him directly, but she had it in her head that he'd be a priest since he was a boy. The funny thing was that none of us really knew him, except Lizzy. I still don't know him. Tom was either off with her or off by himself. Lizzy missed him badly when he left. She went a bit wild, but there was no harm in her. We used to cycle to dances together. She got a bit of a name, but that was spite mainly: men who got nowhere with her and invented lies. I can't tell you what really happened; just that she was seeing someone. On a couple of evenings I covered up for her and told my parents we were out walking together. I'd arrange to meet her beyond the lane. One evening she came running down from the hillside field, her hair wild, scratches on her legs. Somebody had promised her something… or did something… and I couldn't get a word out of her.'

Ellen stopped. How could she explain that world of segregated classes to him? The farm that adjoined her father's farm was bigger, but still barely produced enough food to feed everyone on it. One evening, Ellen had been invited to stay there for tea. Joseph, the farm 'boy', was told to set the table. Joseph was a labourer in his seventies. He had taken out a white cloth, but instead of spreading it over the table he had hung it from the ceiling so that the table was divided in two. Joseph had sat alone, out of view behind the cloth, eating the same food as the family at the other end of the table.

'When Lizzy got into trouble she never told me anything,' Ellen continued. 'I wish she had… maybe I could have done something, though Tom was probably the only one of us who could have helped. He was home during the week her news came out: seminarians were always allowed home to help out at harvest time.'

'What could he have done?' Her nephew leaned forward.

'Maybe nothing,' Ellen backtracked. 'Everything was black and white in those days.' She stopped. 'No. What Tom could have done is get the name of your father from her; he could have made our father confront that man's family. My parents listened to Tom. From the day he entered that seminary it was like he was a priest already. My mother used to take out the good cups when he came home, like he was a visitor. My mother was dying; she knew she would never live to see him ordained. It was to protect Tom that they were so brutal with Lizzy, so there would be no trace of scandal, no talk of shotgun weddings and babies born just six months later or no talk about the whole parish laughing about some flyboy fleeing by boat to England after refusing to marry her. Your father was allowed to get off scot-free.'

Ellen stopped. This had not just been Lizzy's tragedy; it had changed her life too. She had been the one left on that farm, listening to the whispers of neighbours and to the silence in the house.

'I never asked Lizzy who she told first, but I swear it was Tom. Lizzy would never discuss Tom, even when she was dying. I think it was Tom who told my father. Maybe she asked him to tell them or maybe he betrayed her confidence, only thinking of himself. My father was a man of his time. I knew nothing until I came in from the yard and saw the blood on Lizzy's face. I don't think my father had ever struck her before. Tom was standing at his bedroom window, looking out with a white face, not saying a word. My father pulled her into the parlour by the hair and locked the door. I wasn't allowed talk to her. When I tried to shout into her, to see if she was all right, my father hit me and then ordered my eldest brother to lock me into the shed. I kept screaming at Tom to help her or help me, but he did nothing. I knew he was there though, standing at that window, staring out, a terrified coward. All night I was locked out there. I woke at dawn to the noise of a car, footsteps in the yard, the voice of a nun. Then the car was gone and Lizzy and my father inside it. Soon afterwards my mother unlocked the door. I knew that she was dying, but I stood in that yard and spat at her.'

Ellen's voice trailed off. She took out an old photograph of her mother which she still carried in her handbag: a photograph found in her father's wallet. A young girl's face from the 1920s, before thirty-five years of hard labour and bearing children to a man twenty years older than her, had aged it beyond recognition.

'I stood at her grave,' Francis said, 'The old bitch.'

'No.' Ellen grasped his hand tightly. 'You don't have the right to say that.'

His voice was angry. 'It was me inside her womb, me they hated. It was me who was being kicked out of that family.'

'Sean, you can't feel bitter. You were not there, you can't understand those times. I was bitter for decades. It cut our family into ribbons. My mother and I were never close again, even when she was dying. It haunted my father up to his death; it came between all of us. Lizzy never went home again or had contact with any of them. At Tom's ordination, when the whole parish was celebrating with bonfires blazing, my family sat sullen and divided in that church.

People thought we were mourning our mother, but we'd nothing left to say to each other. I don't even exchange a one-line letter with my older sisters and brothers at Christmas. We're all trapped in the past. There's been enough bitterness; I can't allow you to be bitter too. Sean, you've got a duty to understand.'

Francis – she couldn't call him that name aloud or think of him by any other name – picked up the photograph of his grandmother and tilted it carefully in the kitchen light. She remembered Lizzy and herself as girls listening to their mother talk about the locked box of Indian meal that dominated her childhood. Their mother had spent the first decade of her life in a cabin near Tullow, waiting with her baby brother for their father to come home at night. He was a drunken farm labourer whose wife died in childbirth and whose only affection was for the greyhound who followed him everywhere. When he came home, the box would be unlocked and a full scoop of meal taken out. The dog had first serve. The two children shared the leftovers between themselves.

'All my mother knew in her early life was hardship,' Ellen said. 'It was a cruel world, a hungry one, but she managed to marry above herself: a much older man but one with land. I never saw her when she wasn't working, washing, digging spuds out of the frost with her hands. She lived for us children, to give us schooling, respect, prospects. What she did to Lizzy she did to protect the rest of us. My sister working in Carlow was courting a clerk in the sugar factory. That marriage would not have happened if Lizzy had been allowed keep you. My brother could never have gone back to the seminary. I cursed my mother to her grave. But what good will it do if you do the same? My parents were from another age. For your own sake, you need to let any bitterness go.'

'But your brother Tom wasn't from another age. He could have done something to help her. Where is he now?'

'A small parish in Cavan,' she said. 'Kilnagowna. Renowned for lakes of pig slurry and sheds of battery hens. I'd leave Tom alone if I were you. He keeps up contact with no one. He won't want to know you. None of your aunts or uncles will. They'd feel threatened.'

Francis handed her back the photograph. She couldn't tell what emotions he was feeling.

'Where was I born?' he asked.

'Sligo. A convent called St Martha's out in the countryside. Lizzy went back there one time when she ran away. She begged the nun in charge to tell her if you were alive or dead. The nun – a Sister Theresa – told her to mind her own business.'

'How long was I there?'

'Six weeks.' Ellen felt drained. She was tired of opening up old sores. 'It was called "Waiting for the Brown Envelope", for your marching orders. Sister Theresa had the job of making sure that every girl signed the forms.' Ellen tried to remember the invective Lizzy had put into her impersonation of the nun's voice. '"You've no rights to that child," she'd screech. "The child belongs to Christ. You can't deny him a Christian home." In the end it was Lizzy's decision to sign, but what girl of nineteen could stand up to that bullying and try to walk out those convent gates with her baby? St Martha's was miles from nowhere. How could you walk to the train station with every door closed in your face? One girl refused to sign. Sister Theresa kept screaming at her, crushing the girl's wrist as she held her hand over the form for hours. She wouldn't let go until the girl finally signed. Lizzy said that you cried a lot when you were a baby. One night she was walking the floor with you and you kept screaming. She lost control and slapped you. She never forgave herself in all the years after.'

Francis leaned forward and produced his wallet. He took out a photograph of two children, a boy of three being allowed to hold a baby in his arms. It seemed like a peace offering. She held it for a moment and then closed her eyes. It should not be her sitting here.

'For years afterwards Lizzy used to talk about how she should have tried to escape from St Martha's with you,' Ellen said. 'What haunted her was that she'd had the chance to flee and didn't take it. She came back to the dormitory one morning to find you gone from your cot, taken by the nuns to be bathed and weighed. Sister Theresa told her to look on her bed. A brown envelope was there.

'Lizzy insisted on dressing you herself. She always talked about the outfit she dressed you in. They drove her to the station, gave her a ticket for Dublin. One of the nuns bought her chocolate. She cried all the way to Dublin. People on the train must have known. They left her alone. She always said your eyes were pleading with her. She had to stop looking at you and stare out the window, pretending you were already gone. Sister Theresa was on the train too, in a first-class carriage, having nothing to do with her. In Dublin Lizzy stayed on the train until she saw the nun pass, then she walked from the station into Dublin. There was nobody with her, no one to turn to. She longed to keep you. For hours she walked around Dublin making plans to take the boat to England with you that night. But the girl didn't have the courage; she was little more than a child herself. She kept thinking she was being followed. She found herself in Glasnevin near the Botanic Gardens. She went into a draper's and bought a needle and thread. The only address she had was the family farm in Laois. What use would that be? But she sat on a bench in the Botanic Gardens and wrote her name and address on a scrap of paper that she sewed so carefully into the hem that nobody might ever notice. You were crying and she didn't know what to do or how to mind you. She wasn't thinking straight anymore. She went out the gates and walked straight out into the traffic. She wanted to die; she wanted to bring you with her, yet she couldn't. At the last minute she jumped out of the way of a car that had to swerve to avoid her. She ran all the way into town. She would show people the address on the brown envelope and they'd give her confusing directions. It took her hours to find the Catholic Protection Agency. There was a waiting room with four other girls in it. She was called into a room by a Cork woman called Mrs Lacey. She signed a form and then this woman said to her, "Take a last moment now. Kiss your baby goodbye."'

Both of them were silent. Ellen had expected to break down, but found that her eyes were dry, her voice almost expressionless.

'I'm sorry,' she said, as if needing to justify herself. 'I've no tears left in me.'

The sound of the front door opening startled them both. Francis took the photograph from her hands and put it back in his wallet. He looked up as a well-dressed woman in her thirties entered the kitchen.

'Hello, Aunt Ellen,' the woman said, 'I didn't expect to see you here.'

Ellen rose, flustered. 'I was just passing, Sharon. I thought I would clear the last of that stuff out for you. This is...' She looked at Sean and then back at his half-sister. 'This is...'

'Sean Blake.' Francis rose and stepped forward to shake Sharon's hand. 'I was passing. I saw the "For Sale" sign in the garden. Your aunt very kindly agreed to show me around.'

'You really should make an appointment with the auctioneer.'

'I know.'

Sharon looked at him closely. 'You're Irish,' she said.

'That's right.'

'My mother was Irish.'

'I know. I wish I had met her.'

'Don't be silly.' Sharon smiled. 'If she was alive you wouldn't have the chance to buy her house, would you?' She turned to Ellen. 'I'll make a start on tidying upstairs. It's nice to meet you, Mr Blake.'

'Nice to meet you.'

When Sharon went upstairs Ellen walked him to the door.

'I didn't know what to say,' she said. 'I wasn't expecting her. Do you want me to go upstairs and bring her back down?'

'I want you to tell me my father's name.'

'Let sleeping ghosts lie, Sean. Lizzy never told a living soul.'

'She told you.'

Ellen nodded slowly. She felt that they would not see each other again.

'We've gone this far,' he said. 'I have the right to know.'

'I'm not sure if I have the right to tell you.'

'Do you know what this is doing to my life?' he said. 'I'm like a stranger to my own family these last few months. I won't be at peace until I know.'

Ellen touched his hand. She wanted to kiss him but there was a distance between them.

'I can't tell you,' she said, 'because I don't know what Lizzy wanted. You had a good father, you said in your letter, one who loved you dearly. Let that be enough, Sean. Why should a man who never gave you a moment's thought in his life get to meet you, when a mother who longed for you every day never did?'

'Just tell me one thing then,' He asked quietly. 'Do you think my mother and I would have liked each other?'

'Francis... Sean... you're the one flesh and blood.'

Chapter Fifteen

I flew back to Dublin late that evening, intending to go straight home, but I stopped at a bank of public telephones in the terminal to phone instead.

'How was it?' Geraldine asked. Her voice faltered and I realised how nervous she sounded. 'What is your mother like?'

'She's dead, love, she died ten weeks ago.'

The line was quiet for a moment. I could hear Benedict crying to be allowed hold the phone. There was an announcement on the loudspeaker as the luggage belt behind me began to move. Geraldine's voice was low.

'I'm sorry, pet. How are you feeling?'

'I don't really know. I'm confused. I mean, how do you grieve for a woman you never knew? I can't go home just yet, Geraldine.'

'What do you mean?'

'I need a bit of space before Benedict comes at me at a hundred miles an hour. I need time to think. I'm angry.'

'At who?'

'At all kinds of people and maybe at myself too. I'm going to go to a hotel, just for one night. I love you.'

'Do you?'

'You know I do. I just can't be part of a happy family tonight. It transpires that I was part of a bigger and far unhappier one than I ever thought.'

I didn't like lying to Geraldine, but I was not going to any hotel. I couldn't tell her where I was going because I didn't rightly know myself. I was tempted to buy brandy and book into a hotel, to wake up shattered at dawn, my chest burning, my throat raw. This is what I did on the night after my father's funeral when I needed to be alone to grieve. But back then my grief was not fuelled by anger, by a sense that I needed to atone for my sins of omission and that so did other people who had turned their backs on the scared teenager who was my birth mother. I thought of the nuns who ran that convent, the prying neighbours in Laois who had judged her, her parents, her brother – my new-found uncle – who hid behind his clerical collar. I wanted revenge for Lizzy Sweeney or maybe I wanted to forget that I was the one who had failed to find her in time.

I got my car from the airport short-term car park. I was unsure of where I was going as I drove towards the West-Link Toll Bridge that spanned the Liffey valley. I wanted open motorways, unbroken lines of catseyes on the tarmac. I had not driven fast since the crash, but now I raced into the darkness at eighty miles an hour. Occasionally I needed to swerve back into the inside lane to overtake a truck lumbering along in the fast lane, but generally I had the highway to myself. I flicked the buttons on the stereo, wanting loud music. I felt at one with the car, my body shifting in the seat at each bend, my neck pressed on the headrest as I opened up the engine. Naas was bypassed and then Kildare. Monasterevin lay ahead on the border of Laois.

I was closing in on my mother's birth place. In America I would have had two loaded guns as I roared into Dunross. There would be a hamburger bar to spray with bullets, a stake-out afterwards, psychologists to explain my motives on the radio, an actor with good teeth to play me in the movie. Here, the motorway paid for by Europe petered out as I crossed the Curragh. Sheep grazed on the flat grass where thoroughbreds would be exercised at dawn. I was caught up in a slow convoy of local cars.

What could I say to anyone in Dunross? I didn't even know what I was going to do there. I reached Portlaoise and then Mountrath and turned off onto the tiny roads which wound up through the hills towards Dunross. I reached the village, the graveyard where my grandparents lay. There were cars parked outside the pub there, last rounds being consumed before closing time. Now that I was here I knew that I was not meant to stop. I drove on until I reached the laneway that led up to what was once the Sweeney farm. I stopped and got out and looked up at the house lights. Nobody there knew me. Nobody probably knew the story of Lizzy Sweeney. I got back into the car and carefully pressed the counter on the milometer back to zero. I was starting her journey again.

I drove up into the mountains, finding my way along the narrow lane to where it joined the crumbling road that crested the hills and fell away through dark state forests to Kinnitty. I knew where I was going now, although I was unsure of the exact route. This was a pilgrimage, my futile act of atonement. I wanted her somehow to know that I was doing this for her, that – if she still existed in some state beyond the tunnel of light I had seen – Lizzy Sweeney would be aware that I was making our journey again. I drove on through Birr, with the lights of late drinkers coming out from the town to dazzle me, and then through Cloghan, and followed the empty road across the flat bog to Ballinasloe. I had not slept for forty-eight hours and had eaten nothing since having a hurried sandwich in Birmingham airport. In this exhausted state I could easily crash and I knew whose face would be waiting for me if I did. But it felt as if she was protecting me. I drove on, trying to guess what route the nun's driver had taken and imagining the terrible silence that must have built up in that car as she sat between the nun and her father.

I realised that I was off course, but found a side road which led to Athleague and on into Roscommon town. Flags littered the main street, advertising some beer promotion in the closed-down bars. One drunken man sat alone on a bench, staring open mouthed at the empty street.

I drove on towards Boyle. There was no moon and the roads were pot-holed. I was getting low on petrol. Tullsk, Ballyroddy, Ratallen Cross Roads. I thought of a girl's bruised face staring out from a car window. Had Lizzy Sweeney cursed me? Had she jumped down into ditches, praying for a miscarriage? A girl with a bruised face carrying me across this landscape, the pair of us like prisoners handcuffed together. A low wall ran parallel to the road, with a lit building beyond it. Even in the dark its Victorian shape betrayed itself as an asylum. I drove past, wondering if women from that time were still in there, signed away with some doctor's consent, written out of other family histories, slowly going crazy while the world changed outside these locked gates.

The radio station I had been listening to went out of range. There was just static again as I drove beyond the county boundaries of Roscommon. The road climbed into the Curlew Mountains. I found myself nodding, almost falling asleep. I wound down the windows for air. The car plummeted towards the shore of Lough Arrow. I stopped at Ballinafad, climbed down to the lakeside and splashed cold water over my face. The lake spread out into blackness. There was another mountain behind me. I knelt forward and almost fell into the water. I took off my shoe, filled it and poured the freezing water over my hair. I started crying then, hunched stupidly there, with some night bird calling across the dark waters. I could have found her in time if I had bothered. I could have asked her all the questions that were now plaguing me. I rocked back and forth, try-ing to shake the self-accusations from my head.

A girl with a bruised face who had glimpsed the sun rise over this lake. A girl whose brother had been sitting down to his breakfast in Laois, with a tablecloth laid and the good cups put out, before going off to read his breviary while his family collapsed around him. I held the wet shoe in both hands. Maybe he was my father? The thought only lasted a moment, but then I knew it was too neat, too simple. I was assigning my own sense of guilt onto him, but at that moment I would gladly have killed the man.

I climbed back into the car and began to drive. Four miles later the petrol ran out. The car slid forward for a hundred yards, then came to a halt. It was 3.30 a.m. From here on I was unsure of my direction. All Ellen Sweeney could tell me was that the convent was five miles from Castlebaldwin along a side road. She wasn't even sure if it still existed. I wanted to find it in ruins: empty sockets of old windows, tumbledown walls I could deface. I pushed my car as far as possible into the ditch, then took my father's old camera bag from the boot and began to walk.

There was a whitening mist and no sign of the lights of a house on any side. After two hours it had brightened enough for me to see a flat, boggy landscape. I was so tired and disorientated that I was unsure if I was dreaming when I saw a figure coming towards me from a long distance off. He walked rapidly, hands thrust into the pockets of an old great coat. There was something menacing in his walk, the way his eyes never left me. Suddenly I was alert to danger. The man was in his sixties with a peaked cap and the stubble of several days. He came within fifty feet of me and stopped. His stare was manic.

'I'm Barney O'Connor,' he bellowed. 'Do you know that?'

'No,' I said.

'And you don't have a snowball's clue in hell where you are either, do you?'

'No.'

'Hah!' He threw his head back and cackled. 'Well, I do.' He nodded towards my camera. 'Pictures, hah! Do you like pictures, boy? Well here's something you'll not see in a day's march. Take a gander at them!'

His hand came out of his pocket, holding aloft a bundle of tightly rolled newspapers. He came closer and offered them to me. I knew better than to refuse. His bloodshot eyes pressed close to my face.

'Hah!' he cackled again.

I unrolled the papers. They were month-old copies of an English tabloid: *The Daily Sport*. A girl in leather underwear grinned on the cover. *We're off again. Watch her strip all this week,* ran the headline. I looked back at him.

'Hah!' he cackled one last time. It was a laugh without humour, like a shout of pain. I nodded and began to walk on slowly, holding the papers. After ten minutes I looked back and he was still there, a fossilised speck in the distance, staring after me. From that distance he seemed like a ghost from another world and time. Only when he was totally out of sight did I feel it safe to throw the papers away.

I did not so much find the convent as the convent found me. From half seven onwards a trickle of smartly dressed girls on bicycles began to pass by, some giggling to each other as they looked back. They looked so bright that they seemed unreal in my exhausted state. I could hear their voices long after they had vanished. A school bus passed and some cars with parents driving pupils, and then a blue Nissan Sunny came towards me from the direction of the convent driven by a young woman in her late twenties. She stopped and lowered the window. Her amused smile made me realise how bad I looked.

'If you could see the state of yourself,' she remarked gently. 'Is it St Martha's you're looking for? The girls said there was a lost-looking man who seemed like a press photographer. We're used to getting journalists here. Did your car break down?'

'It ran out of petrol.'

She laughed. It was the laugh of a confident woman, aware of her good looks.

'It's a far bigger country outside Dublin than you people in the media realise. You really should at least invest in a full tank of petrol.'

'How long has St Martha's been a school?' I asked.

'Forever.' She shrugged her shoulders. 'It had its twentieth anniversary last year.'

I looked around at the empty fields glistening in early sunlight.

'I am a press photographer,' I said. 'But how did you know what I was looking for?'

'St Martha's has quite a reputation. You don't take a bold step like we have done without getting used to visits from the media. Not only from reporters but from parents all over Ireland. Some put their daughters' names down on the day they're born. We had one father phone us from the labour ward. Of course, our senior girls winning the Aer Lingus Young Scientist of the Year Award three times in a row put us on the map. But it's the Interdenominational aspect that appeals to parents today. It was a bold step, becoming the first Interdenominational school run by the Catholic Church, but that is what our order is about.'

'What?' I said.

'Progress, risk-taking, innovation. We've raised hackles among conservatives in the church, but so be it. I just hope you're not expecting a full Irish breakfast. The girls have decided that for this month the whole school is going vegetarian.'

'What do you mean by your order?'

She climbed out and opened the back door of her car. She wore a purple polo-neck and a white knee length skirt. She held out her hand.

'My name is Sister Anne.'

'Sister…?' I almost let my father's camera drop. 'Well, fuck me.'

She laughed at my surprise and tut-tutted in mock horror.

'You will have to settle for a lift. Our activities have not broadened quite that far.'

*

I suspected that the parlour was one of the few rooms not to have changed since the time I was born here. The old furniture was dark and lovingly preserved. Two senior girls were deputised to serve me a breakfast of cheese, homemade brown rolls and coffee. They chatted away, probing me about the role of political bias in Irish newspapers and the impact of new technology. I got the impression that if I were a fugitive nuclear physicist dropped by parachute, they would have confessed to baking the rolls themselves and then just as easily quizzed me with knowledgeable confidence about new developments in molecular theory.

'Do you know what this convent was before it became a school?' I asked.

They looked at each other and shook their heads.

'Just a convent, I suppose,' one said. 'Nuns cut off from the world. There must have been a clatter of nuns though, because there's dozens of old bedsteads and lockers dumped down by the river.'

'Maybe you should ask what those beds were used for. Maybe you should find out what once happened to girls here no older than yourself.'

They turned, perturbed by my tone, and looked towards the door. Sister Anne had returned. She beckoned the girls to leave. I waited till they were gone.

'What about you, Sister?' I asked. 'Do you know what went on here?'

'That was all a long time ago.' She placed my keys down on the polished table. 'Your car was safe where you left it. We took the liberty of filling it with petrol. Just in case you forget again.'

'Forgetfulness seems prevalent in these parts,' I said.

She held open the door for me. There was a hint of defensive hostility in her voice. 'We're only interested in looking forward,' she said. 'Why are some people in the media only interested in looking back to a time before those girls were born? Mother Superior will see you now.'

The Mother Superior's study overlooked a modern extension where rows of girls could be seen seated in classroom windows. There were framed photographs of former students receiving awards. This nun was older and more traditionally dressed. She looked at me carefully as I entered. Behind me I sensed that Sister Anne's eyes were hinting at trouble.

'Mr Blake,' she said, indicating a seat. 'You're a photographer.'

'That's not why I'm here.'

'I know.'

I looked at her in surprise.

'I saw Sister Anne drive you in,' she explained in a soft voice. 'You got out of the car. The way you looked up at the building. We get three or four callers like you every year.'

'What do you mean, like me?' It felt like a raw nerve being exposed, a flashback to childhood when I had imagined that people could see I was adopted simply by looking at me.

'Babies who saw the light of day here. Sometimes it is the mothers who come back and sometimes the children. Just twice it has been them both together.'

I glanced at the row of filing cabinets along the wall.

'Do you keep all the records here?' I asked.

'Only the records for the school.' It was Sister Anne who answered from behind my back. 'Two of the women TDs elected to the Dáil in the last election were educated here. There's talk that at the next reshuffle we'll have our first minister.'

The older nun looked down for a moment at the heaped trays of paperwork on her desk as if to hide her annoyance.

'Sister Anne is justifiably proud of our recent achievements,' she said.

'How many women TDs did you produce here back in the fifties?' I was surprised at my anger. Maybe it was cloaking my grief but also a buried sense of shame. The shame that my adoptive mother had been made to feel because she could not conceive; the shame bred into me at having been passed from person to person after leaving this convent with the true details of my past sealed away inside a locked filing cabinet. Simply being in this convent made me feel uneasy. 'How many Young Scientists of the Year did you produce back then, or are you part of this collective amnesia too?'

'Mr Blake…'

'My name is Francis Sweeney,' I said. 'At least that's the name you have locked away somewhere. I'm another of St Martha's past pupils, though you are unlikely to stick my photograph on your wall. But how about a photograph of all the scared girls who were locked away behind these gates?'

I stopped, realising how exhausted I felt, how sick inside. I had nothing to be ashamed of, so why did I feel reduced in stature by simply being in this place? Maybe because respectability was the all-pervading cult in the world I grew up in. Any sin was acceptable – drunkenness, domestic violence – provided it was hidden away. Convents and asylums were necessary places where stains on respectability could disappear: places that people pretended didn't exist, not places that you walked into and confronted things. During my childhood my adoptive mother's great fear wasn't poverty, it was losing respectability. For years I had thought I had left behind the mindset of my childhood, but part of my character had been formed by my adoptive mother's fear of exposure and fear of authority. The nun asked Sister Anne to fetch me a glass of water and I heard the door close. When I looked up she was regarding me quietly.

'I am not part of what you call that amnesia,' she said. 'I was a novice at the time. I was from a poor family, so my life was no bed of roses. There was just as much of a class system in here as anywhere else. I spent time in places like this: Magdalene laundries in Athlone and Roscrea where women were often locked up for life. Sometimes they'd had children out of wedlock or had drifted into prostitution. But often – as I later realised – they were simply women who were in somebody else's way, ugly sisters who couldn't be married off or aunts regarded as odd. Some of the nuns in charge back then were among the most stupid, ignorant women I ever met. Not all of them – I met many fine, loving sisters too, women who recognised the system they were trapped in and tried to do the best they could.'

She stopped. The fax machine began to print out a message. The phone rang but she ignored it and, after a moment, somebody outside picked it up.

'But Sister Anne is right about one thing,' she said. 'If you have come in search of records then I'm sorry but I really cannot help you. All the records were long ago moved to a central office in Dublin. They're under lock and key: Fort Knox wouldn't be in it. Also under law your birth mother has the right to absolute privacy…'

'I've found her already,' I said. 'She had just died.'

'I'm sorry,' the nun bowed her head.

'I don't want your sympathy.'

She raised her head and waited until she had made eye contact with me before continuing. 'Things were done badly here. You have every right to be angry. But often mistakes were made out of ignorance, not cruelty. You must understand, we nuns were given little training, we entered the convent while only children ourselves, we knew nothing about the real world. As soon as we donned a black habit we were put in charge of others, presumed to be able to handle any situation.'

'Some of the nuns here were bitches, especially a Sister Theresa who seemed to be in charge.'

'At least we were here. What would have happened to your mother or to you if we hadn't been? What would her family have done, locked her up, beaten the child out of her, drowned you at birth in some lake? Or what if they had allowed her to keep you? Their neighbours would have ostracised the family, made their lives impossible, stoned their house at night.'

'Led by the local priest with his collar concealed for the occasion,' I said.

She shook her head. 'When did a priest have to get his hands dirty back then, Mr Blake?' she said. 'They just needed to plant a few words in a sermon. If there was dirty work to be done we did it for them. We were the pack mules. We were at fault because we allowed problems to be dumped on us, we questioned nothing with our absolute obedience. I pray every night for the girls like your mother who passed through here, girls whose names I will never know. But I pray for those nuns as well. They could be terrifying; they terrified me in their loneliness.'

I knew that she was sincere, but amid the desolation and grief I felt I was in no mood for logic or reason. I wanted revenge. I wanted my mother's name to be spoken aloud here, acknowledged and re-membered. I had felt like a coiled spring ever since I had learned of my birth mother's death. I needed anger to keep that grief at bay.

'I want to see the room where I was born,' I said.

'That won't be possible, not at this time of day.' The nun walked to the window. She leaned her head against the glass and pointed to the side wing of the old convent. 'That delivery ward is a science lab now. Girls are studying there for exams. I can't disturb them.'

'Would they find the past so disturbing?'

'We have a visitors' room,' she said. 'You could sleep for a few hours and then after the school is closed I can show you around the whole building. Those girls are stressed about their exams coming up, their whole future hinges on the results. Disturbing them won't help your mother, Mr Blake.'

'I said my name is Sweeney.'

'Is it really?' She turned from the window to confront me. 'When you walk back out those gates I suspect that Blake will still be the name on your credit cards and the school forms for your children. Rightly or wrongly you were given a second life when you left here as a baby. I can't change that fact and it's a bit late for you to change your name.'

The door reopened. Sister Anne returned. She placed the water down on the desk. The Mother Superior beckoned her to leave. I heard the door close.

'My mother came back here one time,' I said. 'She begged Sister Theresa to tell her one fact about me, even just to say if I was alive or dead. The nun sneered and told her to mind her own business. Maybe I can change nothing here, Sister, but at least tell me where that bitch is buried. If you will excuse the language, I feel a need to piss on her grave.'

'Sister Theresa is still alive, Mr Blake,' the Mother Superior said quietly. 'Why don't you go and visit her? I'll even bring you if you want. She won't know you or your mother: most of the time she doesn't know anyone. She was a right tartar in her day. If your mother hated her so much, then go and see her. Confront your demons, Mr Blake.'

'To hell with her.'

'Are you afraid of her?' the nun asked. 'What good will it do for you to carry around this anger? Lay it to rest. Find out for yourself if she is such a demon.' She paused. 'When did you discover that your mother had died?'

I looked away from her. I wanted to get up and walk out to wherever my car was parked. The last thing I wanted to do was break down in this place, in front of her. 'Yesterday,' I said and then without warning I began to cry. 'I could have found her in time. We all failed her.'

'Have you seen your wife since?'

'I've not even slept since.'

'Phone your wife. Ask her to come down here. Stay the night with us.'

'I can't.' I tried to pull myself together. 'I need to get back: we have children of our own.'

'Then for their sake lose this anger,' the nun said. 'Sister Anne and some of the other younger nuns want to bury the past sins of this place. For them it's all about petitions for human rights in Central America and Travellers' rights to halting sites. They don't want to be touched by anything that happened here. They're wary of people like you who might drag them back. I think that's wrong, I think you have a right to be angry at the way things were, but you can't let it ruin your life. Unless you rid yourself of this sense of shame, you'll pass it on to your own children.'

I took a sip of water. 'Who says I'm ashamed?'

'Aren't you on some level? Isn't that what's eating you? I'm ashamed by the things that happened here. Most nights I walk the corridors last thing. Sometimes I open a door in the moonlight. Instead of rows of desks, I imagine beds and cots. I imagine babies crying and young mothers too. I was just a novice back then with no power. What could I have done to change anything? But I feel guilty because I accepted the received wisdom that these girls were fallen and depraved. I'm guilty, we're all guilty: every person who didn't see because they didn't want to see; every respectable family who sent their tablecloths and sheets down to be starched and made clean in the laundry. In our retreat house in Sligo, Sister Theresa is dying. The younger nuns there think that she's saintly. They won't welcome you, but you owe it to yourself to see her. Only then can you decide whether it's fair to heap the blame for everything on her shoulders.'

A bell rang in the corridor for the end of a class. There was a throng of footsteps outside.

'I'd like to walk in the grounds here, if I could,' I said.

'Would you like me to walk with you?'

'No.'

There must have been a button on her desk, because after a moment the door opened and Sister Anne appeared. I rose.

'Good luck with what you're searching for, Mr Blake.'

The nun held her hand out. I looked at it, then shook my head.

'I'm sorry,' I said. 'I just can't.'

She nodded. I followed Sister Anne down the long corridor in silence. There was a storeroom door open at the end of it. I glanced in at old desks stacked together, tied-up bundles of yellowing ledgers. A crucifix had been removed from the wall, but the outline remained where successive coats of paint had been applied to the bricks around it. There were two high windows. I stopped, while the young nun hovered impatiently. Was this the room where I was born? A group of girls came down the corridor. Now that she had my measure, Sister Anne hurried me along in case I might speak to them. We went outside. My car was parked on the gravel.

'I owe you for petrol,' I said.

'It's okay.'

I forced the young nun to take the money and then looked back at the high convent windows. Would my mother have come here with me if I had found her? What sort of future could she have had as an unmarried mother, shunned by everyone, if the nuns had not brought her here after her family turned their backs on her? These nuns had felt they were giving her a second chance in life. And what sort of life would I have had if she had kept me, the pair of us moving between a succession of cheap flats in London or some other foreign city? For years I had barely acknowledged that I was adopted. Was it hypocrisy for me to feel this grief at her death? If I was honest, wasn't I relieved to have been spared the misery of such an impoverished childhood? These nuns had ensured that I enjoyed a sheltered upbringing with loving parents. I had escaped from poverty and stigma. Sister Anne was waiting for me to go.

'Where are the nuns who died here buried?' I asked.

She pointed to a low wall bordered by yew trees. There was a cross on top of the small iron gate.

'What about the women who died in childbirth or the stillborn children?'

'There used to be a plot for them, but it was the only site that really worked for the new extension ten years ago. We needed to dig up the bodies and cremate them. We planted a tree in their memory.'

'That was big of you.'

If I had been an Aids victim, a rapist in prison or a leper in an oppressed foreign land she would have known what to say to me. Instead she stepped back defensively.

'You have to get it into your head,' she said. 'This is now a school: a school where any parent would be proud to enrol their child.'

*

There were trees behind the convent, which sloped down towards a river. Cows grazed peacefully there. I reached the water's edge and picked up a stone from the bank, breaking the surface of the water with it while the cows grazed placidly beside me. I worked my way slowly along by the river, searching for the dump that the schoolgirls had mentioned. It was in the furthest corner of the grounds. The lush riverbank vegetation had almost choked everything. Local people must have long ago salvaged anything that could be reused. All that remained dumped there were bits of broken beds, the smashed wooden bars of cots and pieces of loose debris so discoloured that it was hard to know what they had once been.

There were six rolls of film in the camera bag. My hands were covered with nettle stings by the time I shot my way through them. When I finished the last roll the sun was high overhead. Far off I could hear the shouts of young voices at volleyball. I felt calmed as I always did after framing the world within this viewfinder. Now I knew I needed to confront the nun who had so terrified my mother.

*

They were waiting for me at the retreat house in Sligo. The middle-aged nun who stood at the doorway looked formidable. Before I was even out of the car she began to explain that Sister Theresa was frail and hardly able to breathe. She was in constant pain and any shock could kill her. If the Mother Superior of St Martha's had asked that I be allowed to see her, then she would not stand in my way, but what possible good could it do me? Bad things had happened in the past, but they were part of the times that Ireland went through. Sister Theresa would not even remember my mother. Could I not just let an old woman die in peace? I was tempted to turn back. Then I thought of Benedict and Sinéad. 'For their sake you must lose this anger.' The Mother Superior had known how to get at me.

'I want to see her.' I said.

'You've caused quite a stir,' she replied. 'Sister Theresa overheard the younger nuns talking. She wants to see you too. She thinks you've come to…' The nun stopped. 'She's confused. She'll be flustered now until she's seen you…' She paused. 'Mr Blake, she is a very ill woman, you can have five minutes and that's it.'

I was led inside in silence, up two flights of waxed stairs and down a long corridor. I could hear doors opening as I passed, and sensed that I was being watched. A young novice sat beside the bed. The old nun under the blankets was shrunken into a child's frame, her head pressed into the pillow as if already dead. She moved her head slightly towards me and smiled. Her whisper was barely audible.

'So pleased you have come to visit me, child. So happy for you. A fine man. How well you've turned out.'

'Lizzy Sweeney,' I said. 'My mother's name was Lizzy Sweeney.'

The nun tried to nod. The novice wiped her mouth with a tissue.

'Yes, a wonderful mother you must have had, a wonderful home. How well you look now, such a gentleman come to visit. I remember feeding you, a sickly baby.'

She began to ramble, her breath coming hoarsely. The novice bent her head close to the old nun's lips. She looked up.

'She wants to touch your hand. She's thanking God for you.'

The novice held up the frail hand. When I took it I felt that

I could crush the bones of her fingers with one squeeze. I leaned across her. There was so much I had intended to say, so many accusations. I looked into her eyes and turned away. I said no words of anger to her because in my heart I knew that Lizzy Sweeney would have wanted nothing angry said here.

'My mother was a good woman,' I said simply. 'Both of my mothers were good women. Both were proud of me and I am proud of them both.'

I don't know if the old nun heard. She was smiling, her fingers aloft as if I was still holding her hand. I could hear her whispering, oblivious to the fact that I had moved away as they closed the door after me.

'So pleased you have come to offer thanks, child.'

Chapter Sixteen

There was building work being carried out on Kilnagowna Chapel. Scaffolding that was flecked with rust rested against the wall nearest the graveyard. The job had the look of being done by local men, unpaid, in their spare time. A long sweep of gravel led down to the single shop with its green corrugated-iron roof at the small turning. There was an old sign in miles for Virginia and a new green one in kilometres for the new hotel which I had passed earlier. A truck sped by, heading for the border. The two young donkeys in the field behind the schoolyard did not raise their heads. An elderly man on a bicycle stopped at the junction beside the shop and stared at me, immobilised, one foot on the tarmac, the other poised on the pedal.

It was half six in the evening. I had pulled over in a lay-by several miles outside Sligo and slept for several hours until I was jolted awake to feel my car being rocked by the slipstream of trucks. My eyes were so sore when I rubbed them that it felt as if glass fragments had slipped beneath the lids. I had started the engine, intending to drive home, but the voice of that nun from St Martha's kept entering my head, urging me to confront my demons. An unspoken impetus propelled me to take side roads through Leitrim and into Cavan, until eventually I found the hamlet of Kilnagowna.

I went into the chapel. A crude spotlight blazed from the ceiling, highlighting the altar and casting the side pews into shadow. 'Confessions from six to eight,' the housekeeper had told me. 'You'll find a queue, though. Father Tom is one of our own.' A line of six people waited in the pew adjacent to his confessional. The sign above his door read Fr Sweeney. A soft light shone from the part of the confessional where he sat, but the small box where the public knelt was in darkness. I had expected all the penitents to be old, but the two girls who waited directly in front of me were in their twenties, while the young man about to go into the box had a punk Mohican hairstyle which seemed incongruous with the black tweed overcoat he was wearing.

How long was it since I had queued to enter a boxed confessional? I could remember my teacher's voice telling us how valuable this period of waiting was as we bowed our seven-year-old heads and searched our consciences for sins we might have hidden from ourselves. The faces of the two girls beside me now were composed in thought or prayer. I wondered what type of understanding they could really expect from this man who felt he had the God-given power to forgive or condemn them? An old woman arrived and knelt beside me. I motioned her to go ahead of me in the queue, but she shook her head.

When my turn came, I entered the box and knelt because it felt foolish to stand. A small wooden slot opened between me and the priest, casting a band of weak light into my side of the box. I could see the outline of his cheek through the golden mesh. I said nothing and I could see his lips puzzling at the silence.

'Do you not remember the words?' he said after a few moments. 'You're a stranger in these parts, I feel?'

'I'm a son come home.'

'Is it confession you want? I don't want to hurry you, but there are people waiting.'

I expected to see irritation on those of his features that I could glimpse through the grille, but his voice sounded genuinely concerned.

'I remember being told there are two kinds of sin,' I said, 'sins of deed and sins of omission? I expect you're a sins of omission man: standing back like a smug Pontius Pilate to wash your hands of all the dirty stuff? But the sins of what you do and the sins of what you allow others to do will both always come back to haunt you.'

'You sound like you have a lot of anger inside you,' he said. 'I don't know what you have done that you want to confess, but if you wish me to hear your confession, I will.'

'I do have a lot of anger at someone: a fair degree of contempt and hatred towards him in fact. How is hatred ranked as a sin?'

'Let's start at the beginning,' he said. 'First you need to say, bless me, Father, for I have sinned. Then tell me how long it is since your last confession.'

'I asked you how hatred is rated as a sin, Sweeney.'

He paused. 'Hatred is a serious sin. Unchecked it can lead to acts of violence. Have you been involved with the men of violence?'

'No. I hate one man. I don't even hate him for the things he did, but for the things he didn't do. I hate how the smug bastard betrayed his own sister.'

'I cannot allow such language in the confessional.'

When I stared in at him through mesh his eyes were looking straight ahead, keeping a professional distance between us. That is the face of my uncle, I thought, the face of only the second blood relative I have ever seen. Maybe in twenty or thirty years I will look like him. I wanted him to turn and be forced to see me too.

'So what sort of penance would a righteous man like you give the two girls who came in here before me if those girls sinned by your high moral standards; if they fell by the wayside? They may peer through this grille and see a kindly old geezer. But I see a moral fucking hypocrite.'

He turned now and eyed me sharply. This is how I would photograph him, I thought, his eyes in shadow, his mouth slightly open in the light.

'What is it you want?' he asked. 'A row, with the guards called? I'm not playing your game. If you wish to talk to a priest, then come and see me at my house or stop me on the street whenever you are genuinely ready to talk. But in the meantime there are sincere people out there waiting to have their confessions heard. I'm closing this grille and I want you to leave this confession box, my son.'

The shaft of dim light narrowed as the slot began to close.

'Wait,' I said. 'Am I your son? Whose son am I? That's what I've come here to find out.'

His hand stopped. There was an inch of light left. My anger dissipated. The closing of the light frightened me somehow. I wanted to talk because he was the only man who might have answers to the questions tormenting me. But it killed me to have to beg for information off a man who had callously watched his own sister being dragged away.

'What if the man I hated was a priest?' I asked. 'What if maybe I hate him unfairly because there were others who did worse things to his own sister, but maybe he is the only bullyboy I can lay my hands on?'

The box filled again with dim slanting light. I could not see his face though and knew that this was because his forehead was pressed against the wooden partition between us.

'It is no greater a sin to hate a priest than to hate any other man,' he said softly. I could hear him breathing. Had he had been dreading an encounter like this for the past thirty-five years? 'Not many cars stop here,' he added. 'It seems an isolated spot for a stranger to pick to have his confession heard. Are there no priests in your own parish?'

'None that I would call uncle or possibly even father.'

There was a silence, then I heard his door open. From his low whisper I knew he was telling the few people left in the church that

211

he could not hear their confessions. I stared in at the empty box where much of his life must have been spent. He returned. There was a click of the light switch and we were both in darkness.

'When people see the light out they know confessions are over.'

'Or maybe you just feel that certain things are best left in the dark?'

'This man whom you appear to hate…'

'This priest.'

'Let's call him a man for now,' he said. 'You have him at a disadvantage. He doesn't know your name or how much you know about what happened in the past.'

'Tell me the bits of the puzzle I don't know: like if you had a hearty breakfast after watching your sister being dragged off in a car?'

He was silent for a long time. The darkness in this box was becoming claustrophobic.

'You have this priest down as a strongman,' he said at last, 'a bully. Maybe all his life he was a coward.'

'Is that an excuse?'

'No.' The voice in the darkness paused. 'I don't know your name. I don't know what to call you.'

'What did your sister call me?'

'I don't know that either.' The anguish in his voice was real, but it only made me angry again.

'Did you never fucking think to find out?'

'When you're a coward the less you know the safer you feel.' His voice was suddenly scared. 'Who sent you here?'

'Don't worry; I haven't come here to drag down your good name. I want nothing to do with you. I just want you to give me the name of my father and let me get the hell out of here.'

'I don't know his name.' His whisper was so low I had to strain to hear it. 'He was older than her, that's all I know.'

'You were the closest to her. If she told anyone she would have told you.'

'She tried to tell me a few days before our parents found out, but I stopped her. I didn't want to know. She wouldn't tell my father though he tried to beat it out of her. Maybe if she had told him something could have been done. Me and Lizzy, we were close, as close as any sister or brother could be.'

'Was it you?' I raised my voice. 'Tell me.'

He laughed – a low involuntary laugh – the loneliest, most desolate laugh I had ever heard. It sounded eerie. Then he was silent again for what seemed like an eternity.

'No,' he said at last. 'Though I wish you were, or to be more precise I wish that at least for a time you had thought you were.'

'I don't know what you mean.'

'I mean that this priest you hate, he has the feelings of any other man – the same need not to be alone, the same sense of growing old. What he is denied are the ordinary things that sustain other men – the sense of belonging to a family, of seeing children grow. I'm not talking about the struggle with sex here, though that has been a battle. I'm talking about the simple joy of sitting down to a bowl of soup with someone you love.'

'Nobody forced you to wear that collar,' I said.

'True. I could have run away: a lot of us did from the seminary. But what if hundreds of neighbours packed the church grounds on the night you were ordained? What if there were pitch barrels blazing and a brass band marching up the lane to your father's farm? What if old women from across the parish were telling you that the prospect of this glorious day had kept them alive for the previous seven years? What if you had made a promise to your mother on her deathbed and you didn't want to shame her?'

'And what if somebody was absent from those celebrations,' I retorted. 'A vanished sister who had spent her pregnancy on her knees scrubbing a convent floor in Sligo?'

There was silence, then a spurt of flame. He inhaled the cigarette, the red tip glowing through the wire mesh.

'The girls you saw tonight and that young punk lad are about the only young people left in this parish,' he said quietly. 'Emigration. They say things will pick up but it feels just like the 1950s again. We won the minor county final two years ago. There was a delay with the medals, they finally arrived last month. It cost eighty pounds to post them to Sydney and Boston, New York, Birmingham, Frankfurt. Just two of that minor team are still living here. The only way I will ever finish the repairs on this church is to burn it down for the insurance and start again. Do you smoke?'

'No.'

'Neither did I until I started going into those convents after I was ordained. You'd need a cigarette afterwards; you'd need a stiff whiskey. I used to dread being sent in to hear the confessions of what the nuns called fallen women. I remember one woman with skin that looked like it had never have been touched by sunlight. You wouldn't keep a dog in the condition she was in. I almost got sick listening to her describing the tape worms she was passing. A nun had told her that it was God's punishment for giving birth thirty years before. So don't try and tell me what those convents were like, because they were worse than you could ever imagine. Would it make any difference to you to know just how much this man you despise has despised himself for years for letting his sister be put into such a place?'

I didn't reply. I didn't want to engage with him. I just wanted a name. A strand of smoke floated like a white ghost through the wire mesh towards me.

'Do you have children?' he asked.

'Two.'

'Do you think I might know their names?'

'There's meant to be anonymity in the confession box.'

'Could you tell me at least if they are boys or girls?' He sounded desperate.

214

'Some nights when I am putting my son to bed, I sit holding his hand in the light spilling in from the landing. He asks me what my daddy was like and I tell him about a quiet man who worked all his life selling postcards from a van. It's simpler that way. I've always kept my life simple. But life isn't simple, I've found that you can't just lock things away. One day I will have to sit down and tell him and his sister all about this.'

'Do you carry photographs of your children?'

'In my wallet. Yes.'

The light clicked on. I could see his face close to the wire mesh.

'Please, can I see what my sister's grandchildren look like?'

'No.'

The light clicked off again. We heard the footsteps of somebody who must have been praying at a side altar. They paused on the aisle outside the confessional as if they were staring in at the box. The footsteps moved on. The church door closed with a soft swish.

'We're alone,' I said.

'Except for God.'

'I don't believe in God.'

'The funny thing is that I do,' he said. 'It's funny because for years I didn't. Once you fall into the routine of a priest the business side of things sweeps you up. It might be a charade but it's a busy one. Every five years I'd attend a reunion of the men I was ordained with, with one or two always whittled away to marriage or cancer, and I could see the change in the faces of men who had once been so devout. Their faith had hardened into something different, had imperceptibly slipped away. They might have started out as fisher-men for souls, but they were now essentially project managers. All the talk would be about parish building programmes and overdrafts and public liability insurance. I drifted along, too scared to leave, knowing I could never hack it on my own. And then, around ten years ago, by some odd chance this whole charade became flesh. I didn't find God, but for whatever reason he seemed to find me. I believe in him, sincerely now. That's funny, isn't it?'

'I didn't come here to laugh,' I said quietly.

'Why did you come?'

'I want to know the name of the man who left Lizzy Sweeney in that state.'

'Can you not call her what she was to you?'

'Lizzy Sweeney was a stranger to me. She died before I found her. Besides, who are you to tell me what to call her? How often did you try to contact her in the years since you watched your parents fling her out?'

'I didn't try for years. I was too much of a coward. Then I tentatively tried through my sister Ellen but Lizzy wanted nothing to do with me. I can't blame her.' He went quiet again. I could hear his breathing in the dark. 'It would have meant a lot to her if you'd found her in time. I said a mass here for her soul on the morning of her funeral.'

'That was a safe enough distance, was it?'

I was consumed by anger and grief. I had wanted this man to be callous and evil, to be a substitute for my own nameless father who probably never even bothered to think of my existence, who – if he remembered my mother at all – boasted about her late at night in pubs as an early conquest. But I knew also that my anger was really directed at myself. I could have found her in time. The accusation kept returning. I could blame nobody else for that. I opened the door of the box. The light still shone on the main altar. A few candles flickered in memory of the dead in front of a cheap statue on a side altar.

'Please wait. Please.'

I stepped out onto the side aisle. The station of the cross on the wall beside me depicted the Crowning of Thorns. The whisper came from the box again, near tears: pleading, yet dignified.

'Please… whatever your name is… stay. I loved your mother. There has never been anyone on this earth that I was ever so close to. Mock me or reproach me or even strike me, but please, do not desert me just yet. For years I've prayed that you and I would meet face to face. I have no family. After the business with Lizzy I turned my back on all of them except Ellen – and I can barely bring myself to meet Ellen because – even though she tries hard not to – I know she blames me. Call me Judas, call me any name you want, but just stay for a few minutes more.'

I turned to address the closed wooden door of his confessional.

'Open that door so and walk out of this church with me. Walk with me to the shop on the bend below and introduce me there as your bastard nephew who was born in a Magdalene laundry.'

'What good will that serve? I am the confessor of the woman who owns that shop. I buried her husband two years ago. I sat with her in the hospital in the hours before he died and the hours after he died. I am someone she feels she knows, someone she feels she can talk to her in her loneliness. What will you achieve by making her a part of your vendetta?'

'Maybe I need to be acknowledged.'

'Then why won't you even tell me your name?'

'Let's be clear here,' I said, 'you're the coward hiding in the box.'

'And I have the courage to admit it. I've been a coward all my life. I don't know if I have been a bad man, but I'm a weak man who saw bad things done that I did nothing about because I felt powerless and I was scared. I'm still scared. I've wanted to meet you and yet I've been scared to meet you all my life.'

I walked away from him, my footsteps loud on the waxed aisle. I reached the church door. I felt tired and lost. I looked back up at the altar. I wanted a response. I wanted Geraldine and Benedict and Sinéad to put their arms around me. But I knew I had to make peace with the past before I could ever hope to fit back into the warmth of their world. Slowly I walked back up along the aisle. My footsteps were quiet, but as soon as they stopped outside the confessional his voice came softly through the wood.

'All my life I've made false confessions to other priests, telling nobody the truth. Hear my confession, then you can damn me to hell.'

'It was you who told me not to mock this place.'

'I have come to know God only very slowly. Let me decide what constitutes mockery.'

'Come out here and face me.'

'No,' the voice said. 'The priests of this parish change, but this wooden box does not. Sometimes I think it is not us who absolve sins but these wooden walls that must be intimately acquainted with the human heart.'

Reluctantly I re-entered the box and closed the door. Behind the thin wooden partition he was waiting for my permission to speak.

'Do you know what a false confession is?' he asked.

I leaned my head against the wood and said nothing.

'I was eleven when I made my first one. Every confession I have made since then has been a false one. At the age of seven, boys start to enter this box. Week in and week out I listen to the same banal prattling. Then one week their voices are different… awkward, fearful… and you know it has begun: adolescence. The sudden weight on their shoulders like they were the biggest sinners in the world. "I hid under my sister's bed the night she had a bath… I read a magazine a boy brought into school… I had bad thoughts, impure deeds that just came flooding out of me." It's hard on those young boys stammering away. They're in a cage and I'm in a cage too, with absolute rules that I'm meant to hand down. I speak to them kindly. I tell them to kneel at the altar and say three Hail Marys for their sins. But think of how much harder it would be for a young boy in Laois in the 1950s to say, "I knelt in front of the altar, Father, I gazed up at Jesus's alabaster limbs on the crucifix, naked except for a white loincloth. It was an occasion of sin."'

'This has gone far enough,' I said to the darkness. 'I'm not your confessor. Whatever you have to say, come out and say it to my face.'

'Do you not think I've tried to talk about this in the open, to not spend a life trapped by secrets and lies?' his voice answered. 'Afterwards you can walk away but just listen to me now. There were two sorts of boys in Laois: footballers and priests. When I was six, my father brought me on his crossbar over the mountains to see a hurling match in Birr. There was a field of young men stripping for the game behind bushes by the river. I've never forgotten the feeling I experienced, the marvellous joy at the way the winter sun gleamed on their ribs and naked legs. It was during The Emergency, a time of rationing. One young man gave me a piece of orange. I bit into it and felt the juice run down my tongue. I think perhaps I never felt so happy again. At first on the way home, crossing the mountain in the dusk, with the road so pot-holed my father's bike had to keep swerving, I could sense Dada's amusement as I talked away about how lovely the men were. Then his amusement turned to unease and after a while we were freewheeling down by Roundwood, with neither of us speaking and him annoyed and me not knowing why. On the following Sunday he brought my other brother and you could hear them laughing and joking in the dark for over a mile before they got back to the farmyard that night.'

As I listened to him I felt flooded with exhaustion. I didn't want the burden of hearing about his life because it tied me too much to a past that didn't truly feel like mine. I was not really the Francis Sweeney he was addressing: I had spent my life avoiding being that disgraced baby passed from hand to hand. I tapped my knuckles against the wood as if to drown out his voice. He ignored the noise.

'You grow up and find that you're different from other boys: gentler, not getting into as many fights. Your classmates start to roam in packs, hungry for the sight of girls. If you're not with them it's hard to avoid rumours of sanctity, especially when you see how much such rumours please your mother and you want no other rumours started about you.'

My name is Sean Blake, I wanted to tell him. I should not have sought you out here: your life has nothing to do with me.

'Take a small parish in Laois,' his voice continued, 'three pubs, a shop, a church, a bridge for men to gather on in the evenings. A parish is like a closed fist: even when walking out through the fields in winter somebody will always see you. At first I thought there was no one else like me in the world; that I'd wind up in an asylum. Then one day I found out, from listening to stories and twisted jokes, that there were others like me out there and the asylum wasn't my worry anymore. I realised that I could very likely be found kicked to death.'

'So you run off and hide behind the priesthood?'

There was silence from the far side of the partition. I wondered had he been in other cubicles like this, in cubicles with men who had not looked into his face while water gushed from the urinal behind them.

'Would I have been better to hide behind marriage like most men like me did?' he said then. 'What type of husband would I have made for Lizzy? What kind of father would I have made for you?'

'What are you saying? Lizzy Sweeney was your sister. What are you trying to tell me?' I was suddenly ready to drag him from that box.

'Listen to me… I didn't mean it like that. Your father was some flyboy. I don't know who he was or if he forced himself on her or if she gave herself willingly. I'm talking about my stupid, stupid plan to look after you both.'

His voice dried up, as if he had touched on a memory so raw that it was impossible to continue.

'Put your light on,' I said.

There was a click. I reached into my wallet and held a photograph up against the grille.

'The boy is aged three,' I said. 'The girl is fourteen months old.'

I expected him to ask for names or details of their personalities, but finally all he said was 'Thank you' in such a way that I knew he had been crying. The light was switched off again. It was some time before he spoke.

'My parish sensed that I was different and so they collectively decided to have my vocation for me. Dunross had never raised a priest before. It was easier to just get caught up in that public acclaim than face whatever sort of uncertain other future I might have alone. I told myself that because a priest is celibate anyhow it would be no harder for me than for anyone else. In fact it would keep me out of harm's way. The trouble was that in my heart I didn't want to be a priest. I wanted an ordinary life with ordinary things. Lizzy had a special magic about her. Every boy in that parish dreamed about her. I have a photograph of her taken one summer if you would like to walk up with me to the parochial house?'

'I have a life of my own,' I said. 'There are people I need to get back to.'

'Lizzy and I were always close. She'd talk to me about boys she liked and now and then I'd try to hint to her that just maybe I liked them too, but… how could she have understood when nobody wanted to understand such things in that place and time? The only thing I found hard about leaving Dunross to enter the seminary was leaving her. The seminary was no lonelier than life had been for me at home. In fact I felt safe behind those walls, not allowed to read a newspaper or listen to the wireless except for the All-Ireland Final. It was said that even if you didn't have a vocation, once you lay prostate at the altar to be ordained God would grant you one. A few years ago I looked at a photograph in the newspaper of young Iranian boys in their bare feet holding up holy books as they walked through minefields to clear a way for the tanks. That was us back then, I thought, led by blind faith, brainwashed to trust in God and keep walking through minefields no matter what. Most evening in that seminary I prayed to God to show me a way out, but I knew I hadn't the guts to run away on my own.'

I closed my eyes as he spoke. I was visualising the face of the young man who had blocked my path when my heart briefly stopped after that crash. I found myself trembling. From the far side of the wooden panel his voice continued.

'Then in the autumn I was allowed home. Lizzy didn't seem herself, she was anxious, pale. I caught a glimpse of her behind bushes in the high field one morning and realised that she was getting sick. I didn't understand why. I asked her at dinner if she was feeling better. The look she gave me across the table… it was a look of pure terror.'

Footsteps entered the church. He paused until they turned and walked out again. That young face which had haunted my sleep was so clear, only it no longed look surly. It was frightened and pleading. I knew now that it belonged with the voice on the other side of that box, that since the crash it had been leading me here.

'I could never get Lizzy alone to talk to her,' he said. 'It was like she was avoiding me, avoiding all of us. Then one morning when we were making hay in the lake field I deliberately nicked my hand, knowing that our mother would send Lizzy back to the empty farmhouse with me to bathe it. "Tell me what's wrong," I said in the kitchen. "Whatever it is I can help." Gripping my hand tight, she started to cry. She told me she was three months gone. This is God's sign, I thought, he's showing me what path to take. Lizzy and I would find the strength to flee together. I hushed her and told her not to worry. I told her that the pair of us would go to England and pretend to be man and wife; that I'd find work and I'd mind her and mind…' He stopped, as though frightened to say the word. '…you. I told her I didn't want to know who the father was, that you'd be mine – mine and hers…'

He stopped again. There was a scraping noise. It was his nails on the wire mesh. He did not seem aware of it.

'Lizzy kept shaking her head, terrified, saying that it would be a greater sin to take me away from God, that she couldn't do that, she would manage alone. But I told her that this was what God wanted. Eventually I convinced her, I wore her down. She told me how she'd tried to kill herself. She had gone to the man – your real father – and he'd wanted nothing to do with her. Not all men are like that, I told her, from now on I would mind her and she was to trust me. Every man in that parish dreamed of her, yet I abused her far worse than the dirtiest old man ever could because I gave her hope and she gave me her trust. Such plans we made, what we would bring, how to get the suitcases down from the attic when no one was around. My father had money in a biscuit tin from the sale of calves. It would pay our fares all the way to London, it would give us a start. There was a big mart in Mountrath, the whole family planning to go there when the harvesting was done. We'd get the bus when they were all there. We'd be in Dublin before anyone noticed the money was gone, then on the boat to England. I still remember lying upstairs in my room, listening to her singing in the kitchen. Sometimes I wake at night and I think I still hear her.'

The scraping had stopped. I had never known a silence as deep. It was some time before he began to speak again.

'The evening before we planned to go,' he said, 'I waited for our mother to send her out down the lane with the bucket for water. I could hear my father joking with Lizzy as she passed him while he scraped his boots out in the yard. It would never have worked out: it was sheer madness. God knows how long we would have lasted but only God knows because, when it came to it, I was just too scared. All the plans in the world were grand, but when the time for action came my only thought was to save myself. Maybe I could have faced the running away and the scandal, but what I couldn't face was the inevitable moment when Lizzy – who trusted in me fully, who was convinced I was her saviour – saw with her own eyes that I was simply a coward, shivering with fright on the Dublin quays or some London train station, a scared boy without any real clue about what to do next. So I walked downstairs and, with every step I took I hated myself more, but I knew I was going to tell our mother that Lizzy was three months pregnant. I betrayed her and then, like the coward I was and the coward still am, I went back up to my room and closed the door. I lay on the bed with the pillow over my head, but I could hear her screams after she came in. She was calling for me to protect her. The awful thud of my father's belt as he tried to get the man's name from her. Ellen started pounding on my bedroom door for me to help until she was dragged away. All I had to do was walk downstairs and I could have stopped the beating at least. But I did nothing. Lizzy vanished behind one set of walls and I retreated back behind the safety of another. But Sweet Jesus in Heaven, not a day passes when I don't think about what I did to her.'

He stopped speaking. My eyes had grown used to the darkness. I could see the shape of his hand pressing against the wire mesh.

'Are you still there?' he asked, his voice suddenly fearful. I tapped very softly on the wood in reply.

'People come into this confessional,' he said, 'and they think that all sins can be forgiven. But I know they can't. I give absolution to dying people and I feel so privileged to give them that peace of mind. But I know that when I come to die, I will turn my face away from the priest because there are certain sins that you bring with you to the grave.'

I opened the door of the confession box and looked out at the darkened church. If I drove quickly enough I could be back in Dublin in time to read Benedict a bedtime story. I wanted to put my arms around him and Sinéad and Geraldine. I wanted bright lights and music and streets filled with people. I wanted to be gone from this man's pain.

'Will I ever see you again?' he asked.

'I don't believe so.'

'It would never have worked for us in England,' he said. 'Legal documents, jobs, birth certs. God knows what I spared you, but I did it for myself.' He paused. 'No matter how much you hate me for what I did to your mother, it will always be less than how much I hate myself.'

'I'm sorry,' I said, 'but it is not within my gift to condemn or to forgive you.'

'I condemn myself fully. It is only within your gift to try and understand.'

He had taken his hand away from the wire mesh. I turned and placed my fingers lightly against it. I could feel the slight pressure when his hand pressed back against the other side. Long after I had driven away, when I had passed through Navan with the lights on at the dog track and the straight flat road had consumed me inside the lines of unblinking catseyes, I knew that he was still sitting there, his fingers pressing on that wire mesh, trying to cling on to the last trace of human warmth.

Chapter Seventeen

On the night that I finished working on the St Martha photographs I took Benedict to his first football match. After a twenty-one year absence, Shelbourne were back in a European Competition. Two weeks ago in the Ukraine they had lost the first leg away to Karpaty Lviv by an unlucky late goal. Tonight the second leg was being played in Tolka Park. When I came down from my darkroom in the attic I heard on the radio that Shelbourne had pulled a goal back in the opening minutes to level the tie. I scooped Benedict up into my arms as Geraldine was about to undress him for bed. Ignoring her protests, I pulled on his coat and told her that we would be back before ten. He turned to wave at her and then put his arms around my neck, delighted to be carried off on a late adventure.

It was a source of pride to my father that he had brought me as a child to every home game that Shels played in Europe, back in the glory days of the early 1960s when we lost to Sporting Lisbon and Barcelona. I could remember little about those games, except the joy of being allowed to stay up so late. But I could still recall the only occasion when I ever saw my father in tears. It was 1964 – the first and, so far, the only time that Shelbourne won a European tie – against Belenenses in what was then called the Inter Fairs Cup, with Ben Hannigan and Mick Conroy scoring the goals that put us through.

There had been a storm that night, lightning splitting the sky, rain spitting down like darts of crystallised light in the haphazard floodlights, as the huge crowd screamed around us. To me as a child it had felt like the electric storm was pulsing through our bodies as I swayed on my father's shoulders, and cried at the final whistle too, because he was in tears of joy.

The glory didn't last long; we were beaten in the second round by Athletico Madrid. After that Shelbourne went into decline, with just one more European outing, seven years later in 1971, in the UEFA Cup against Vasas Budapest. I was thirteen years old then, standing with my own friends behind the goal where Shelbourne's late chance of a winner rebounded off the crossbar in the one-all draw that knocked us out. I had been staking out my own independent space, away from my father and the men he knocked around with, who went off to relive their past over pints afterwards in the Hut Bar.

Since then Shelbourne had been forever on the move. Twenty years in seemingly terminal decline, itinerants and nomads with no real home ground of their own. Years spent playing in the wilderness of Harold's Cross Dog Track, struggling to avoid relegation every season, rumoured always to be on the verge of extinction. Two decades lit by the optimism of occasional cup runs, as their dwindling band of supporters sustained each other with memories of Sundays in the 1960s when all of Dublin was stilled by the roars of packed local derbies against Shamrock Rovers or Bohs. I once found an archive photograph in the sports department of the paper. It showed three elderly figures standing slightly apart on the terrace of Harold's Cross stadium. On every side there was empty space around them. I could recognise my father in the middle, with almost all his friends having passed away, shouting himself into a lonely old age.

He had not lived to see the revival of Shelbourne, with the club returning to Tolka Park, where they were tenants in my childhood, this time to buy it and finally own their first ground since 1895. Under their owner, Ollie Byrne – part hectoring despot, part romantic dreamer – they had turned Tolka Park into the best stadium in Ireland and finally brought the championship back to the ground that my father had almost regarded as his spiritual home.

When I arrived there with Benedict he paused on the street to stare at the huge television cranes leaning across the stand from outside the ground. He was both excited and scared by the shouts coming from inside. Gently I picked him up and the steward at the turnstile nodded for me to lift him over it. We entered into a tumult of noise and I placed Benedict up on my shoulders. Being there with my own son made my father's death painful again. He would have loved to be here tonight with the grandson he never knew, his heart bursting with emotions he would not have known how to express.

Benedict was restless, thrilled to be out so late and yet frightened by the large crowd. I carried him up to the corner overlooking the river where there was some space. He ran among the rows of plastic chairs behind us, pulling at the seats and then turned to stare in wonder at the full moon in the sky that seemed a richer blue beyond the plume of floodlights. It was still one-nil for Shels. How long was it since I had heard a crowd this large chanting for Shelbourne? Not since I had been small enough to fit on my own father's shoulders on this terrace when men queued on freezing nights for steaming Bovril.

I sat down and Benedict tumbled onto my knee, tired of the novelty of being here and simply wanting to be held and told stories. Shels were pressing forward frantically. They won a free just outside the box. Ken Doherty lay on the ground, the Ukrainian player was booked.

'Benedict visits the farm,' Benedict suggested as a story title. Mick

Neville took the spot kick. It struck the underside of the crossbar and was scrambled away. Benedict tugged at my jacket as I rose to join the chorus of screams. 'Hello farmer,' he said, trying to get my attention. 'Has your tractor broken down? Me and Gary the Goat will fix it.'

He began to busy himself with imaginary spanners, waiting for me to improvise a story around him. The French referee blew for half-time. I stilled his hands.

'Let me tell you a different type of story tonight,' I said. 'About when I was a little boy and my daddy – your granddad – used to bring me down here.'

Benedict settled down on my lap to listen, asking questions about the man I had never talked to him about before, with his grandfather becoming real for him. I had blown up an old photograph of my parents when they were young and hung it in the downstairs bathroom. So far he had shown little interest in it, but now he wanted to go home so he could look at their faces. I realised that if I had died in that crash outside the Botanic Gardens he would not even have had a photograph to remember me by. How could I have ever felt any regret at having survived that crash? I hugged my son tight, flushed with the euphoria of being alive.

It was a euphoria that I regularly felt ever since I crashed for a second time, on the journey home from Kilnagowna in Cavan. Perhaps it was inevitable that I would crash again that night, with my body so pumped up with emotions and my mind wrecked from lack of sleep. I had just wanted to get away from the dark intensity of that confession box as quickly as I could. I had so badly wanted to be back home with Geraldine, to turn the corner of our street by the cherry-blossom trees by the library and glimpse the light on in our kitchen window across a row of back gardens.

All that evening it had threatened rain. Beyond Kingscourt it came down with ferocity, my windscreen wipers barely able to cope. At Dunshaughlin I decided to try a shortcut by taking the twisting side road that led to Ratoath. There were dangerous bends but I pushed on, desperate to make up time. I came around one steep bend and braked as I hit a pool of rainwater. Once again the crash seemed to occur in slow motion, but this time it was different.

Outside the Botanic Gardens I had watched the crash unfold with a mesmerised fascination, like a rendezvous I had been secretly racing to keep. This time I watched with pure horror, scrambling at the steering wheel as the car spun, willing myself to live. Death once again became a genuine and absolute terror. I fought with all my strength against meeting that host of welcoming faces again.

There had been a crash and I was jerked back. The car had spun off the road, narrowly missing two trees as the boot ploughed into a five-barrel gate. I heard the tinkle of glass as the rear lights shattered. The boot burst open. I opened the door and stepped out into the heavy rain. The clouds were so low that the road was almost dark. I was utterly alone. I hunched down, shaking. Then gradually I had felt the shock dissolving into euphoria. I was okay, I was alive: I had just written off my second car in a year, but I didn't care. The wheels had missed those trees by only a matter of inches. The windscreen could have shattered, the car turned over. I had come so close to dying again. I lifted my head into the rain. It tasted like champagne. A truck came round the corner. I held up my hand and he stopped to give me a lift. I was so giddy the driver thought I was in shock, but I was simply celebrating the miracle of my survival.

I phoned Geraldine from Healy's pub in Ratoath to say I would be home within the hour in a taxi. She had kept asking me where the car was and why I hadn't called her before now.

'I'll explain when I get home,' I had told her. 'I'll explain every-thing. Just keep Benedict up until I get there. I'm dying to get home to you.'

Dying to get home. I remembered the phrase now as the teams came out for the second half. I hugged Benedict tightly before I lifted him up on my shoulders.

'Let's stand where your granddad would have stood,' I said and walked up into the heart of the die-hard Shelbourne fans standing among the seats at the Ballybough End. There were other small children there, their fathers knowing that they might not remember this night in later years but wanting them to be able to say that they had been there. Benedict was tired but I could sense the crowd's adrenalin starting to work on him. Twenty minutes into the second half, Neville won the ball and released Brian Mooney. He moved forward – Ukranian defenders backing off him – and then, from thirty yards, he unleashed the finest right foot drive I had ever witnessed. It curled in under the post. I threw Benedict up in the surge of screaming bodies and caught him in my arms. He was frightened by the deafening noise but reassured when I hugged him. It was the first Shels goal Benedict had ever seen. He would not remember it, but he would never see a better one. I looked up at the sky which had turned a deep blue.

'What are you thinking, Daddy?' Benedict asked.

'I was just wishing that your granddad was here.'

'And your mammy too?'

'I had two mothers.'

'I didn't know you could have two mammies.'

'They never met but each one loved me as much as the other. I'll tell you about it one day, when you're ready to know.'

'Had you two daddies?'

'Just the one. I have no need of the other fellow: I'm beyond caring about him, whoever that stranger was. I have you and Sinéad and Geraldine, that's all that counts.'

Then we both got caught up in the game, terrified that Shels would concede and go out on away goals. But when the next goal came, after seventy-six minutes, it was scored for Shelbourne by Izzi, a young Italian part-timer who worked by night in his uncle's fish and chip shop. Against Belenenses, when I stood with my father, we had scraped home, but all these years later we were winning in style. It had been a decade since an Irish side had won in Europe. My father had supported them all in European competitions. How many times had he dreamed about a night like this? The crowd began to whistle for full time.

I took Benedict down from my shoulders. He curled up against my jacket. I had been his age when my father first brought me to games here, his mates pressing sixpenny bits in my hand, plying me with bars of chocolate which they told me not to mention to my mother. His mates had known exactly who I was. That was why they had gone out of their way to make me feel so special here as a child. I realised now that I had not just been adopted by him, but, on the Sundays when he took me here, I had been adopted by every one of those fathers.

The final whistle blew and the ground erupted. Old stewards whom I recognised from my father's time were dancing and blowing kisses at the crowd. The crowd stood to applaud the team off and Benedict was excited enough by the noise to climb back up onto my shoulders and join in the clapping. I began to make my way down through the crowd and a hand gripped my shoulder. It was an old friend of my father's who hugged me in silence. I nodded in understanding. The crowd were climbing over onto the pitch. I lifted Benedict down onto the floodlit turf and he ran around in a circle, excited by the magic of the floodlights. The terraces were almost empty. A scarf had been dropped by some kid running after the players. Benedict raced towards me. I caught him up in my arms and put the scarf around his neck. Shelbourne's owner, Ollie Byrne, stood near the centre circle, simultaneously hugging people and telling them gruffly to get off his pitch. He recognised me from years ago and stopped.

'A great night,' he said. 'Your old da would have loved to have been here.' He looked down at Benedict. 'Still and all, isn't this fellow the spit of him. Your da will never be gone from this world as long as this young scut is knocking around.'

'You know well that I was adopted, Ollie,' I told said. 'Everyone in the club knew that.'

He ruffled Benedict's hair as the child buried his face shyly in my jacket. 'Listen,' he said, 'I'm busy running a football club; I haven't time to be arguing with you about genetics. This fellow is the spit of your old man and always will be. Now get off my fecking pitch, will you?'

I walked past him towards the empty terrace that bordered the river. If ghosts did exist then I knew that my father would be standing on those concrete steps. I wanted my father to know that it was his name and his wife's name that Benedict was carrying, and that, despite my grief for my birth mother, his name was being carried on with pride. He's your grandson, I said in my mind, not the grandson of some nameless bastard who ran away. I reached the touchline and lifted up Benedict on my shoulders like a trophy for his grandfather to see.

*

Benedict was exhausted when we left Tolka Park and I had to carry him. He dozed with his head against my jacket as I cut through back lanes and up by the side of All Hallow's College. We reached the gates of Drumcondra Churchyard and Benedict woke. He gripped the railing and stared in at the moonlit headstones.

'We used to walk there, Dada.'

He leaned his head back against my jacket. Those March mornings seemed a lifetime ago, when I had walked with him here, afraid to venture back out into the world, tormented by a face that I could not place. Ever since the journey back from Cavan, that young man's features were gone from my mind. What often haunted my thoughts now was my uncle's profile glimpsed through a mesh of gold wire in a dark confessional, in his eyes the desperate pleading to be understood.

There was a movement among the tombstones, a ginger cat crossing the gravel path. Having being officially dead once – if only for a few seconds – death could never frighten me as much again. What I dreaded was one day having to explain to Benedict what the word death meant. I looked down at him half-asleep in my arms. His was a world without death, his future was still just an infinity of fresh mornings. He no longer cried out at night, but would climb in beside us at half seven every morning. Soon Sinéad would discover this pleasure and clamber into our bed too. Let her come and join our raft of love. These last months had taught me to treasure every sleepy caress, every elbow against my back, had taught me to appreciate being able to reach out and know that your child is there and nobody can take him or her away.

I walked on and paused by Drumcondra Library to watch the light shining in our kitchen window. Benedict stirred and I pointed out the light to him across the back gardens. He looked around, a little scared by the darkness, and asked to go home. Geraldine had biscuits and hot milk waiting for him.

I had left the St Martha shots in an envelope for Geraldine to look at. She had them laid out on the kitchen table. How long was it since I had worked on photographs with such utter engrossment, enhancing or bleaching colours, waking up each morning for the past three weeks with new ideas about exactly where the crop should occur? Although I had taken the photographs very quickly that afternoon by the river I was surprised at how I had intuitively worked complex elements into each composition. There was a disturbing ambivalence about how the blue unpolluted water and the lush riverside vegetation awash with flowering rush and green figwort drew the viewer's eye into a pastoral setting, only to be then confronted by the intrusion of dumped, obsolete objects so tangled amid the undergrowth that they no longer looked like themselves. The iron tops of bedsteads; rusted by twenty years of weather and now embroidered by a lattice of green weeds. The distorted reflection of the broken bars of a wooden cot half submerged in the river. An ancient horsehair mattress colonised by flowering nettles. Camouflaged by time, each item only slowly betrayed the secret of its past.

I had found myself honing in on displaced items: the knob of a bedside locker half buried in the mud, the sole of a tiny child's shoe camouflaged in the colour of the earth. They were man-made objects, but so distorted that they seem like part of the natural landscape. Yet although the earth had almost claimed them, they still clung to their identity and their past. These objects had once been precious, because they were all that we knew. How many babies like me had woken from our first sleep behind the broken bars of this cot, how many mothers had gripped that iron bedstead in terror when they felt their waters break? These beds and cots had been all we once had to call our home before we left that convent to commence the second lives we were given.

These photographs were my elegy for the forgotten, the only monument to my past I could create. During the last three weeks I had often sat in the darkroom unable to work anymore as I cried for the mother I never knew or was engulfed by anger at what had happened to her. Then the creative impulse that had first driven me to take photographs would take over: my compulsive need to be in control of what I saw, to cut away everything superfluous, to stop life for one millisecond so that I could try in my limited way to understand it. By the end there were dozens of different versions of each shot, the differences barely noticeable to anyone else, but those solitary hours in the darkroom had given me the space to gradually come to terms with and accept the past.

I stared down at them now as Geraldine fussed over Benedict, listening to him telling her about his great adventure. There was a noise from the baby monitor and we both instinctively listened for any sound of Sinéad shifting in her cot. But the machine had just picked up the noise of somebody passing on the street. Geraldine put on a tape of Benedict's favourite songs and walked over to the table where I was staring down at the photographs. She nuzzled against my shoulder as if to say that she understood.

'They're wonderful,' she said, 'I'm proud of you. I always was.'

'These last months I haven't been easy to live with.'

She kissed the back of my neck softly.

'You'd swear to God you ever were.' She paused. 'He called when you were out.'

I fingered one of the photographs for a moment.

'I still can't forgive him,' I said quietly, 'for what he did to her.'

'Sean, it was you who phoned him first. You started the contact, he phoned you back.'

'I know.'

'Have you decided what you are going to do?'

I nodded and turned to put my arms around her. Benedict came over and tugged at my arm for attention. He held out his empty palm with an imaginary offering.

'Look,' he said, 'Benedict has taken a picture of Gary the Goat.'

I leaned down to inspect the tiny fate lines criss-crossing his palm and smiled.

'It's lovely,' I said, 'you captured him just right.'

In another year Benedict would start school and forget all about such imaginary friends. I could remember my own first day in school, my terror when a black-robed nun reached out to take my hand and how my mother had been reduced suddenly by that outside power. Benedict was so young. He loved me so much, I was so essential in his life and yet if I had died in either of those car crashes there would have been nothing of me that he could remember. In the years to come we might argue as fathers and sons do. But when he reached my age I wanted him to be able to look at my face as it was now and to know that I had felt the same things as him. The only photographs of me were on my passport and my driving licence. Geraldine and I had fought bitterly before our wedding when I said I wanted no photographs taken. That mistrust of photographs had lasted since my eleventh birthday when I tore up those pictures of myself as a baby because I felt they told a lie, they fooled me into believing I was somebody I was not. Since then I had always needed to be in control, safely behind the lens, where I could be sure that the picture would tell no lies. Whose son was I? Which mother had shaped me most? I would never know the answer, but in truth I was not anyone's son anymore, I was a husband and a father. It was time to let go of everything else, time to focus on the miracle of being here and being loved. I looked across at my father's old camera bag lying behind the couch.

'Benedict,' I asked. 'Will you take a photograph of Dada?'

He peeped through his fingers and made a clicking sound, then held his empty palm out again to show me the imaginary picture.

'No,' I said, 'a real photograph. I'll teach you how to do it.'

I took out the camera out and showed him how to look through the viewfinder. He was tired and for a long time protested that he couldn't see. But then, by the look on his face, I knew that he had discovered how to gaze through it. Geraldine watched us in stunned amusement.

'I've seen everything now,' she said, 'Mr Control lands over his lens. Hang on a minute; I think I still have my wedding dress somewhere.'

I walked away from Benedict to sit on the floor where I knew that I would be in focus. I stared at the lens and found that my throat had gone dry.

'Show him how to press the shutter,' I told her. 'Go on, hold his finger for him.'

Every time the camera flashed Benedict looked up and laughed, then bent again in deep seriousness to peer at the condensed image of me. He shrugged Geraldine away, wanting to do it himself. His delight made me smile as I stared into the lens. Suddenly I was not afraid of it any more. This was how my son saw me, this was who I was: a father sitting on a floor to amuse his child. My studio contained thousand of contact sheets, but these were the shots that I would always treasure most. Benedict looked up again and laughed.

'Get Sinéad down,' I asked Geraldine. 'I know that we'll be up half the night quarrelling when we can't get her back to sleep, but please just get her down.'

I put a new roll of film in the camera and placed it on the table on automatic self-timer. I sat Benedict down on my knee.

'Now,' I said, 'Gary the Goat will take our photograph.'

The camera flashed by itself. Benedict jumped, unsure whether to laugh or cry. He looked back at me and I smiled to reassure him. He stared at the empty space behind the camera with huge eyes. Geraldine entered the room and sat down beside us with Sinéad still asleep in her arms. The camera flashed once more. Sinéad blinked, then closed her eyes again and began to suck her thumb. Geraldine snuggled closer to me. The camera flashed again and this time Sinéad opened her eyes wide and gave a gurgling laugh. Benedict turned in delight and hugged Geraldine.

'Mammy, Gary the Goat is taking our photograph!'

He laughed and we laughed with him as my father's old camera flashed on by itself to the end of the roll.

Chapter Eighteen

Oblivion briefly claimed her before the pain drove her back towards consciousness in the hospital ward. There were lights above her and beyond those lights there were faces waiting for her to die. Lizzy wanted those strangers to be gone, she wanted to be alone. For thirty-seven years she had essentially been alone. Ever since the day the whole family had waited by the roadside for the Dublin bus, with her beloved brother going away from her with his new suitcase and freshly cut hair. Only she had seemed able to sense the terrible fear within Tom that day.

Above her the lights of the ward blurred and merged into each other. The beam became so bright that it burned against her eyelids and dissolved into a core of darkness. The drip in her arm began to hurt and she became aware of where her skin had broken from lying there so long. But it was the searing pain inside her that pulled her briefly back into consciousness. It felt like a thread of copper wire twisting through her body, holding her back when she should be gone. Darkness awaited her: bereft of the suffering of souls in hell or the bliss of paradise. Those hallow childhood beliefs had long died. Instead all that she could expect was a numb unknowingness: an end to these years of waiting and of hope.

How long was it since the last injection? But what did time mean here? The faces leaned over her again, blurred and as indistinguishable from each other as the years of waiting for him to find her had been. An eternity of afternoons spent in the kitchen when her daughters were at school, with the radio playing for comfort: peeling potatoes, scraping carrots with that sharp black-handled knife passing so close to her wrist. Trying to focus and not succumb to dreams.

She found herself back at that sink, staring out at the shed which her husband kept locked. The radio blared out tinny music. She turned and the music stopped: the kitchen vibrating with the hiss of static. She was forty-one again. She dropped the knife and stared at the fate lines on her palm. If she was forty-one this made him twenty-two, wherever he was. Did he ever even think of her? Did he know her name? There was a shaving mirror beside the sink. She picked it up and stared at it, trying to imagine something of her own features in a young man of twenty-two. She closed her eyes. *Lord or Devil, Demon or Christ: I don't care who can answer my prayer; I don't care what your price is – just let me glimpse my son's face when I open my eyes.* She held her eyes closed for a long time, knowing the pact was foolish but scared by the desperate hope that surged inside. She opened her eyes and stared at herself. She closed her eyes again, desperate to imagine his face. The face she saw in her mind was Tom's. Lizzy dropped the mirror. When it shattered the noise came from a great distance off. She bent down to pick up a shard and let it prick her palm. The afternoon was heavy with grey clouds; Coventry clouds she called them. She closed her eyes again and smeared the blood in the sign of the cross on her forehead, ready to make a pact for her soul with any devil or God if she could just see Francis for one second.

She opened her eyes quickly as she felt a gloved hand cover her face. Was it a rapist, a burglar after breaking in? The fingers pressed hard as she fought in panic against his grip but he was strong as he suffocated her. He opened his fingers wide and fresh oxygen was pumped in. She could see through his knuckles now, they curved in hard transparent plastic. An oxygen mask. Each noisy inhalation of breath drew her back into this mesh of present-day pain. The faces were still above her: strangers, daughters, a low babble of English accents. Was one of them crying? No, that was the trickle of water running down the rocks beside the ruined cottage beyond the farmhouse in Dunross: the cottage abandoned after the famine. She lay on the mossy stone wall beside them on the hill that overlooked Dunross, with scrawny mountain sheep grazing around her. She closed her eyes to enjoy the sun's heat as she lay there, at nineteen years old, her flower-patterned dress blowing up over her thighs in the wind.

Rustling grass, rushes blowing beside the stream, midges filling the air. Below her, the valley seemed like a shimmering black sea in the heat. When she opened her eyes to gaze up the sun was blazing down and overhead a bird of prey hovered, huge black wings outstretched as he bided his time to swoop. He had the face of the man who had used her body on this hillside: Brylcreem and cajoling, force and broken promises. She opened her mouth to scream but a plastic oxygen mask prevented her, a hand pressed down on her face. She heard crickets in the rushes, their chirp growing unnaturally loud before it dissolved into the ticking of a watch on the wrist of the nurse attending to her. Then the copper wire twisted inside her again, tearing through her flesh. Her body jerked and fell.

Where had she landed? She smelled turf. She was twelve-years-old: lying out up on the bog the morning after a neighbouring boy had left for America. Her limbs were jaded from the dancing all night at the American wake in his parents' house; from walking among the crowd going to see him off at the station, their songs turning to silence in the dawn light. Afterwards the men went straight to cut turf, throwing up long wet sods for the children to stack. The sun was high and merciless as they stopped to eat. Her sister Ellen lay down beside her and drifted into an exhausted sleep. Lizzy turned to stare at her sister's breasts beginning to press against her cotton dress, then stared at Tom sitting a small way off, separated from the other boys but intently watching them. Then everyone went silent as Ellen rose, still in a dream, and began to repeat the dance steps from last night, her eyes closed, her face expressionless, dancing in her sleep across the surface of the bog.

The sun grew in brilliance, lighting up the dancing girl until she burst into flames. But still Ellen danced on, burning as bright as the sun. Then she split into four shimmering discs that gradually came back into focus: the four lights in the hospital ward. The copper wire twisted in Lizzy's bowels again, cutting into the lining of her stomach. Those same watchers would not leave her alone, though she sensed that Ellen too was there. The mask was being lifted away for one moment, then steadily lowered over her face again. The pain was all-consuming and then it ceased. She could see a wedding ring on the finger of the nurse holding down the mask and the tubes which fed into a machine.

It took Lizzy a moment to realise that she was looking at the wrong side of the mask, and that she could see her own sunken face in the bed and the nurse's hat, which covered her dyed hair, as the medical team began to frantically press buttons and the watchers stepped back, lifting up their faces to reveal tears.

Lizzy felt sorry for them in their sorrow. She wished to stay and watch, but her own momentum was carrying her away. She seemed to reach the ceiling and glide along it. She felt no sense of fear, just a disconnected fascination. She was in the corridor now with figures moving beneath her, a trolley being quickly wheeled along. Then she was out of the hospital; she didn't know how, just that it was dark in the car park and even darker now that she was looking down on the whole city of Coventry. The darkness wrapped itself around her until she was twirling through it: with all the pin-pricks of city light shrinking into one single orb; a distant, brilliant luminosity that she was drifting towards.

She felt herself being buffeted about in this warm tunnel as the light beckoned her. She had to decide whether to allow her death to occur or to try and force her way back down into that bag of bones and pain. Francis had never found her. Every other aspect of her life seemed distant already, but this yearning remained and the regret seemed to trap her in this tunnel between two worlds. The light was drawing closer, but it seemed to have become a globe of speckled faces: faces that she had never thought to see again. All she had left to do was to pass through this globe where the faces were merging into the luminous core.

But how could she leave behind her living son? The thought made her fight against the pull of the light, but then she saw him: the one unblurred face amid that throng. For a moment she thought that he was her son but then she knew that this young man could not be Francis. But he was somebody close to Francis though, a shadow of Francis, someone who had watched over Francis's life. The young man's face seemed surly at first but then he smiled as if to reassure her. It was a smile of welcome and recognition before he vanished into the swirl of faces that she now felt able to plummet through.

The globe broke apart and she found herself walking across the hillside overlooking Dunross. Trees in the valley began to change colour as if months were passing in an instant. She reached the top field and stopped at the dry stone wall her father had laboured to build. Lizzy sensed that the young man was walking beside her, guiding her although she could no longer see him. Her father waited at the gate where a sheepdog barked.

'You'll like it here, Lizzy,' he said. But she was still frightened of his anger. She climbed the wall and jumped down, knowing that her father was following at a distance. Her mother was waiting for her in the lane that led to the lake field overlooking the church and the shops in the village. The woman opened her arms, but Lizzy backed away and turned to find that the young man was still beside her. For a moment she wondered again if he was her son, but he silently shook his head. He had something of her son in him, that was all she knew, and something of Tom's gentleness. His feet were bare, his clothes ragged, but he was welcoming her, taking the place of someone else who could not yet be there.

He held out his hand and she accepted it. She looked back, but discovered that there was only darkness behind her. With every time she took a step, the ground where she had just trod seemed to vanish. How long had she been in this state? She knew that time meant nothing in this place.

Her father and mother walked a little way off to her left; keeping their distance as if waiting for her to decide to forgive them. Cloud shadows passed quickly across the ground she was covering. She reached the wall of the lake field and looked down at the two cars coming to a halt beside a blue car that was already parked outside Dunross graveyard. A man got out of the first car and took off his jacket before opening the doors to help two women out from the back seats. She saw that one of them was her sister Ellen who was pointing out landmarks to the frail old woman beside her. A solitary figure emerged from the blue car and walked towards them. She recognised her brother, even though the decades had greyed and saddened him. He fingered his stiff white collar awkwardly.

And she knew at once who her son was when he emerged from the other car and walked over to shake Tom's hand. A woman was carefully lifting a baby from the back seat, having undone the safety harness on a young boy who ran from the car towards her son. Her son picked him up in his arms and climbed over the stile into the graveyard. The child gazed around, pointing excitedly towards a tractor which had stopped in the field across the road. Tom opened the gate so that the woman could wheel in the buggy into which she had placed the sleeping baby girl.

A fourth car now pulled in: a Mercedes driven by a man in a suit with broad shoulders. He opened the back door and two women got out. She knew from their faces that they had once been like her: scared young mothers in a convent. They stood awkwardly, a small distance off. The farmer had stopped his tractor in the field and walked to the gate. Several local women emerged from the post office and began to talk. The small group of strangers walked up through the graveyard.

*

And the funny thing was that it seemed like I could almost feel my mother's presence there, for the first time in my life, as we left the gravel path and began to make our way carefully among the graves. Behind me, my two aunts walked together in silence: Cissie and Ellen. They had both borne witness to the lives of the two women who were my mothers. Gerry stopped and put on his jacket, removing a tie from his pocket. For him that was a rare mark of respect. He walked beside my Uncle Tom who seemed unable to control a tremble in his hand. I had not expected Peter McHugh to be here, and had only left a message for him at the last moment, at Geraldine's suggestion. The two women I had met in his office walked beside him. I wondered if their husbands knew where they were.

Perhaps it was the sight of Tom, sitting alone in his car, which caused the local women to gather outside the post office. He had not returned to his native parish since his ordination. But when I looked back, I found that the women were following us from a distance. The farmer and some other old men were walking behind them. We reached my grandparents' grave. The evening sun cast shadows from the crooked tombstones. When I looked down at the grass I could still see the motionless shadows of a dozen local people blending with those of the stones. I stared up at them. My own nameless father might even be standing here. They were all of an age to have known my mother. From their faces I knew that each of them was acutely aware of who I was. Ever since my mother vanished in the nun's car they had known about me, I had been part of the secret history of this village, spoken about in whispers.

Benedict was scared by the circle of people. Aunt Cissie came over to lift him from my arms and soothe him with her gravelly voice which had so often soothed me. Geraldine pushed the buggy back and forth as Sinéad sucked her thumb in sleep. I nodded to Aunt Ellen who took the urn from her bag and placed it into my hands.

It was the strangest sensation. The urn weighed little more than a new-born child. It was the same time of evening as when I had first searched for this grave, the time of evening when my mother had once been allowed to stand here and mourn for her own dead mother, while carrying me inside her. No words had been spoken on either of those occasions and there were no words that could be said now, although some of the local men glanced at Tom, as if expecting him to lead them in prayer. But he kept his eyes fixed on the urn in my hands. I looked down at the grave of my grandparents. Leaves had blown in to cover the grass. My family – my two families – stood in silence. The local people remained at a distance, the men defensive and slightly hostile, the women staring at me with frank curiosity.

I opened the urn and began to scatter the ashes. The wind blew some of them away from the grave before they had time to settle. Before dark they would have blown into every corner of this graveyard. Some ash would be blown out onto the road where the tyres of cars would carry it off to villages and farmyards, while more ash would be lifted by the wind and borne across the fields up towards the empty hillside where sheep grazed.

I wanted her to know that I had brought her home. Maybe she never would know, because perhaps after death only oblivion exists. But all that mattered just then was that I had made this journey here, to be with her spirit if she was presence or to represent her absence if she was gone. After all the ashes had been scattered I stood there in the silence, feeling drained and forlorn, holding the empty urn. Then after a moment I heard footsteps approaching. I did not look up. I knew that the local men would still be standing awkwardly in their places watching as their wives placed their arms gently about me. I leaned my head forward. It touched some old woman's cheek which was damp with tears. I nodded and felt the arms of the other women pressing against me, each one taking away some tiny part of my grief with a mother's certain and quiet caress.

Also Available in the Modern Irish Classics Series from New Island

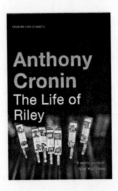

Anthony Cronin, *The Life of Riley*

Anthony Cronin's comic novel centres around the literary scene in Dublin in the 1950s, and follows occasional poet Riley's misadventures after he has resigned from his job as assistant to the secretary of a Dublin grocers' association, in favour of beggardom.

'I have laughed more at *The Life of Riley* than at any other book I have ever read' Benedict Kiely, *The Irish Times*

'A comic triumph' *New York Times*

'Gorgeously funny ... True, crude, raw, rude, nude ...' Elizabeth Smart, *Queen*

'A splendidly comic imagination' *Times Literary Supplement*

NEW
ISLAND

Also Available in the Modern Irish Classics Series from New Island

Benedict Kiely, *The Cards of the Gambler*

A wonderfully imaginative and dark tale from master storyteller, Benedict Kiely. A doctor loses everything to gambling and finds himself making an extraordinary pact with God and Death.

'Not only is *The Cards of the Gambler* Benedict Kiely's best novel, but it is one of the finest novels that has been written in this country in years' Brian Friel

'An astonishing book. …What is uniquely Kiely's, his thumbprint, is his easy mastery of the lyrical, and the feeling of felt life, felt experience, just beneath the surface of his prose' Thomas Flanagan

NEW
ISLAND